I0699227

rival summer

JESS BRYSON

EDITED BY
SARAH WATERMAN, A3W EDITORIAL

EDITED BY
KADY ESHLEMAN, KEY EDITS

To my mother who gave me everything I ever wanted growing up, and never let me know how much she struggled to do it.

RIVAL SUMMER
playlist

1	Don't Pick Up Sadie Bass	**11**	Eyes That Ain't Yours 2 Lane Summer
2	Guess We'll Never Know Mitchell Tenpenny	**12**	Between Us Austin Williams
3	Wish I Never Felt Nate Smith	**13**	Silverado Tanner Adell
4	the 1 Taylor Swift	**14**	For Me Levi Hummon
5	Forget Me Celina Sharma	**15**	Cowboy Songs George Birge
6	Love Makes You Blind Kaylee Rose	**16**	Summer Night Supercuts Josh Kerr
7	The Story Of Us Taylor Swift	**17**	'tis the damn season Taylor Swift
8	What I'm Missing Timmy McKeever	**18**	Worth It Danielle Bradbery
9	What If I Don't Shaylen	**19**	Healing Kaylee Rose
10	Worst Way Riley Green	**20**	Cowgirls [feat. ERNEST] Morgan Wallen

RIVAL SUMMER
playlist

21	Before You David J	**31**	Ride [feat. Macy Maloy] Chase Rice
22	Mind On You George Birge	**32**	Bad Blood Taylor Swift
23	Who I Am With You Chris Young		
24	Sittin' On Empty Warner & Spencer		
25	When She Goes Josh Mirenda		
26	Left Right Carson Wallace		
27	Love on the Line Warren Zeiders		
28	Holding On Bailey Zimmerman		
29	Still Do Josh Kerr		
30	Ends of the Earth Ty Myers		

prologue

BOSTON

"Bro. You're still here?" Parker's voice was light but I still felt his concern as he leaned against the chain-link fence. "You're always the first one in and the last one out. You gotta give yourself a break."

"I'll be done soon," I responded, quick and sharp. I set my jaw and took another swing, the ball shooting off into the net.

"Okay, man," Parker said disbelievingly, as if he knew full well that my definition of "soon" was not what he was suggesting. "Just don't burn out."

I nodded without looking back, my mind already recalibrating for the next pitch. There was comfort in the repetition, in the solitude of the cage where the only expectations I had to live up to were my own. I swung again and again, the echo of the ball against my bat a constant reminder that for now, this was all I allowed myself to feel.

The crack of a bat against a fastball was the only sound that made sense anymore. I stood in the dim glow of the batting cage, my hands calloused and raw from swings that were just as much about releasing stress as they were about form. With each pitch, I tried to obliterate the truth that had shattered my world into a million fucked up little pieces.

It wasn't supposed to be like this. Baseball—the game—was where life made sense, where I was no longer just the person everyone could count on, but an unstoppable force that no one could mess with. Now, even here, surrounded by the smell of dirt and leather, I couldn't get rid of the feeling of betrayal no matter how hard I tried.

There's a darkness in me that never used to be there. I didn't want anyone to see it—to see me like this. I couldn't bear the thought of pulling anyone down into this shitstorm with me, so I pushed them all away—friends, anyone close to me. Every cheer from the stands, every high five from my teammates—all background noise. The roar of the crowd was a reminder of what I'd lost inside, how isolated I had become despite the chaos around me.

"Oh and hey," Parker called out, breaking through my thoughts. "I know you hardly go out anymore, but Saturday is Chandler's birthday party. We'd love to see you there." His voice carried that familiar lightheartedness, but I felt the concern in his tone.

My grip on the bat loosened slightly. I acknowledged Parker with a nod, feeling the weight of those words. A party meant people, laughter, and an inevitable confrontation when I saw her. Chandler.

"I'll see what I can do," I managed to say. I wasn't sure if I was ready to step out of the shadows I had grown accustomed to.

Parker shot me an encouraging smile before making his way out of the batting facility, leaving me alone once again with the echo of the ball and my thoughts.

It had been nine months of the same routine—baseball, drills, and working out. I filled any free time from school or baseball with training. Every workout, every run, was an attempt to shove away the revelation of what my mother was hiding from me. I'd always known there was a silent war raging between me and Reese, my rival on the field. A war of his pitches vs. my hits; stolen bases and strikeouts. It was one thing to discover that the girl I've always loved was slipping away and drifting toward him, the very person who represented my unraveling world. But what came after that... it was a cruelty I hadn't been prepared for.

I couldn't absorb the reality of the situation, yet somehow it still clung to me, like heavy chains I couldn't shake off.

I took a staggered breath as another ball hurtled toward me. I swung with ferocity that sent the ball tearing through the air, slamming into the net with a satisfying clang that resonated through my bones. This was my sanctuary, the one place I could pour all of my confusion and anger into something powerful—something that mattered.

But as I waited for the next pitch, my focus shifted. It was always in the quiet moments that I thought about Chandler. She was on my mind in the spaces between drills, during the stretch of tired limbs, in the pause before sleep. The girl who had grown up before my eyes, who cheered the loudest at my games, the one who always saw me.

I shook my head, trying to dislodge the thought of her, but it lingered, persistent and gentle in a way nothing else was anymore. I tried to force those thoughts out of my head when they happened. I was confused and broken, and baseball was all I had left. It was no longer a game but a lifeline, keeping me tethered to something—anything—when everything else had slipped through my fingers. I clung to it—the routine of practice, the adrenaline of games, the predictability of each inning. Unexpectedly restless, I swung my last bat at the cages earlier than usual. The metallic echo of the cage door clanging shut behind me punctuated the end of a long, unchanging chapter.

I headed toward the showers, and once I was done, I wrapped myself in a towel and approached the foggy bathroom mirror. I lifted my gaze, taking in the taut lines of determination etched into my face. Eyes that once held dreams or hope were now clouded with an internal storm. I exhaled slowly, trying to purge the image of Chandler's smile from my mind. Deep down, though, I knew she was the one light I couldn't extinguish, no matter how dark the world became.

But this was my life now, and I'd continue to carry it all—the hurt, the love, the uncertainty—because that's what you do when your whole life changes and everything you thought you knew was ripped out from beneath you.

ONE

chandler

THE WORLD WAS FLIPPED UPSIDE DOWN, and my wavy hair dangled toward the floor as I fixed my eyes on the bodies surrounding me. Their hands were steady on my ankles to keep me from falling. I tasted the metallic tang of the keg's nozzle pressed to my lips. I opened my mouth and the beer rushed out—bitter and unexpectedly warm.

"Chug! Chug! Chug!" The chant reverberated through the room. As the last drop of beer trickled down my throat, the hands holding me up guided me to the ground, and I readjusted to the upright world.

"Chandler, seriously?" Kristina offered me a water bottle, slightly judging. "Look, I know it's your birthday, but I'd be doing you a disservice if I didn't at least make sure you make it to the candle blowing part of the night."

Her concern, genuine and grounding, was in severe contrast to the wild energy of the party. But it was so Kristina, the mom of the group. She was always looking out for me.

I smiled, accepting the bottle and the memory of the last time I drank more than I should have with equal reluctance. "Thanks," I said before taking a sip of the cold liquid as it promised to shield me against the headache I knew was yet to come. "You should be celebrating too, you know? It's not just my birthday—finals are over!"

Kristina's eyes sparked in agreement. We both knew the pain of countless study nights on top of reciting lines together. She gave a noncommittal shrug, the corners of her mouth turning up into a reluctant smile. "Fine," she conceded, "I will take one shot, but only one."

All around me people were laughing, dancing, living in the moment. It was my birthday and the end of another school year. It should have felt liberating, a release from the relentless pressure of essays and exams. And yet I couldn't shake the worry creeping up. The weight of last summer's memories were closing in on me, heavy like the humidity outside. I tried to lose myself in roles onstage, in the academic grind, hoping to outrun the confusion and hurt that crept up when I least expected it. As the room swirled around me, I allowed my mind to drift back to last summer.

It was an intoxicating blend of sunny days by the lake and wild nights, and a very naïve me had thought she'd discovered the hidden depths of bad boy Reese Carrington. I'd felt like I was unraveling the mystery of him, only for it all to crumble. The thought of falling under his spell so quickly stung, an uncomfortable feeling of regret that kept me awake at night. The sad part was I didn't think I could even call him my ex-boyfriend. A summer fling, maybe. I don't know what he was to me, but most importantly—I don't know if my brain could ever understand the fact that he was Boston's brother. What in the Lifetime movie kind of story was I living? How could their mother have kept that secret?

And then there was Boston Riley. My childhood crush, the boy who seemed impossible to get over when in reality, he was never even mine. Our relationship was complicated, and that was putting it lightly. I pried as much information from Parker as I could about how he'd been doing, but it was no substitute for the real thing.

He hadn't just grown distant, he'd shut me out completely, leaving messages unanswered, leaving questions and confused feelings swirling in his absence. Occasionally, I stalked him through the baseball team's social media and saw most of their home games. He looked undeniably good—more than good. His hair looked shorter and lighter, almost as if it had been sun-bleached; his shoulders seemed broader, arms more defined—like he'd spent every moment since last summer lifting weights on top of playing baseball, just to stride on the field and unintentionally command it.

He seemed different. It was almost like we were just strangers, not that he was my brother's best friend and that we'd known each other practically our whole lives. It stung more than I expected knowing that Boson and I were in this place. Not to mention the boy who broke my heart last summer—Reese, Boston's rival—was who turned out to be his brother. Like I said, complicated.

I tried to fight off the thoughts as Kristina and I maneuvered through the crowd, heading for the kitchen. I could hear the sharp pitch of an argument as we approached my brother standing at the center of the fire. The girl in front of him had her arms crossed, eyes sharp, shooting daggers at him. "You never called or texted me back."

There was genuine surprise on his face. He blinked as if trying to remember which girl this was, which was deeply disturbing. "Oh, did I not?" Parker scratched the back of his neck, not quite hiding the awkward recognition.

She scoffed. "I can't believe I cried over you and your shitty hair-cut," she spat out. Without waiting for a response, she turned sharply and left the room.

I rolled my eyes at the spectacle. Kristina nudged me, a signal to turn my focus on the shot. I reached for the bottle of vodka and uncapped it before pouring it into two shot glasses waiting on the counter.

I glanced over at Parker who was still watching the space where the girl had been standing. I couldn't help but insert unwanted sarcasm into the moment. "My brother, always the gentleman."

"Do I really have a shitty haircut?" he asked, turning to me.

I shook my head and poured another shot, lining it up with the others.

"Come on, you need this more than we do," I said, nudging the glass toward him.

Parker raised an eyebrow, accepting the shot with a grateful nod. "Here's a shot to..." he paused, eyes twinkling with a familiar mischievous glint, "me getting the hell out of this town."

We laughed and raised our glasses in unison before throwing back the shots, the vodka burning a trail of warmth down our throats.

Kristina chose right then to make her announcement. Her voice cut through the chatter. "Okay, now is a good time before everyone gets too wasted. Let's do cake."

Kristina reached for the cake, a pink masterpiece she baked herself, complete with my name in cursive across the top. She didn't fumble as she carried it across the room to the battleground of red cups and half-empty cans on the dining room table. With practiced grace, she cleared a space and gently set down the cake. She struck a match igniting the candles, their flames flickering in anticipation.

"Everyone, gather 'round!" Kristina commanded, her grin wide and infectious. "It's time to sing to the birthday girl."

I felt a buzz in my pocket and pulled out my phone. The screen lit up with a message I wasn't expecting.

REESE

Happy Birthday, Beautiful

I blinked once, twice, making sure the words were truly there and not just figments conjured by the alcohol.

With a press of the side button, I banished the message to darkness, locking away the words and the feelings they stirred. Slipping the device back into my pocket, I turned to face the group that had begun to converge around me.

My cluster of friends closed in around the table, forming a semicircle of excited faces. The first notes of the familiar tune began, tentative at first but soon swelling with volume and cheer. I stood at the epicenter of it all, cheeks warming not just from the candlelight but from the love that surrounded me.

As the melody wrapped around me, my eyes drifted shut. Flickers of orange danced against my eyelids, casting shadows on the wishes swirling through my mind. This summer... This summer was going to be different. I wished for strength, to stay focused on myself. No boys. No tangled emotions to trip over. No giving my heart away only to have it handed back, broken. I'll never be in the center of some twisted brother rivalry. No getting hurt again.

I drew in a breath, my chest rising with the weight of my silent wish. As the song faded, I leaned forward, the warmth of the candles kissing my face, and blew with all the hope a year older Chandler could find.

My eyes flickered open to the sight of wisps of smoke curling upwards, the remnants of my resolution ascending to whatever universe wishes float off to.

And then, as if planned by some evil wish-rejecting asshole with a twisted sense of humor, the energy shifted and all eyes flew to the front door as Boston walked in.

Seriously? Was the universe playing a joke? Did they hear me wrong?

"Happy Fucking Birthday to me," I murmured under my breath.

boston

EVERY PART of me was screaming to turn back, to retreat into the solitude that had become my refuge. But the thought of her expectant eyes searching for me in the crowd was something I couldn't ignore. My thoughts had consumed me lately, but the birthday girl was a persistent whisper in my mind. Even though I tried keeping to myself this year, I'd be there for her in a heartbeat, no questions asked. I'd drop everything, even baseball.

The party was buzzing, and I could see Chandler's roommate cutting a cake in the kitchen. It may have been the first college party I'd actually seen a birthday cake. If I had, it was usually for the aesthetic. No one actually ate said cake.

I caught sight of her. Chandler. Pure beauty in human form, surrounded by admirers, a smile lighting up the room just like I'm sure the candles did on her cake before she blew them out. Our eyes met briefly and there was a flicker of something—recognition or maybe surprise—before she quickly concealed it. She turned away, looking interested in a story one of her friends was telling.

"Yo, my boy!" The familiar voice, warm and excited, shook me out of the trance I was in. Parker bounded over with open arms.

"Didn't think you'd show." He bear-hugged me, almost taking me down.

"Didn't think I would either," I managed to say before he released me.

"Thanks for gracing us with your presence," Parker retorted with a chuckle, scratching his head sheepishly. "But seriously, glad you're here. Shit has been weird. There's a girl lingering around who keeps saying I never called her back. Bro, I don't remember her at all."

"Parker, are you serious?" An annoyed voice trailed into our conversation. A girl appeared behind Parker, giving him a look that quite frankly terrified the shit out of me. Then she stormed off.

"Whoops," Parker whispered with an alarmed look.

I patted Parker's shoulder reassuringly and took a deep breath, feeling the weight of being here heavy on my chest. I was unsure where to rest my hands, so I found comfort in the depths of my pockets. It was a small comfort, a momentary anchor amongst the turbulence of my conflicting emotions.

Laughter and conversation filled the room as I shouldered through. Chandler was in the thick of it, her eyes sparking in the dim light every time she laughed. Some guy was standing too close for comfort, his lips barely touching her ear as he whispered something that made her laugh. A flare of irritation tightened my jaw. It wasn't jealousy—that much I had relinquished—but maybe the protective instinct I always had over her refused to loosen its grip.

I'd known her since she was a kid, tagging along after her brother and me, with that wavy chestnut hair bouncing behind her. But it had become more obvious as I got older that those innocent childhood memories were intertwined with an awareness that left me restless and on edge, always battling the feelings I had about her. She'd always been off-limits. She was my best friend's sister—and who knew what was going on with her and my mother's other son? I wasn't ready to say the B-word, not even close.

And despite the dark cloud that had taken up residence directly over me, it was impossible not to feel the faintest flicker of warmth around her. It wasn't happiness or the rush of excitement that I used to feel, but it was something. Something other than numbing coldness and all-consuming resentment. I couldn't afford to listen to those feelings, though. Not now. With a mental shove, I barricaded my emotions. I wasn't going to pretend I was available emotionally —I had a giant list of other items consuming my mental capacity.

Taking a deep breath, I closed the distance between Chandler and me.

As I inched closer, a surge of familiarity coursed through my veins, so potent it almost had my arms reaching out to pull her into a hug. But I froze, held back by my inner demons. The man who would've swept her up in his arms and spun her around until dizzy with laughter... he felt like a stranger now. It wasn't that I couldn't remember how to be him, I could. I just wasn't ready to pull him out of his darkened space.

Chandler's circle opened subtly as her friends noticed me, almost as if they all knew I was there just for her. Stepping into the space, I caught her eye, and time stopped. For a heartbeat, there was no one else, just her and those bright hazel eyes. They held a question, a flicker of recognition, and surprisingly no sign of anger or resentment.

"Happy birthday," I whispered as I gently pressed a kiss on her cheek. It was a small gesture, one that felt achingly familiar yet painfully distant.

Then I slipped away, dissolving back into the party. But Chandler's gaze lingered on me, a weight I felt even without looking back, as did the stares of her friends. They saw me walk away, they saw that moment between us, but none of them knew what it took—the force it took to do just that and nothing more.

Eventually I found Parker again outside. He sat alone on the wooden porch steps. I settled beside him, the wood creaking under our combined weight. I nudged his shoulder with my own.

"You ready for another summer in Bayside?" I asked, trying my best to infuse some lightness into the question.

Parker exhaled, a half-hearted chuckle escaping him. "Ready for baseball and seeing the boys—definitely ready for the wild nights," he admitted, running a hand through his hair.

"Same, buddy." I clapped him on the back. "So, what's your sister up to this summer?" I asked casually, observing my surroundings as if I might catch a glimpse of her.

Parker leaned back on his hands. "She's in charge of the chaos at my parents' place," he said with a chuckle. "Mom's got this whole game plan to revamp the house, paint colors and all that. I think they're going to tackle it together."

"Sounds like quite the project." I nodded, then hesitated for a second before treading lightly on the subject weighing on my mind. "Is she... still with... him?"

He picked up his beer to take a sip. "No," he said finally, shaking his head. "I don't think they've talked since last summer. Love the guy now that I know him better. Badass pitcher. But I don't know if he's the one for her, you know?"

I felt something inside me loosen, a tension I hadn't fully acknowledged until then. I always cared about Chandler more than I let on, and the idea of her and Reese together had left a bitter taste in my mouth. But hearing they were no longer together was a relief.

"How about you, man? How are you doing with all that, by the way?" He put his beer down on the step next to him. "We've chatted a few times, but I still can't wrap my head around how it's all possible."

"Yeah, you're telling me," I agreed, the weight of the entire dilemma pressing down on me. The twist of fate that had revealed my baseball rival was my brother; the tangled emotions involving Chandler. I hadn't fully processed it all yet.

"Life's a trip, isn't it?" Parker sighed, and I couldn't help but agree.

"One big trip to hell, as my grandfather used to say," I said, as I shook my head.

"Now that's dark," he snickered.

The screen door creaked open, jolting us from our laughter. "Parker, I've been looking for you," a girl I hadn't seen before announced. Her tone was sharp, and it drew our attention immediately.

"Some scroungy guy just tried to talk to me and spit in my eye," she explained, her disgust palpable. "Take me to your place?"

I couldn't help but smirk at her request. Parker had brought plenty of girls home this year, and it seemed like he was enjoying every minute of it.

"Sure thing," Parker said as he shot me a wink and rose from the wooden steps.

I stood up alongside him, brushing off the remnants of our conversation. "On that note, I'm gonna head home, too."

"Sounds good, man." Parker nodded, as he reached for her hand. "I'll catch you back at our place."

Before I left, I stole one final glance at Chandler—she was dancing, enjoying herself—radiating beauty. I couldn't help but think about the texts she'd sent me, all left unanswered as I threw myself into running or working out. I knew she was checking in on me through Parker. The guilt weighed heavily on me.

Retreating into the shadows, I found a hollow quietness where I could breathe through the ache left in me at seeing her. She made me feel like I was suffocating and breathing for the first time all at once. Maybe I pushed her away and ignored her messages because I knew deep down if anyone could reach into the depths I'd sunk into, to pull me out of this darkness I was in, it was her. It was who she was —kindness, loyalty, unwavering belief in the good of those she cared for. Despite the walls I'd built around myself, a tiny piece of me couldn't help but wonder what would have happened if I'd allowed her in this year now knowing Reese wasn't in the picture.

chandler

"THIS IS what's out in the dating world right now," Kristina declared, her voice a pitch higher than usual. She turned her phone screen toward me, pointing to a profile with the username "Papi Likes Butts." Appalled, she shook her head, still trying to decipher what she was seeing.

I pressed my lips together to keep the laugh from escaping, watching as Kristina scrolled dramatically through the photos of a man who was clearly more in love with his own abs than any potential date.

"Can you believe this?" Her tone was incredulous as she dissected each photo—the flexing, the abs, the lack of any actual face photos. "I even extended the radius from here to Bayside, hoping to find better options."

"He could be really nice," I offered, which earned me an eye roll from her.

But as I tapped absentmindedly on my phone screen, my amusement faded, replaced by curiosity, and I wasn't sure where it was coming from. I suddenly wondered if Reese was on dating apps, or with anyone new. My thoughts quickly started spiraling. Reese

Carrington—the bad boy with so much more depth than people knew. I saw glimpses of what lay beneath that carefree exterior. I wondered if he had a dating profile. Would he be shirtless, flaunting those piercing green eyes? Or would he have candid shots of him on his boat—reading, revealing the depth I was only just beginning to understand?

My fingers acted of their own accord, keying in his name. Flicking through Reese's Instagram grid, my thumb paused on a photo of him sitting in an empty stadium, his green eyes looking into the distance, a half-smile playing on his lips. No sign of his ex-girl-friend, Blair, or her polished presence in any frame. Just Reese, alone or with friends, in landscapes and cityscapes. It was a strange relief that there weren't girls draped all over him, no evidence of a romance for me to agonize over. Yet it also left an unsettling void, a space where answers should have been but weren't. I never responded to his text message on my birthday. He cut off whatever fragile connection we'd cultivated at the end of last summer—and it now seemed drenched in unreal memories. Checking on him through these glimpses online hurt—it was a reminder that I was just another spectator of his life.

Thank goodness for Kristina, the one who endured my relentless analysis of every moment spent with Reese last summer. Her patience never wavered as I recounted each smile, each touch, each word that passed between us. She had become an unwitting partici-pant in the tangled web of emotions and revelations last summer had left me with.

Kristina had been there through it all, listening to my shock, my confusion, my heartache as I tried to reconcile the two versions of Reese I knew: the boy who Parker and Boston said he was, and the man who'd shown glimpses of something deeper. From Boston's unexpected confession of his feelings, to the bomb that dropped on top of it all... I thought back to the kindness she showed me while I struggled during the school year.

* * *

The stage lights dimmed, and the final notes of the closing song played as the curtain shut slowly. I made my way to the dressing room and there, on my vanity, sat the most beautiful bouquet of roses. The vivid red was striking against the bright white of the tabletop.

I picked up one of the roses, feeling the velvety smoothness of its petals between my fingers. The faintest smile touched my lips as I placed the rose back among the others. Kristina pretended they weren't from her when I thanked her, but I knew they must be.

It was a ritual at every show. Her silent gesture spoke louder than words ever could.

* * *

Kristina squealed, jolting me out of my memories. Her face contorted in horror as she recounted the dating app atrocity unfolding on her phone. "Papi Likes Butts just asked me for a picture of my feet. He said that feet tell him everything he needs to know about a woman. And even worse... He sent me a picture of his feet," she shrieked, her voice hitting a pitch that could shatter glass. "Why would I want a picture of his feet? A dick pic, okay, I can deal with that, but his rugged big feet?" In disgust, she threw her hands up in the air. It was the foot that broke the camel's back.

I bit my lip, struggling to keep my own laughter from spilling out. It wasn't that I found his request particularly humorous—it was the unfiltered terror on her face that I couldn't stop myself from laughing at.

Just then my phone dinged, a gentle chime that tore my attention away from Kristina's rant. She continued to ramble about the absurdity of modern courtship, but my gaze drifted down to a message from Willow that flashed across the screen.

WILLOW

Are you coming to Bayside this summer?

My thoughts drifted back to Bayside, where the sun danced on the water's surface and the days stretched into even better nights. But, I had no intention of going back there this summer.

ME

No. :(

WILLOW

Seriously?! Ugh need ur help!

ME

With what?

I'm going to my parents. Helping my mom tackle some projects around the house.

WILLOW

Dad is making me work my way up on the coaching ladder. He says I need to be on the Blue Devils committee this year. Was hoping you'd be my saving grace and join with me.

You could even stay with me for the summer…

Doesn't pay a ton, but has some nice perks.

ME

Sounds exciting. Wish I could help!

WILLOW

I get it

Offer stands if you change your mind! love u.

A sigh escaped me. The offer was tempting. It would be a summer with Willow, uncontrollable laughter, and memories I'd probably never forget. But I couldn't be around Boston or Reese— not just in their presence, but pulled into the same orbit as Reese, who'd ended things with me last summer. The thought of facing him again twisted my insides into knots. And there was Boston, who I didn't recognize at the moment. I quickly typed another response before putting my phone back down on the couch beside me.

ME

love u too!

How could I step foot in Bayside, knowing the chaos it would create? Attending some of Parker's games and hiding in the shadows was one thing. Actively participating in the committee and being forced to hang around both of them was an entirely different situation.

"Chandler!" Kristina's voice pulled me back. She was peering at me now, her earlier rant forgotten, replaced by a look of concern.

"Foot guy still bothering you?" I asked Kristina, redirecting the conversation back to her and away from my own internal conflict.

"Ugh, his username should really be Papi Likes Feet," she groaned, but the sparkle in her eyes told me she'd already moved on. I couldn't help but smile at her playful teasing, a signature of her charm.

But Kristina caught the flicker of my fading amusement. "Hey," she said, her tone softening with concern. "How have you been doing since your birthday?" Her eyes searched mine, seeking the truth.

"I've been fine," I shrugged, trying to appear nonchalant. Being around Boston stirred up more emotions than I'd expected. "It just… brought back memories, you know?"

"Memories," Kristina echoed, her voice laced with understanding. She knew the depth of it all without another word.

"Yeah," I sighed. "I didn't expect Boston to show." I honestly wasn't sure why he came. After spending the entire year hidden away, why had he chosen my birthday to finally make an appearance?

Kristina's expression warmed, her confidence unwavering. "I knew he'd show," she said, her belief in him—and perhaps in us—

was clear. "You're the Topanga to his Cory, Chandler. If you said jump, he'd dive off a mountain without a thought."

"I'm the what?" I asked.

"Seriously? You've never heard of Cory and Topanga?"

I shrugged. "No, who are they?"

"They're like..." she paused, searching for the words. "The epitome of childhood sweethearts. My mom made me watch this show... Basically two people just destined to be together."

A tiny laugh escaped me, despite the turmoil inside. Boston was the king of mixed signals, the type of person to confess his feelings at the most inconvenient moment, or disappear for months then suddenly appear on your birthday. Case in point.

I forced my eyes up to meet hers under the weight of my next thought. "That's not true, Kris. I don't think there's much he cares about besides baseball these days." My throat tightened at the admission. "He looks like Boston—well, a more toned Boston—and he smells like Boston, but it's like he's just disconnected from everything else."

Kristina leaned forward, her elbows on the table, expression soft yet serious. "Think about what he went through, Chan," she urged gently. "Knowing your mom kept a secret brother from you your entire life? How could he not be disconnected?"

I nodded slowly, absorbing her empathy for him. She was right. Boston's world had been turned upside down, the ground beneath him shaken by secrets and lies. But the Boston I knew, sweet-natured, always protective—that didn't just go away.

"Yeah, I get it," I murmured, tracing the rim of my coffee mug with a fingertip. "I just hope he doesn't lose sight of himself."

"Maybe he's just a different person now," she said gently.

I shook my head. "I don't even know if the old Boston is still in there," I said quietly, more to myself than to her. My conviction surprised even me, yet it was unshakeable.

"Well, if anyone can find out, it's you," she said, not a question but a statement—a belief in my strength and in the childhood bond that tied me to Boston Riley.

My mind drifted back to the moment he'd walked into my birthday party, to the unexpected softness when he kissed my cheek. For an instant, as his lips brushed my skin, there was a flicker in his bright blue eyes, a flash of warmth that transported me back to all the special moments we'd shared as kids. In that fleeting encounter I saw the Boston I'd grown up with, the one whose laughter was a melody that resonated with the rhythm of my own heart.

FOUR

boston

DROPLETS OF SWEAT slid down my temples. My body was still trying to cool down from my earlier workout. My shirt clung to my chest as I carried bags of groceries to the cool marble countertop in Mom's kitchen. If it weren't for these routine deliveries, I often wondered if she'd remember to eat anything at all.

I cracked open the fridge, strategically arranging the fresh produce and dairy where she could easily spot them. I was always careful to place her favorite Greek yogurt front and center—if nothing else, she wouldn't miss that.

From the dining room, I heard faint voices—Mom's, punctuated by the almost hypnotizing sound of her psychic. Dr. Finkle, with a soothing intonation that could sell our jerseys to opponents, was delivering guidance through the laptop screen. "Greatness is just around the corner," he reassured.

"Greatness is just around the corner," Mom repeated obediently, her voice a reverent echo. I smirked to myself, shaking my head slightly as I tucked away the last of the canned goods. It was hard not to find amusement in the ritualistic way she hung on his every prediction.

"You will feel relief from your worries by the fall," continued Dr. Finkle.

Her faith in his words was unshakeable, and though I may have harbored my doubts, her hope made me smile.

With groceries put away, I leaned against the counter for a moment, allowing my body a second to rest. As their Zoom call ended, I arched an eyebrow as I watched her close the laptop with a satisfied sigh.

"Are you *sure* this isn't some kind of cult, Mom?" I asked, unable to mask my disbelief. She looked up at me, a playful glint in her eyes as she lightly tapped my arm before reaching into a bag of chips.

"It is not a cult, Boston," she took a sip of coffee. "Dr. Finkle knows exactly what he's talking about."

"Sure, Mom," I stretched the words out in gentle skepticism.

I knew she was searching for answers—for help with our family situation. Mom and I were okay, but things hadn't been the same since last summer. When I stopped by her house, I felt the weight of change—a distance between us that never used to be there. My gaze shifted to the living room. I hadn't stepped foot in there since the day she opened up about everything.

* * *

It was my first stop when I got back to town from Bayside. The house had been unsettlingly still—no noise from the television, no movement. Mom sat on the couch alone.

She said tenderly, "Honey, I could tell you were upset when we talked on the phone earlier. I'm so sorry. For everything."

"Mom, please," I urged her, sinking onto the couch across from her. "No more secrets. I need to know everything."

She had looked at me, really looked, and something in her expression shifted, like a dam breaking. The truth was ready to spill out, raw and unfiltered like skeletons locked away in her closet, ready to be released.

"I'm not sure where to begin," she'd started, her voice quiet, as if the

walls themselves might betray her trust. But I could tell she was finally going to lay all the cards on the table.

"Just say it, Mom. All of it."

"There was nothing I could do," she whispered, her gaze holding mine with the fierceness of a mother's love. "Reese's dad was a lawyer, a very successful lawyer."

Her fingers trembled slightly as she brushed a stray lock of hair behind her ear, her eyes lost in a distant memory.

"Mom," I finally said, breaking the silence. "Were you in love with him? With Reese's dad?"

She hesitated and then let out a slow breath, exhaling the weight she had held onto for years. "Maybe," she shrugged. "Or perhaps we were just... caught up in it all. The parties, the Bayside ball, the glamor of those events." She offered a wistful smile, but it didn't quite reach her eyes. "After Reese came into the picture, nothing was the same. We became strangers under the same roof, arguing over everything."

"Couldn't you have left?" I asked, trying my best to understand.

Her smile faded completely. "I wanted to. I told him I wanted to take Reese and move to Stillwater because your aunt was here. But he..." her words faltered as she swallowed hard. "He was ruthless. Said he'd fight me tooth and nail—and he did. He said his child was destined to grow up in Bayside. He was already the most prominent lawyer there, Boston. And now? He's untouchable. What chance did I stand? No money, no influence. He stripped me of all rights—he got full custody. I couldn't stay in Bayside after that, knowing my son was in the same town, but I could never see him. When I got here I was so depressed. I was drinking a lot, I had a summer fling with your father, and then I almost lost you. I knew from that moment on I'd do anything to protect you. I wouldn't have survived losing you, too."

I absorbed her words, a surge of protective anger building towards the man who'd caused her so much pain. She rarely ever discussed my father, but according to my mom, after she gave birth to me early at 30 weeks, the doctors thought I wouldn't make it. My father came to see me in the NICU at first, but then he stopped coming altogether. She always said his heart couldn't handle seeing me in such a fragile state, thinking I wouldn't make it. And then he left town. To this day, I don't think he knows I lived. My mother always called me her miracle baby.

"Why didn't you tell me?"

For a moment there was only the sound of her shaky inhale. "I just wanted to protect you from it all." Her hands clasped together tightly, knuckles white. "I was embarrassed and didn't want anyone to know I'd lost custody. I feel like a failure. I am a failure."

Pieces of a puzzle I hadn't even known were missing suddenly clicked into place, reshaping the landscape of my life. Everything would be different now.

"You're not a failure." My eyes searched hers for something, anything, that might help me understand. "But you should have told me."

"Everything I did... Boston, it was never meant to hurt anyone," she said, her voice laced with emotion so raw I thought she might cry. Her gaze held mine, pleading silently for me to understand.

"I'm sorry for keeping it from you," she added, her lips quivering. "Believe me, I thought about it every day."

For years, she had carried the burden alone, and I could see now the toll it had taken on her.

"Mom," I started again, my heart clenching at the sight of her distress. I wanted to be angry, to let the betrayal wash over me, but as I sat there watching her crumble under the weight of her own secrets, all I could feel was a deep, aching sympathy.

"I wish you didn't have to deal with that on your own," I said softly, closing the space between us. I reached for her hand, and squeezed gently. "But I get it. You did what you thought was best."

She looked up at me then, her blue eyes swimming with unshed tears, and in that moment I saw not just my mother, but someone who had battled demons I was only just beginning to comprehend.

"Thank you," she whispered, her hand squeezing back, conveying a lifetime of love and sacrifice in a single, fragile embrace.

* * *

Standing in the house, now, with the ghost of that conversation lingering between us, I couldn't help but feel a wave of grief for the simplicity of our past. For a time when my biggest worry was what was for dinner, not this tangled web of secrets.

My mom's arms wrapped around my frame, pulling me back from the edge of my thoughts. "Thank you for taking care of me, hunny," she squeezed even tighter. "I love you."

"Love you too," I replied, the weight of our shared struggles momentarily lifting in her embrace. "But I've got to get going. I need to shower and head out for another training session soon."

"Okay, but you better let yourself rest," she said gently, but there was a twinkle in her eye. "Ruth next door said your muscles are getting a little too big. She asked if you're training for one of those Magic Mike things."

That coaxed an involuntary chuckle out of me, a brief pause from the heaviness in my chest. "I told her yes, just to see her reaction," she confessed with a grin. "You should've seen it, Boston—I swear she almost dropped her watering can."

"Goodbye, Mom," I said, giving her an eye roll. "And quit messing with that poor woman."

Stepping outside, I closed the front door behind me with a soft click, sealing away the sanctuary of my childhood home. A deep breath filled my lungs, the outside air refreshing even though it was warm.

I lingered on the threshold for a moment longer. Being near my mom was still hard for me. It was a task to keep it all together for her when every cell in my body felt broken.

With a final exhale, I released some of that burden into the breeze and sat in one of her porch rocking chairs. I traced a crack in the white wood. The world outside felt distant, like I was peering into it from some strange dream as my thoughts drifted.

* * *

The sharp thud of knuckles against wood jolted me awake.

In an instant, I stumbled to the door half asleep, and yanked it open. It was her, Chandler Hartford, the moonlight creating a spotlight just for her. Her hazel eyes were wide with concern.

"Chandler," I managed to say, feeling suddenly conscious that I wasn't wearing a shirt, gray sweatpants hanging from my hips.

She had barely acknowledged my disheveled state, her brows furrowed as she launched into her rant. "Why is no one texting me back? Parker dropped me off and promised to keep me updated, but nothing. And you— you haven't answered your phone at all."

Her words tumbled out in a torrent, each sentence filled with frustration. "Your coach dropped that bomb on us this morning, and I couldn't even think straight the whole drive back. Why is no one else flipping out right now? I'm flipped out!"

I watched as she paced before me, hands flying expressively as she spoke. The rise and fall of her voice, the slight quiver of anger mixed with worry, twisted my heart. But my thoughts were shackled by Reese. He was unraveling my life; his presence in hers wasn't something I could ever get on board with.

So I did what I had learned to do best—I hid my emotions, locking away the warmth of wanting to reach out to her. I kept calm, my stance rigid as I rested an arm on the doorway and let her finish. It took everything within me not to pull her into my arms, to tell her everything would be alright, even though my own world was shattered.

"Chandler, it's late," I finally said, my voice low and steady. "I don't want to talk about it—not to you, not to anyone. I just want to be left alone."

It was a lie, at least in part. I craved her presence, I wanted her there, but lines had been drawn in the sand, and she was on the side with him. And even if she wasn't, I couldn't pull her into my fucked up situation. There was nothing good I could offer her. She was too good for me, and definitely too good for him.

Her lips parted, ready to protest, but she paused, biting down on her lower lip—a habit I knew all too well. "Boston," she whispered, walking up the steps and inching closer. Her voice trembled slightly. "I want to be here for you. We can talk, I can sit with you—just let me be here."

I looked down at her and she looked up at me, our height difference pronounced. My hand came up instinctively, fingers gently brushing her cheek. The contact, a touch connecting us in the quiet night, sent an ache through me. My thumb traced her softness, lingering on her cheekbone.

"It's not your problem," I whispered, trying my best to push her away. "Why don't you check on... him? He needs you more than I do."

Her eyes locked with mine as if searching for something, Maybe the truth, buried beneath. But I couldn't give it to her. There was nothing for me to give.

"Please, Boston," she urged softly, her voice more tender. I stepped back and the night air swept in, filling the space where our bodies had almost met. "Go home, Chandler," I said, my voice steady despite the fucking dumpster fire burning inside me.

And I turned away, leaving her standing in the darkness. My chest tightened with the effort of pretending I hadn't just shut the door on her, on my entire world.

chandler

KRISTINA and I sat across from each other at our small kitchen table, stuffing our faces full of twirled forkfuls of spaghetti. I had just taken a bite when my phone started to vibrate on the table.

With a mouthful of pasta threatening to spill from my lips, I clumsily swiped at the screen, answering the call. "Hey, Mo—"

The moment the video call connected, I knew something was off. She wore the same face she used to tell me I was grounded and not happy with me. My heart sank a little at the sight.

"Chandler? How is everything?" she asked weakly.

I quickly swallowed my mouthful of noodles, feeling them slide down somewhat awkwardly. "Yeah, all good here," I replied, trying to keep my voice even. "Kristina made spaghetti." I gestured with my fork to the dish in front of me, hoping maybe I was reading her facial expression wrong.

"That's good, honey," she said. Her thoughts seemed elsewhere, though. The lack of enthusiasm was unlike her, and I felt a knot forming in my stomach.

"Mom?" I pressed, leaning forward slightly. "What's up?"

"I have some bad news," her voice was gentle, but the gravity in her tone made my heart drop into my stomach. "Your dad was laid off, unfortunately."

"Oh, no. Is he okay?" I asked.

She gave a small, reassuring nod. "You know we've been here before, sweetheart. He's trying to stay busy." She paused and gave me another unhappy look before continuing. "He called a friend and there's a construction job he can help with for the summer. In Texas. We're hoping he can do this big project and it'll give him some time to find another job back in Stillwater."

The spaghetti on my plate suddenly seemed like an insurmountable mountain I couldn't climb. The fork clattered softly against the plate as I set it down, my appetite vanishing into thin air. "That sucks, Mom," I mumbled through my fingers. "I hate that he'll have to be away for the whole summer."

"That's the thing, Chandler..." her voice trailed off for a moment, while I braced for the additional blow. "I'm going to go with him. I don't need to be back to start planning lessons and setting up for the school year until August."

I remembered summers when I was younger, how I'd once envied my mom's long breaks from work. I loved the freedom she had when we were out of school.

"Wait," I blurted out, the news sinking in. "What about our plans?"

"There will be plenty of time for that in the future, honey. With everything that's happening, I think it would be a good idea for you to get a summer job. Just in case we're unable to help with school next year. Luckily your brother has the scholarship, so he'll be okay."

The thought of spending my summer cashiering or pouring coffee wasn't what I had planned, but I also didn't want them to stress about finding a way to continue helping me.

"Okay, Mom." I nodded, still feeling disappointed. "Well, give Dad a hug for me."

"Of course, sweetie." She managed a brave smile. "I will. And don't worry, I'll keep you updated."

"Love you, Mom."

"Love you too, Chandler."

I stood up, feeling defeated as I scraped the now unappetizing mound of spaghetti into the trash with a dull splat.

"Can you believe that?" I sighed, placing my plate in the dishwasher.

"No, that sucks," Kristina said, tapping her fingernails on the table. "But I do seem to remember you telling me someone in Bayside offered you a job."

I let out a long sigh. Even though that was the last thing I wanted to hear right now, she was right. Could I really do that, though? Go back to Bayside? Into the heart of Blue Devils' territory.

"And I seem to remember Papi Likes Butts asking you for feet pics. Maybe we could profit off those," I said sarcastically.

"Now that's an idea I can get behind," she said, rubbing her chin. "But you should probably still get a job while I'm waiting for that compensation."

I swallowed hard as my mind raced. Could I really take a job in Bayside? That small town was more than just a place—it was a reminder of painful memories and secrets I wanted no part of. Could I keep my heart guarded when it had already been so recklessly exposed?

And Boston and Reese... how could I be around them? I'd be forced to hang around the two guys I wanted most to avoid.

"Kristina," I murmured, her name slipping out like a call for help. "I don't know if I can survive another summer in Bayside with... with them. Both of them."

She raised an eyebrow, her stern expression devoid of empathy. "You're not going to just survive the summer. You're going to face it head on," she urged. "You need to get closure with Reese. And you should mend things with Boston. He came to your birthday, that has to mean something. You can't spend your life running from things."

I swallowed hard. "But what if they don't want me around?" The vulnerability in my own voice caught me by surprise.

"Who cares?" Kristina's retort was swift, shoving away my doubts. "You're there for a job, remember? A good friend offered you this opportunity, and you're taking it. Don't fixate on anyone else— or how they feel about it."

Maybe it was possible to face both Reese and Boston, to sort through the tangled web of emotions that bound us all.

"I can get through this," I whispered under my breath, trying to convince myself. "I'll just focus on work." But even as I said it, I knew it would take every ounce of strength not to feel anything when I got around them. I let out another sigh and sent a text message I never expected to send.

ME

so how much does the job pay?

WILLOW

SCREAMING! If I lie and say you have
experience they'll start you at a decent rate.

ME

Get that spare bedroom ready

Guess I'm in

WILLOW

YAY! I'm so excited. This summer is going to
be epic, Channy!

I wasn't sure "epic" was how I'd describe it. But Kristina was right, I could make this summer about reclaiming the pieces of myself I'd lost last summer. Willow could be my sunshine in the Bayside darkness—a lifeline to cling to when things were hard. I wouldn't be there for Boston or Reese, or any man for that matter. I would be there for myself and for Willow.

I glanced at my reflection in the mirror, searching for any sign of the fortitude I'd need to navigate this summer. Boston's shining blue eyes came to mind. They mirrored the ocean on a summer day, always so full of warmth, something I wasn't sure he still had. And then Reese, with his hypnotizing green eyes that seemed to know too much, always challenging me. Others had warned me about him for a reason.

Fuck my life. I really was going to do this. Going back to Bayside, into Blue Devils' turf, and hoping I'd find some strength to get me through. Maybe, just maybe, everything did happen for a reason and the unexpected detour could lead to something good. It could be a redemption, a summer that I could be proud of, one where I discovered myself—and I held the power not to let anyone distract me.

I thought back, lost in the reflection of how broken I felt back then. We'd been on the road back to Stillwater after leaving Bayside. I'd opened up to Parker about everything. Back then, my heart had been shattered, the fragments still raw from the abrupt ending of a summer romance.

* * *

I stared out the passenger window, tracing the raindrops with my eyes as they raced one another down the glass. My thoughts were a tangled mess —between Boston and Reese, and now this bombshell of a secret that had detonated everything I thought I knew about both of them.

The silence in the car was overwhelming. We were still in shock—both trying to look back at all the signs we'd missed over the years from the boy next door, and his mother who we thought we'd known so well.

"You doing okay?" Parker's voice finally interrupted the quiet. "You've been staring out of that window since we left. Talk to me."

I turned my head slightly, meeting his concerned eyes before they shifted back to the road. How could I explain the hurt in my heart, the confusion? Words seemed inadequate, but the weight of them needed a release.

"Everything's just... a mess, Parker." My voice broke as the tears started to blur my vision.

He reached over, resting his hand briefly on mine before returning it to the wheel. The gesture was simple but overwhelming. Like when you're sad and someone hugs you, which sometimes opens the floodgate of tears you were trying to hold back.

The reality of the situation was beginning to settle in. Parker and I were still reeling from the revelation that Boston's mom had kept Reese, her other son, a secret all these years. The magnitude of it had us both feeling like we were in some kind of parallel universe—even Parker's usual jokes were blunted.

"Can you believe she kept that secret all these years?" I whispered, the question rhetorical, voicing the shared shock that had rendered us speechless.

Parker shook his head, his jaw tight. "No, I can't. It's... it's insane."

As he drove, taking us further away from a town filled with memories and secrets, a sob escaped me. I had tried to hold it in, to remain composed, but I couldn't do it any longer. Tears streamed down my cheeks.

Parker spared a glance, worry creasing his brow. "Chandler, are you...?" His voice trailed off, understanding that I was crying without needing to finish the question.

"Everything's just so overwhelming," I managed, my voice a whisper between sobs. Parker didn't say anything, but the car slowed down as he gazed at me, switching out of the fast lane as the rain continued its relentless drumming.

"Take your time," he murmured, giving me the space to let out the hurt and confusion Reese and Boston had unwittingly caused.

At that moment, Parker wasn't just my brother, he was the shoulder I needed to cry on. I shook my head, pressing my fingers to my temples as if I could physically hold back the suffocating emotions. "It's just, everything." I exhaled a shaky breath. "I should have listened when everyone warned me about Reese. They were right. He hurt me—just ended things, like it wasn't even a big deal to him."

Parker's expression softened and he looked back at the road, as if he couldn't stand to watch my heart break all over again. "Chan..."

"And you know what's crazy?" I continued, a bitter laugh escaping me. "All along, I've had this thing for Boston. Since I was five years old." There, I said it—the secret I'd clung to for so many years.

Parker's mouth fell open in genuine surprise. "You did?"

"Did you seriously not know?" I asked.

"No, I... I just thought you were always trying to follow us around because you wanted to be around your badass older brother," he said, attempting to inject a little humor into his voice.

"Parker, love you, but no." I rolled my eyes, leaning back against the seat, fatigued from the emotional rollercoaster of the day. I felt raw and exposed, but there was a certain relief in finally telling him the truth.

He shook his head. "I knew something strange was going on between the three of you at the ball."

"Look," I blurted out, turning towards Parker. "This summer it felt like for the first time there was a chance, you know? To see if there might be something real between us. But I really liked Reese, and... and now I don't even have him. It's just all so messed up, especially now that we know they're brothers."

"First off..." he started, hesitating as if he was going to tell me something I didn't want to hear. "I'd really prefer if you didn't date my teammates. There are plenty of other guys out there. Football players—actually, forget I said that. Your drama club friends, that nerdy school president kid... anyone else."

He paused, taking a deep breath, and when he spoke again, his voice was lower and filled with a sincerity I rarely heard from him. "And secondly, it would probably freak me out if you dated Boston. He's been my best friend, like, my whole life. So maybe it's a good thing nothing happened there."

The silence was interrupted only by the rain pattering against the car. Then, in an even softer tone that I barely recognized as his, he added, "But last, and most importantly, you deserve the world, Chan. Nothing less. Don't ever let any guy make you cry, and don't ever let them make you feel like you aren't good enough. Okay?"

I swallowed hard, moved by the protective warmth radiating off him. For a moment, we shared a look, a silent understanding passing between us. Then, a subtle half-smile appeared on his face. "Besides, if I'd known Reese was ending things like that, I would've kicked his ass."

His attempt to lighten the mood worked. A small laugh escaped me, and I shook my head, the tension easing ever so slightly. "Thanks, Parker." I smiled, feeling a small fraction better as we continued our drive.

Raindrops continued to fall across the windows like tiny, fleeting tears, the sound a soothing backdrop to the unexpected moment we'd just had. I glanced over at Parker who was now smirking, clearly pleased with coaxing a smile out of me.

"Okay, okay," I admitted. "You know, you're not the worst brother in the world."

His smirk widened into a full grin, and he shot me a sideways glance, one eyebrow raised. "Not the worst? Thanks for the glowing review."

I rolled my eyes, but couldn't suppress another smile. "Well, you're certainly not the best brother either. But definitely not the worst... Oh, and Park? I think I need to try to speak to Boston tonight."

"Why?" he asked.

"Because," I hesitated, choosing my words carefully, "I just need him to know that I'm here for him if he needs me." There was more to it than that —unspoken feelings, regret, and unacknowledged moments—but this was neither the time nor the place.

Parker exhaled slowly. His hands were relaxed on the steering wheel now. "Okay," he said finally, "just don't be surprised if he needs space. I know that you've known him as long as I have. I get it, but he probably won't be in a great headspace."

"I know," I whispered. "But I won't sleep tonight if I don't at least try."

After everything, after spending the summer with the one person who could cut him deepest, I couldn't blame him for not wanting to speak to me.

The rest of the drive was lighter as I acknowledged the odd comfort of having Parker by my side. The car hummed along, tires splashing through puddles as we settled into silence that didn't need to be filled.

* * *

It was time to face my dilemma head-on. My fingers trembled slightly as I picked up my phone again and sent a message to Boston, so frustratingly distant lately. It was his team, but I had a right to be there too, damnit.

ME

Boston Riley, I know you're seeing my text messages. We need to talk. Coming by your place tomorrow.

The next day, I pulled up to Parker and Boston's place, my heart drumming an anxious beat against my chest. I'd rehearsed the speech replaying in my mind all night. The words had to be just right —firm yet nonconfrontational. He needed to understand where I stood.

I gathered my courage, stepped out of the car, and approached their front door. But before my knuckles could tap against the wood, the door swung open. Parker's face greeted me, his brow arching mischievously.

"Whatever you're selling, we don't want it," he quipped.

"Very fun–," I started to say, but he shut the door, leaving me standing there. A bit deflated, I crossed my arms, contemplating whether to knock again or turn around and leave. But then the door reopened.

This time it was a girl I recognized from my party. She looked displeased and her hair was a mess. "I've been trying to tell him his jokes aren't funny," she sighed, casting a pointed look at Parker, who only smirked in response. She gave me a tight smile before nudging him gently. "Let's go, I'm hungry."

They brushed past me, and Parker paused, his humor subsiding into genuine concern. "What do you need, Chan?" he asked, dropping his usual antics for a moment.

"Oh, nothing," I lied, my voice nonchalant. "Just stopped by to say a few words to Boston."

Parker studied me for a heartbeat longer, clearly curious about what I might have to say. "Are you okay? Need me to stay?"

"No, I'll be quick," I responded.

He nodded toward the living room. "He's all yours," he said, stepping outside.

As I closed the door behind them and ventured further in, I found Boston sitting at the kitchen island, a bowl of cereal almost to his lips. His surprised gaze locked onto mine.

"Hey," I began, forcing my feet to carry me closer despite the butterflies fluttering in my stomach. He set down his bowl and waited. For a moment neither of us spoke, the silence stretched between us.

"Look, I need to say a few things," I started, then hesitated. This was Boston, after all. No matter what he was going through, he was still the boy who'd grown up next door, who had the kindest heart. And here I was, finally alone with him for the first time in what felt like an eternity.

"Go ahead," he encouraged, his voice gentle but wary. He stayed seated but there was tension in his shoulders, a readiness for whatever I might unleash upon him. I took a deep breath, ready to release my rant.

"I get that you're going through something, Boston, I do." My words came out in a rush. "But, unfortunately, I happen to be in need of a summer job." I clasped my hands together, fighting to keep them steady.

"Willow offered me one on the Blue Devils' committee," I continued, trying to read his reaction, but he didn't show a single emotion. "And I'm taking it." I swallowed, pushing on despite the tightness in my throat. "I appreciate that it's your team, and you obviously don't want me around."

I could see the tension in his jaw, but his eyes, those bright blues that I'd looked into for years—remained unreadable. There was so much history between us, so many unspoken words hanging heavily in the room.

"There are a number of reasons this isn't ideal," I admitted, feeling a knot forming in my stomach. "But it's not about that. Trust me, I don't want any drama this summer." I paused, waiting to see if he would interject, but he didn't.

"I am staying away from boys, especially those in a blue jersey." My voice faltered just a bit as memories threatened to surface. I shook them off with a deep breath. "I just didn't want you to be surprised when you see me there." My gaze locked with his, daring him to challenge my decision. "I'll be there to do my thing, and you should do yours."

With my rant over, relief washed over me, even though my heart still hammered in my chest.

Unexpectedly, a trace of a smile flickered across Boston's lips—a rarity as of late. It caught me off guard, and my defenses momentarily wavered.

"Wait, what do you mean, 'those in a blue jersey'? So you'd be with a guy in another color?" He gave me a teasing look before picking up the bowl again. "I hope it's not red—the Titans. Those guys are the worst."

I blinked, taken aback. Then I shot a deadly glare at him. "That's your response to what I just said?" My voice was laced with disbelief. Without waiting for an answer, I pivoted on my heel, ready to walk out.

"Wait a sec," Boston said, a casual lilt in his tone that didn't match the intensity of his gaze.

I paused as he reached out and grabbed my hand, pulling gently. The warmth of his touch sent an unexpected jolt through me. In one fluid motion, he spread his legs slightly in his too-familiar gray sweatpants and drew me into the space between them. The close proximity felt dangerously intimate, like playing with fire. There was power in his touch, strength in his thighs pressing against me. Our bodies were so close I could smell his cologne, feel every beat of his heart, every rise and fall of his chest as our breaths mingled in the silence of the room.

He tilted his head, and met my gaze with such intensity that it rendered me momentarily speechless. "I'm glad you'll be in Bayside," he began, his voice low and genuine, each word carefully measured, as if he knew the effect they would have. "Not just because I'm glad there'll be someone else around to keep Parker in check... but because it's you."

His words lingered. The weight of what he'd said rooted me in place for a moment—longer than I intended. Those words were like honey, sweet and slow, tempting me to believe I could break through the wall he had up.

"Sure, Boston. You've just been avoiding me all year." The response came out breathier than I intended, betraying the flutter in my chest. With reluctance, I withdrew from his grasp, feeling the loss of his warmth as our fingers slid apart. "I'll see you in Bayside."

I tossed the words over my shoulder and didn't look back. I felt the weight of his gaze on me, heavy with things unsaid. Once outside, I inhaled deeply, air filling my lungs and chasing away the heat of his proximity.

My heart sank as the weight of the situation settled in. From that brief interaction it was clear this summer was going to be more difficult than I thought. They say you never forget your childhood crush, and mine was etched deep into my bones. But I could handle it. This would be a chance to find closure and maybe even happiness. At the very least, I hoped to emerge stronger and embrace whatever the future held for me.

boston

THE DOOR swung open and Parker appeared in nothing but a towel slung repulsively low on his hips. "What time are you leaving?" he asked.

"A couple of hours," I answered, despite my reluctance to commit to even that small certainty.

His gaze drifted to my open and empty suitcase lying on the bed. "Sure about that?" he questioned. "You're not backing out on me, are you?"

"Nah, I'll get it done." I replied, pushing myself up from the chair.

"Alright." He nodded before continuing. "I need to get away from the women in this town. Last night, the girl I hooked up with told me she likes it rough and I thought, okay, sign me up," he said, a half-hearted chuckle escaping his lips. "But at one point, I think I begged for my life." He rolled his shoulder in a slow rotation. "She almost broke my arm."

"Jesus, Parker..." I exhaled, trying to get that image out of my head. "Where do you find these women?"

"Obviously the wrong places," he chuckled. "Maybe I'll find better options in Bayside."

"Let me know how that goes," I teased.

"You know I will," he said with a small smile as he shut the door with a soft click.

I turned back to face the open suitcase. It was like staring into a void, one that mirrored the unease twisting in my gut. The question wasn't whether I could pack the bag—it was whether I could handle another summer at the lake.

The thought of being around Reese again tightened a knot in my chest. And Chandler—she was a different story altogether. A chapter I wasn't sure I was ready to revisit.

But none of that mattered, not really. I was going for one reason, and one reason alone: baseball. It was my future, my ticket out of here, and the one constant that never failed me. On the field, every-thing else fell away—the cheers, the bullshit, the weight of expecta-tion. It was just the game.

"Focus on that," I whispered to myself, dragging the suitcase closer. "On the drills, on practice." That was how I'd tune everything else out, how I'd survive the summer. How I'd escape this dark place that clung to me like a shadow.

I grabbed a handful of clothes and began to pack. Each item placed in my suitcase was a silent vow to keep my head in the game. Because baseball wasn't just a sport—it was my lifeline.

And I was determined to hold on.

A few hours later, gravel crunched under my truck tires as I pulled up to my grandpa's cabin. Numbness had become a constant lately; it was there during every moment of the day. But stepping out into the fresh air was almost comforting for a moment.

The cabin was a reminder of good days, of the best summers, of so much laughter. Its wooden walls still held the smell of my grand-pa's famous barbecue drifting in the breeze. I stared out at the land-scape, letting the sunlight glimmering off the water wash over me. I breathed in the scent of pine and earth, threading through the emptiness inside me. Here we fucking go. A new summer.

I turned to see Parker in the driveway, grinning from ear to ear as he unloaded his bags.

"Hey, man," Parker yelled on his way inside. "You wanna run down to the Blue Devils' clubhouse with me? Check out our trophies on the wall this year?"

"Sure," I shrugged. "Bet they've already got our names on the lockers, too."

"Fuck yeah," he chuckled, clapping me on the shoulder as we headed toward the car. "No one should be there today. It'll be badass seeing the place again."

The clubhouse loomed into view, commanding as ever, surrounded by the freshly manicured field. "Here we are," I sighed.

"Time to get in the Blue Devil spirit," Parker added, his eyes lighting up like a kid's on Christmas morning.

The air was thick with the scent of freshly cut grass as we approached. The facility looked just as glorious as I remembered, unaltered by the last year—walls probably had a fresh coat of paint. We stepped inside, the echo of our footsteps filling the hallway leading to the trophy wall.

"Look at that," Parker whispered in awe, nodding towards the gleaming trophies. Our names were etched alongside legends, a physical representation of hard-earned glory. We shared a look, a silent acknowledgement between us. It was badass—there was no other word for it.

Energized by the sight, we made our way to the locker room, the door swinging open to reveal the space that kick-started the summer and made it feel real. There they were—our lockers, with nameplates gleaming under the harsh fluorescent lights.

 Our new jerseys hung neatly inside, the fabric crisp and untouched.

"Man, they've outdone themselves," Parker remarked, running a hand over his jersey. "Badass doesn't even begin to cover it."

Before I could respond, a familiar voice echoed off the tiled walls. "Look who it is. The dynamic duo is back."

I spun around at the sudden intrusion. The excitement that had filled the room moments before shifted with the presence of someone I hadn't expected to encounter—not yet, at least.

Parker and I turned in unison. Two figures leaned casually against the doorframe, Reese with Bailey just beside him. He wore a smirk and his voice lacked any edge—it was almost welcoming, which defused some of my dread.

"Bailey," Parker greeted, stepping forward with a nod and fist bumping him. Then, shifting his attention, Parker moved toward Reese, and for a fraction of a second Reese extended his arm to shake with him. But before their hands could clasp, Parker's fist shot out, connecting solidly with Reese's manhood.

"That's for breaking my sister's heart," Parker said with a satisfied smirk.

Reese crouched down, trying to hold himself up with one hand on his knee. "Good to see you too, man," he managed to say though pained words edged with humor and understanding.

Parker, satisfied with the delivery, clapped a hand on Reese's back, a sign that the hit was more brotherly discipline than enemy fire. Bailey and I exchanged an amused glance, the corner of his mouth twitching upwards as we both tried—and failed—to stifle our laughter at Reese trying to regain his composure.

"Nice," I quipped to Parker, offering Bailey a more sedate handshake. We all knew this summer was going to be interesting, and I wasn't mad at how it had just started.

I was still slightly entertained as Reese straightened, trying to fight a grimace. The memory of my last conversation with him after the season ended came to mind, erasing all humor.

* * *

I had to make a stop before I left Bayside, even though it was the last place I wanted to go. I needed to clear my head, to get this shit out in the open before my thoughts consumed me.

"Okay, Boston, just say what you need to say. Get it over with," I

coached myself. But it wasn't just about saying it—it was about finally making a change.

I strode purposefully towards Reese Carrington's over-the-top house, a structure that seemed as impenetrable as the man himself.

"Reese!" I called out, voice slicing through the quiet morning while I stood at his door, banging defiantly. "Get out here. We need to talk!"

There was a momentary pause, then the front door swung open, revealing him in the bright sunlight. His expression was unreadable, but I sensed his annoyance from where I was standing.

"Hang on a sec," his voice held an edge, a hint of irritation, or perhaps resignation. He grabbed a gray hoodie draped over a hall chair, pulled it over his head in a fluid motion, then stepped outside.

I walked back to my truck and hopped onto the tailgate with an air of casualness I didn't feel. My fingers drummed on the cool metal as I waited for him. Reese walked toward me, hood up, hands buried in his pockets.

"Alright, Riley. What's so important that you're showing up at my house?" He leaned against the side of my truck, arms crossed, looking unfazed.

"We need to talk," I said simply. His eyes narrowed slightly, a flicker of curiosity breaking through his guarded demeanor. I needed this, needed to clear the air, though my mind was racing with doubts. Could anything even be done at this point?

"Talk then," Reese prompted, his voice softer now, the façade of indifference faltering as he waited for me to continue.

"I need to know," I started, voice low. "Why'd you keep silent all these years about our mom? About everything?"

He shifted, looking away into the distance. "Who wants to talk about that shit?" he said. "It's fucked up. It's not something I ever want to talk about. She walked out, she left. What do you want me to say?"

I watched him closely, saw his jaw clench, the way he shifted uncomfortably.

"Look, I called her," I confessed, my hands tightening on the cold metal. "She told me she'd be there, waiting to talk when I got home."

"And?" His head snapped up, eyes piercing mine. "I could care less what she has to say about it."

I pushed on, urgency rising. "And I need you to know that I never knew, Reese. I never had any idea. But there's gotta be a reason, right? I know you don't know her, but Mom—she wouldn't just leave a child behind without one hell of a good reason."

The air hung heavy between us as I searched his face for something, anything that might signal understanding. Despite the wind, sweat gathered at the back of my neck from the anticipation of this conversation.

"Didn't take you for the naïve type," he said, finally breaking the silence. His response lacked its usual bite. His gaze dropped to the ground. "But you find out the information you need... let me know how that goes."

"I do need to know the whole story," I echoed with determination. This felt like it was more than just a conversation, it was a small olive branch, tentative and unsteady, but a connection nonetheless.

Reese leaned back against the side of my truck, his hands still tucked into his hoodie, and I could see the tension in his shoulders as if bracing for a blow.

"Look," he began, his voice sounding softer then, "I know you didn't know the truth." He exhaled slowly, "And I've been an asshole for holding it against you when it's not your fault."

I blinked, surprised by the apology that seemed so foreign coming from Reese. I didn't think he was capable of an apology. His admission hung between us like a fragile truce.

"Thank you." My voice faltered, emotions clogging my throat. Years of stress and animosity seemed to dissolve in that confession, even if it was only for a moment.

He nodded, a half-smirk appearing for a fleeting second. "It's a shitty situation," he continued, shifting again. "But it's not an excuse for how I've treated you."

"Or Chandler," I interjected, steeling myself for his reaction. Reese's eyes narrowed slightly at her name, but he didn't interrupt. "I know you were trying to use her to get to me. She doesn't deserve to be involved in any of this."

The silence stretched on as he digested my words. "Yeah..." his voice trailed off, and then he sighed, nodding once. "You're right. She's got nothing to do with our shit, I know that. But, just so you know, I care about her. It may have started out as something else, but it's not like that now."

His eyes softened for a moment, reflecting a sincerity that was rare and a little disarming. Then our gazes locked, and for the first time in what felt like forever, there was an unspoken agreement between us. It was clear that we both cared about Chandler, and it was a touchy subject. We both needed to tread lightly.

"I know what you mean," I added. "I've loved her since we were kids."

For a second, it seemed like he had stopped breathing. His eyes searched mine, probing for the truth in my words. "Loved her?" Reese echoed with an edge of something like surprise.

"Yeah," I shrugged. "I always hoped she'd be the one. Someday." But hope was a dangerous thing, a flame that could either warm you up or burn you to the ground. And the truth was, Chandler was with him. That thought alone was enough to bring me to my knees, the pain of knowing that dream was scorched was unbearable, but my resolve was pushing me through.

It was clear that my confession had hit a nerve, stirring something within him. He stood up straight and let out a long sigh, heavy with something I couldn't quite figure out—regret, maybe. "Damn," he shook his head. "I knew you liked her, but I didn't know it was like that."

I shrugged like it didn't matter, keeping the storm inside from showing. How could he possibly get it—what Chandler meant to me? No chance.

"Look, Riley," he paused. "I'm not going to be in your way anymore. She's... she's a great girl. She deserves someone like you."

There was raw honesty there, but I could see the internal struggle on his face, the weight of his decision pressing down on him.

"Honestly, it might've been possible for us to get there. I like her a lot," Reese confessed, a flicker of wistfulness passing through his eyes. "But I'm not where you are. Plus, I'd be selfish to put her through the long-distance thing in college."

I sat there listening, processing. It was clear he actually liked her, and even though he was throwing out other reasons for stepping aside, I knew the truth—it was me. Maybe, after all these years, he had a conscience. He'd been a shitty person, but maybe this was the line he didn't want to cross.

"I don't need you to do any of that. It's her decision." *My thoughts were a whirlwind, but one thing was clear—I had my own demons to battle, my own shit to figure out.* "And I've got other shit on my plate I need to deal with."

His shoulders relaxed slightly, then, as if I had taken some of the burden from him. But the look in his eyes told me everything I needed to know: this wasn't just about stepping aside. It was about making amends, in whatever way he could.

"I wouldn't be doing it for you," *Reese said.* "She deserves better than me."

"She deserves better than both of us," *I added quietly, my thoughts flickering to Chandler's bright hazel eyes that held stories of their own— stories I could read over and over again.*

"One last thing... Why now? Why did you decide to tell me at the ball after all these years?"

He looked down, scratching the back of his head. "I was tired of being her secret," *he finally admitted.* "I didn't want to be that anymore."

I sighed, sort of understanding. "I'm sorry you had to carry that alone."

"Well, anyway, you know where I live if you need me after your talk," *Reese said, and for a moment his eyes softened, reflecting a rare glimmer of hope.* "And I guess you aren't that bad of a ball player either."

"Yeah, yeah," *I agreed, pushing off from my tailgate before making my way to the driver's side.* "I'll see you around."

* * *

"Alright," Reese grunted, pulling me out of the memory. He

straightened his shirt as if realigning his scattered dignity. "Guess I deserved that one."

After taking a moment to regain his composure, he glanced at me, nodding. "Boston." His tone was nonchalant, but I could tell he was cautiously navigating this conversation.

"Reese," I acknowledged him with a nod.

It was a brief exchange but it spoke volumes. The rivalry that had defined our relationship seemed trivial now, overshadowed by this new, uncharted territory we found ourselves in. No longer enemies, not friends—not ready to say what we really were.

"Right," Reese finally said, breaking our silent communication. He ran a hand through his dark hair, and adjusted himself—almost as if he was checking to make sure all parts were still there.

"Guess we've got some work to do if we're gonna win that championship this year, huh?" he added, a half-smile playing on his lips.

"Yeah," I breathed out, the word barely audible. "Guess we do."

Our shared uncertainty was obvious, a bridge still yet to be crossed. But for the moment, we could be in the same room, silently acknowledging the complicated ties neither of us asked for but that nevertheless unexpectedly connected us.

chandler

I BELTED out a song on my Taylor Swift playlist with the carelessness that only solo car concerts could inspire. I danced in the driver's seat, the steering wheel my only witness to the horrendous performance, thank goodness. I glanced in the rearview mirror, catching a glimpse of the clothes and boxes obscuring my view. It was clear I'd packed every single thing I owned. If I hadn't, I would still be standing in my room, trying to decide what to bring with me.

I sang louder, tapping the steering wheel in time with the beat, doing my best to fight away the anxiety of returning to Bayside. My phone interrupted the music, blaring through the speakers. The screen flashed "Willow" in bold letters. Willow rarely called without good reason.

"Hey, Will," I answered, pressing the answer button on the dash.

"Channy! How far out are you?" Willow asked, her voice a mix of excitement and urgency.

"About thirty minutes away. Why? What's up?"

"Okay, listen, I need you to come straight to the Blue Devils' clubhouse."

I almost pulled the car over. "What? I can't. I'm wearing no makeup, and my hair is..." I reached up to feel the messy bun on my head, suddenly self-conscious.

"No one cares about your crazy hair right now. No one but the staff is here. But Caroline is losing it. She's president of the committee this year, and someone just bailed. With the welcome event for the team and their families tomorrow, we're gonna be chained to decoration duty all night."

I sighed. "Alright, I'm on my way." I could already hear the commotion of preparations in the background.

"Thank you! You're the best. See you soon!"

The line went dead, and the song resumed. I turned down the music and focused on the road ahead, the landscape zipping by as I made my way to a place I wasn't quite ready to see again. The Blue Devils' clubhouse.

"Alright," I reluctantly conceded to the empty car, a frown tugging at my lips as I caught my reflection in the rearview mirror. The girl staring back was not the same girl as last summer. I veered off the main road, steering towards the clubhouse, my heart beginning an erratic dance.

I pulled into the gravel lot and the sight of the familiar facility sent unexpected sadness through me. I parked and switched off the ignition, allowing the silence to envelop me. It wasn't just the building that flooded my mind with memories—it was him. Reese Carrington. His image was etched into every corner of this place. My first glimpse of those piercing green eyes had been in that building, setting the course for the rest of the summer.

I let out a shaky breath, thinking about the way my heart had leapt in his presence. After things ended, Reese's attempts at communication had been sporadic—a few texts here and there. It seemed like he just sent them because he felt bad for breaking up with me and wanted to maintain some form of contact so I wouldn't think he was a dick. I kept my distance.

I would often wonder about him—if his voice still sounded the same, if he still smelled as good as he did when I pressed my head against his chest. But nostalgia was a bitch, one I needed to close the door on—actually, slam the door on. That was in the past and it was staying there.

"Stay strong," I whispered to my reflection in the mirror. "New summer, new rules," I affirmed, gripping the steering wheel before finally pushing the door open. This summer was about moving forward, not looking back. No summer flings, no heartbreaks—just pure, unadulterated fun, starting with surviving Caroline's decorating debacle.

The door to the clubhouse swung open with a familiar creak, and I was instantly surrounded by the controlled chaos of pre-event commotion. Vibrant streamers danced from the ceiling, balloons scattered, and committee members were running all around, absorbed in their respective tasks.

"Chandler!" Before I could look around, a tornado of golden curls was on top of me. Willow attacked me with such a force that it made us both tumble to the floor. It had been months since I'd seen her, but the warmth of our embrace bridged the gap of time.

"God, I missed you," I breathed out. Willow's hug was a reminder of the unspoken bond we shared, a friendship worth being in Bayside for.

We might have stayed lost in our reunion if not for a sharp voice interrupting our bubble. "I'm not paying you to cuddle."

Looking up from our spot on the floor, I saw Caroline standing over us, arms crossed, gaze as stern as her tone. A box thudded beside me, overflowing with rolls of paper towels, glass cleaner, and a pile of sponges and brushes.

"Your first mission: make the entrance bathrooms sparkle like the Fourth of July." Caroline's lips twisted into a tight smile, though it held no warmth at all. "Everything needs to be top-notch for tomorrow."

Willow and I exchanged a glance as Caroline strode away, leaving a trail of intimidation in her wake. Our smiles held a mutual conspiracy, eyes twinkling with silent awareness at the absurdity of being tasked with bathroom duty.

"Up you get," Willow chirped, extending a hand to help me off the floor. Together, we hoisted the box of cleaning supplies.

"Thanks, girl," I said, brushing off the dust from my clothes. "Let's knock this out. Then onto the next ridiculous task Caroline comes up with."

"Got your back," Willow replied, her grin infectious. "Bathroom duty now, and a much needed margarita later." Arm in arm, we took on the bathroom shitstorm together.

The next day, Willow and I got ready for the welcome event together. I twisted a silver tube, watching as the dark red shade of confidence emerged. I glided the lipstick over the contours of my lips, trying to hide my turmoil. My stomach knotted knowing I'd see Reese and Boston at the Blue Devils' welcome event. But this lipstick—bold and unapologetic—was my armor. It made me feel invincible, or at least that's what I told myself. As my grandmother would have said, "Lipstick and the right pair of heels can carry you through any battle."

"So, how has Reese been?" I asked casually, my eyes meeting Willows in the reflection.

"Same old Reese," Willow responded with a small smile. Pausing, she added, "Well, maybe not entirely the same. Wait till you see him."

Curiosity piqued, I turned to face her directly. "What do you mean?"

She flashed a knowing grin. "Oh, you'll know when you see it."

"Whatever," I muttered, brushing off the vague response. "Is he with anyone?" I said, changing the subject.

"No, I don't think so," she replied, applying the final touches to her makeup.

"Have you guys talked much since last summer?" she prodded gently.

I shook my head. "No. He tried to send me a few messages,

maybe called once, but I didn't really get the feeling he wanted to actually talk."

Willow's expression softened. "I'm sorry."

"It's okay," I said, forcing a smile. "Everything happens for a reason."

"Are you nervous to see him?" she asked, her curls bouncing as she tilted her head.

"Yeah, can't help it—but I'm staying away. Not repeating last summer."

"I have an idea," she said with a wink. "I know exactly what you need."

"What do I need?" I echoed, puzzled.

"You need a hot girl summer." Her eyes twinkled mischievously.

I couldn't suppress a laugh at the absurdity. "What does that mean?"

"Oh, Chandler," she rolled her eyes playfully. "It just means that you do what you want this summer, no boys bringing you down! No worries."

"Hmm... that doesn't sound so bad," I admitted.

"And I will totally help you execute this plan."

Despite the playfulness of the exchange, a knot of worry still settled in my stomach, heavy and persistent. Tonight loomed over me like a shadow I couldn't escape.

When we got to the welcome event, I beamed, proud of the work we'd done the night before. We'd outdone ourselves. The tablecloths draping over the long tables glimmered with an elegance last year's linen couldn't match, and the banners swayed grandly above us, commanding attention.

I plucked a flute of champagne from a passing tray, the bubbles tickling my nose as I settled into a chair next to Parker. Who, when food was involved, always showed up early.

"Seriously, what is this?" Parker said with dramatic disgust as he held up some sort of meat from his plate.

"I was planning on drinking my way through this," I replied, lifting my glass in a half-hearted toast to the gourmet mystery in front of him. With a deep breath, I rose from my seat, the need for a quieter space pulling me away. "I'm going to make sure the committee doesn't need any extra help."

The clubhouse still felt like stepping into a portal that led to last summer. The trophies still glistened under the soft lighting, probably polished daily. My gaze lingered on every shining surface until I was drawn, inexorably, to the shadowed hallway where Reese had once stood last summer when I first laid eyes on him—a memory permanently etched into my mind.

I remembered how he looked that day, the intensity of his green eyes, the carelessness in his stance as I unknowingly insulted him. Reese, who played the bad boy so well, unraveling a part of me I hadn't known was wound so tightly. He'd forced his way into my heart, only to leave it cracked like I'd never felt before.

The ache of it, the ghost of him, still clung to me. But the Chandler standing there wasn't the same girl who had fallen for his charm. This summer was a clean slate, a promise to myself that history would not repeat its painful cycle. Reese Carrington had taken his final bow in the theater of my affections. This time, my heart was locked away, and he was coming nowhere near it.

My eyes scanned the trophy wall again as I moved toward the exit—none of the committee members were in sight. Then my eyes locked on something new—a glinting addition to the collection. It was Reese's MVP trophy from last year, his name engraved in bold, assertive letters. Another reminder of the season he dominated the field and, unwittingly, my every thought back then. The impulse to turn away, to deny the trophy any more attention than it deserved, was strong. Then I smiled, realizing a few smaller trophies had also been added. Parker, Boston, and a few others had been put on the wall too.

"Never learn your lesson, do you?" The smooth voice cut through the silence, as unmistakable as the trophy I was fixated on. It curled around me like smoke, insinuating itself into the space I had regret-fully walked into again.

I stiffened, the words ricocheting through my bones. I didn't need to turn around to picture the smirk that would accompany his taunt, or the green eyes that would be sparkling with mischief and charm.

"Reese," I said, allowing his name to acknowledge his presence without betraying the tremor I fought to keep from my voice. There was no turning back now; the past had stepped into the present, and I braced myself for the moment I had been dreading.

I turned, my resolve wilting under the weight of his gaze. There he was again—Reese Carrington—leaning casually against the club-house wall, as if he had all the time in the world to unravel my knotted together composure. He rolled up his sleeve and readjusted the watch on his arm as he waited for my reaction. Something about him was different. My eyes traced the intricate tattoos covering his right arm—an annoyingly sexy addition on his tan skin. I knew then it must have been what Willow was talking about.

"Should have known better," I managed, hating the way my heart skipped as if trying to leap out of the fortress I'd built around it. The tattoos were mesmerizing, each one wrapping around the curves and veins in his arm. I caught a glimpse of one that stood out—an adorable little dinosaur on his wrist, almost like a cartoon character. I wanted to inspect them closer, but I knew better than to step into his orbit again.

"Not happy to see me?" The corner of his mouth quivered, reading my lingering glance with ease. That smirk, those piercing green eyes—he was an alluring danger trying to lead me back to the wreck I'd barely survived.

"Thrilled," I said, sarcastically. "New ink?" I asked, hoping my voice sounded nonchalant.

"A friend of mine worked on it this year," he replied with a tilt of his head, the light catching on hints of mischief in his eyes. "Wanted a change."

It was in-fucking-sane how both Reese and Boston were the very reasons last summer was chaos for me; how they both stirred up so many emotions; and now they both were—somehow—even more fucking attractive than ever before. It was like the universe had conspired to test the limits of my sanity. Both guys were even hotter than last year. Cool. Universe- 2, Me- 0.

Without warning, he pushed away from the wall, closing the distance between us. I was unprepared for his presence, wrapping around me like an inevitable storm, impossible to ignore.

"I texted you a few times," Reese said, his low, rough voice in contrast with the smooth lines of his face. "Even called you once."

I kept my gaze steady, though I felt the weight of his stare trying to dissect my carefully curated indifference. "Sorry, I was busy," I replied, my tone clipped.

The corner of his mouth twitched into that signature side smile. It had once quickened my pulse. Now it was just a reminder of the hurt he had caused, and all the damage he was capable of. His eyes narrowed, as if he was peering straight through my thoughts, seeing through the layers I'd built up since last summer.

Undeterred by my short response, Reese leaned in slightly, the faint scent of his cologne teasing my senses. "So, how've you been? You look good," he offered. His words were stained in charm and the ease of someone who knew the effect they had on people.

"Reese, can we not make small talk?" I interrupted, irritation threading through my voice. I brought the champagne glass to my lips, taking a sip to have something to do other than acknowledge the flutter in my stomach.

His gaze lingered on me for a moment too long before responding. "That wasn't my intention," he said, that smirk playing across his lips as he stood there, tall and self-assured. "Nothing about me is small."

His words didn't phase me, not now, even though the Reese that so many, including myself, found hard to resist was right in front of me. But I was determined not to fall into that trap again, not when I knew the cost all too well.

I rolled my eyes and turned on my heel. My heels clicked against the polished floor, echoing around me as I strode towards the door, eager to end the conversation. "Maybe not," I tossed over my shoulder, my voice cold. "But you sure know how to make others feel that way."

I didn't look back to see his reaction; I didn't need to. I could imagine the slight tilt of his head, the way he'd run a hand through his hair in that casual, self-assured manner. But the Chandler he knew—the one who blushed at his every word—was gone.

"Chandler." The raw edge of his voice snagged me, like the fading colors of a vanishing sunset still painting the sky with lingering, quiet beauty.

His tone alone threatens to unravel me, reminding me of whispered promises, of intimate moments we shared. "Glad you're back," he said, words hanging heavy behind me.

With little effort, I lifted my hand in a dismissive wave, not trusting myself to face him again, or even respond. The champagne flute, now light in my grip, came up to my lips as I forced down the remaining bubbles.

As I reached for the door, his voice, confident yet hopeful, carried across the hallway. "I'm sure I'll see you at Willow's later tonight."

Without a backward glance, I stepped out into the evening air, the cool breeze wrapping around me like a much-needed embrace. Inhaling deeply, I tried to shake off the lingering intensity of him and the frustration it brought. At Willow's tonight, I'd be ready. Ready to prove that I was no longer the naïve girl from last summer.

I sank against the clubhouse door, trying to shove away the emotions Reese had stirred up. As I shut my eyes, I was unwillingly dragged back to that day. Reese had dropped me like a summer fling, tossing me aside right before the leaves started to change. I remembered it with excruciating clarity—the casual shrug of his shoulders as if it was just another task during his busy day and he wasn't dismissing me from his life.

I closed my eyes tighter, willing away the images, the sounds, the scents—all the tiny, insignificant details that seemed so important back then. But most of all, I clung to the crushing weight of the realization. Because when he ended it, we were over. The hollowness that followed, the numbness... It had been a bold awakening. I wasn't the same Chandler who melted at his compliments, who had hung on his every word. That Chandler was replaced by someone stronger, someone who knew better than to fall for his bullshit. Not again. Not ever.

Gathering myself, I pushed away from the door and navigated through the dimly lit area toward the laughter and light spilling from the gathering.

And then time froze. Boston appeared, walking up at exactly that moment, his presence commanding attention even without intent.

I could see it, the hint of something unspoken flickering across his features—almost like he was happy to see me. It was there and then gone, replaced by a shadow of disappointment as Reese emerged from behind me, the door behind him shut with a click that echoed louder than it should have.

Reese paused, then stepped into the light. Boston's gaze shifted from me to Reese, and I could almost hear the silent conversation passing between them. With every second that ticked by, an invisible tension flickered around us.

The subtle tick in his jaw and the look in his eyes said it all— Boston was piecing together a false narrative. There I stood, caught in the middle of something I had been fighting hard not to be part of at all. It wasn't what it looked like, but the truth was often lost amongst assumptions that rushed to fill its place. I wanted to say something, anything to dispel the tension, but words failed me. I could only stand there, watching the silent exchange between two men who had each, in their own way, etched indestructible marks on my heart.

EIGHT

boston

MY IMPECCABLE FUCKING TIMING. There we were, the three of us caught in a moment so tense it could shatter with the slightest movement.

Chandler walked out, her hazel eyes avoiding mine. Reese followed her, trying to act casual, but I could see the guilt all over his face. The sight of them cut deeper than I wanted to admit. I should have been numb to this dance by now—should be used to Chandler choosing him—but witnessing it again after all this time? It was an entirely different ball game now.

A muscle in my jaw ticked involuntarily, the only visible sign, I hoped, of my internal turmoil. Chandler stood there not saying a word. I swept my gaze over her—the soft glow of her cheekbones down to the dress hugging her figure in all the right places. I was fighting hard to keep my cool, to hide how much this bothered me.

The silence between us stretched on for what felt like a century, until Reese finally broke it with the gravel of his voice. "I'll see you over there, man." His eyes flickered from me to the crowd gathered around the buffet tables.

I gave him a nod, the slightest dip of my head, but my gaze

remained locked on Chandler. He left without a backward glance, and we were alone—together, but miles apart.

"You okay?" The question was all I could come up with at that moment.

"Fine, Boston. Not like you care." Her eyes flashed with hurt, and that surprised me, cutting deeper than I expected.

Fuck me. Despite her reaction, I reached out, fingers gently grasping her wrist, bringing her to me. "I'm sorry," I said, genuinely. "For not responding to your texts, for pushing you away."

"The entire year, though?" she shook her head. "We haven't talked in months. You didn't care about me then, so just keep ignoring me, Boston."

"You're impossible to ignore." My eyes held hers, hoping she would understand the truth behind my words. "It's not you. I've had a lot going on in my head, and I'm working on it."

Her gaze locked onto where my hand held hers, and for a second I hoped she might understand. But then she pulled her wrist free from my grasp, her movement swift and cold. "Glad you're figuring it out," she shot back.

She placed her champagne glass on the table nearby. I wanted to reach out—no, I ached to—but I stayed still. Adjusting my tie, I thought about the hurt in her eyes, how I was the reason for it. She had every right to feel the way she did after all the times I'd retreated when I should have stepped forward.

I needed to be better for her. It was time to pull whatever I could from the depths of myself, to stop pushing her away, or—even worse —back into his arms.

The old Boston seemed like a stranger now, a ghost, even. But if there was a chance, any chance at all to be with her, I had to get out of my own way and fight for her.

A hush fell over the crowd as Coach Levy rose from his seat. Clutching a flute of champagne that suddenly seemed too delicate in my hands, I leaned back against the doorframe, my gaze drifting from Coach to the reason my heart was thumping so erratically.

"Welcome, welcome everyone!" Coach Levy's voice boomed, his smile as wide as the ball field. "To another year we hope is filled with victories, teamwork, and unforgettable moments."

I should have been listening, nodding along like the rest of the room, yet all I could see and think about was Chandler. Her smile drowned out Coach's words, her eyes sparkled brighter than the twinkle lights on the tables, and the way she threw her head back in amusement with Willow... the air vanished from my lungs. She was extraordinary. She'd been there all along, right in front of me. And then harsh reality hit me—there was a possibility that she wouldn't always be. My heart clenched in a painful ache as I realized what I could lose if I didn't do something.

"Here's to making this season one for the history books," Coach finished, raising his glass high.

A chorus of applause echoed around me, glasses clinking in celebration. I remained silent, my thoughts too loud to share space with anything else. I needed to get my shit together—for me, for the team, but most of all, for her—for Chandler.

Parker snapped me back to reality as he clapped me on the shoulder with a carefree grin. "You meeting us at the after-party?"

"No, I'm going to bed early tonight," I said, hoping my voice didn't betray the inner turmoil his sister had just stirred within me.

Parker scoffed playfully, giving me a look that told me he wasn't letting me out of this one. "No way, man. You've done this all year. It's summer. You have to go out with the team tonight."

A couple of our teammates overheard the conversation and chimed in. "Boston, come on, man, don't be a party pooper."

"Fine, I'll think about it," I conceded.

"Plus, you have to be my beer pong partner," Parker persisted, then whispered, "Everyone else kinda sucks."

"Okay, I'll go for one game, and then I'm leaving."

"Deal!" Parker exclaimed, slapping me on the back with enough force to make me lurch forward.

When I pulled up to Willow's, I took a deep breath before

opening my truck door. People were scattered around the porch and in the front yard as I walked up.

"Riley! Come take a shot with me!" Bailey's offer was a welcome relief. I desperately needed a drink knowing Chandler would be running around somewhere. He waved a bottle in the air, and I couldn't help but smile at him.

The porch's wooden boards creaked under my feet as I walked up the steps and accepted the bottle Bailey thrust into my hand. With a nod to him, I tossed it back. Liquid fire seared down my throat, leaving a trail of heat that settled in my stomach. Bailey clapped me on the back with a grin, oblivious to my internal grimace.

"Ha, that'll rip hair off your chest!" he chuckled.

"Oh buddy, the expression is that'll *put* hair on your chest," I snickered. He shrugged and took another sip.

"Come on, Riley," Bailey said, nudging me toward the house with his elbow. "Let's get this party started. Parker just got here, too."

Willow smiled and greeted us when we walked in, but her gaze stayed locked on Parker. It was clear there were unspoken words and feelings hanging between them, leftover from last summer. She took measured steps toward him, her bubbly demeanor giving way to something more pensive.

"Hey, Parker," Willow said, her voice a blend of warmth and caution as if she was testing out the situation.

"Willow," he replied, looking surprised to see her. His stance softened.

They shared a long hug. A little bit too long. And then Willow planted a kiss on Parker's cheek.

"It's good to see you," she said, rubbing his arm, "but we're definitely going to have a discussion later."

"Sounds good, Will," Parker nodded, a hint of humor flickering in his eyes.

I gave him a knowing look and he shrugged, downplaying what everyone else clearly saw as more than just a friendly greeting.

Crew tilted the bottle back, finishing what was left of it. "Well," he drawled, "guess that's our cue to get this party started."

The television's neon glow flickered across Parker's face, deep in concentration as we sat hunched over, controllers in hand. Mario Kart—the only game Willow owned—had been set up in the living room. My attention was pulled away from the game by the sound of laughter as Chandler walked by. She had that kind of beauty you could get lost in, and those shorts she was wearing hugged her hips just right. I swear I caught the drift of her perfume—something light and fresh with a touch of coconut.

I forced my gaze back to the screen in time to see Parker's car go flying off a cliff. He was distracted too—his eyes had been locked on Willow.

"You gonna go talk to her or what?" I set my controller down with a smirk. His eyes met mine for a split second before he put his controller down too, a short laugh betraying his cool exterior.

"Yeah," Parker agreed, nodding toward Willow, her curly blonde hair bouncing as she chatted animatedly with Chandler. "Let's go see what they're up to."

"Lead the way," I said, as we rose from the couch.

Parker snatched a beer from an innocent bystander, who gave him a strange but understanding look. He took a long sip, his Adam's apple bobbing as he swallowed it down.

Willow spotted him first, her face lighting up with surprise mixed with suspicion. "There you are! Way to keep in touch with me this year, you jerk," she said, playfully.

"Woah, I sent you a picture," Parker tilted his head. "You never responded."

I looked at Parker, wondering what kind of picture would elicit such a response—or lack thereof.

"Because, Parker," Willow retorted, hands on her hips and trying to hold back a laugh, "you sent me a picture of your grilled cheese sandwich."

"What kind of picture did you want, baby girl? A dick pic?"

"Honestly, that would have been more entertaining than your burnt sandwich," she said, playfully.

"That's where I draw the line," he shot back with a smile. "It was not burnt. It was golden-brown. My best one yet. That's why I sent you the picture."

I leaned against the wall, nursing my drink and shaking my head at their antics. But then my gaze drifted to Chandler.

She was standing next to Willow with her arms crossed, her hazel eyes tracking every movement Reese made across the room. She was subtle about it, but I'd known her long enough to understand what she was doing. A pang, sharp and unwelcome, twinged in my chest. After so much time, I thought the stupid feeling would stop.

"Hey," I nodded toward Reese. "You keep looking at him like that, he's gonna catch on. Just go talk to him."

Her gaze snapped to mine, a flash of surprise flickering across her face. "No," she said, firmly. "I'm staying clear of him this summer." She turned away slightly, looking back at the crowd, not quite meeting my eyes. "He ended things. He made his choice." Her lips pressed into a thin line.

I caught myself staring just a little too long at the way her hazel eyes shimmered under the soft glow of the string lights hanging on the wall nearby.

"Reese might be related to me," I began, the words smooth despite the flutter in my chest, "but you know there's one huge difference between us."

She raised an eyebrow, her gaze skeptical yet curious—a look I'd come to appreciate over the years. "What? I hope you're not about to brag about your batting averages. I've heard it many times."

It was easy talking to her like this, even if my heart hammered against my ribs with every word. "Nah," I said, before taking a small sip of my drink. "If I had you, Chandler, I'd never let you go."

The air seemed to still around us, thick with the weight of my confession. She looked intently at me in the dim light and took a step back. There was a vulnerability in that suspended moment that told me my words had landed right where I'd intended.

I wasn't sorry for telling her the truth that had been swelling inside me for far too long. This summer things needed to be different; I needed to be different—braver, stronger. And as I watched Chandler's lips part slightly, her eyes searching mine for sincerity, I knew I wasn't going to hold anything back. Not anymore.

After she had a moment to take in what I said, her eyes darkened and narrowed, pinning me with an accusation. "Well, you had no problem shutting me out this last year," she spat.

I clenched my jaw. I should have seen that coming.

"Isn't that kind of the same thing? Actually, worse?" she added.

"How is that worse?" I shot back, struggling to keep my voice even. The memory of that time was raw. It was the most fucked up situation. What was the right way to handle it? "I thought you were still with him, anyway. I was sorting through shit."

"Well, maybe I'm sorting through shit, too," Chandler retorted, her frustration palpable.

She abruptly turned away, still mad, I could tell, but looking cute as ever. She stepped into Willow's ongoing conversation with Parker, who was deeply engaged, his animated hands punctuating each word.

"Did you say we're going to the bar soon?" Chandler interrupted him, not bothering to hide her urgency. She clearly wanted to escape. "I think I've had enough of this crowd."

Willow blinked, focusing on the interruption, but before she could respond, Parker's gaze flicked to Chandler, a knowing twinkle briefly overshadowing his usual mirth. He sensed the undercurrents swirling around us, and his protective instincts were rising to the surface.

"If you're going to the bar, then I'm going to the bar," he declared with a determined nod towards his sister.

I took a deep sigh, the weight of inevitability settling on my chest. This meant one thing for certain—I was going, too. In Parker's presence, the air was always lighter, but tonight, even his humor felt like it wouldn't be enough to bridge the distance between Chandler and me.

chandler

I SLIPPED into the backseat of the Uber and felt my crop top stretch, the material pushing everything up just right. I went for a pair of tight shorts that hugged my hips like a second skin. Tonight wasn't just about celebrating the start of summer—it was about feeling confident and shoving it in the guys' faces. Boston and Reese had been a constant loop of frustration in my head, and a small part of me wanted to prove that I could do just fine on my own. I didn't need either of them.

"Have fun," the Uber driver called out as Willow and I stepped onto the curb outside the bar. We waved at him before he took off.

The door swung open to a wave of distant music and clinking glasses. The team's laughter came from the right side of the bar where they had congregated, basking in their excitement of a new season. But I didn't head towards them. Instead, I veered left, headed straight to the bar.

"I need to use the bathroom. I'll meet you at the bar," Willow said over the music. I nodded as she walked in the opposite direction.

I slid onto a barstool, my fingers tapping lightly on the smooth counter as I waited for the bartender. He reached for my card as I ordered a cranberry vodka, but the guy next to me—a stranger with an easy smile—waved cash in the air.

"Let me get that," he said, his voice smooth as he paid for my drink.

"Thanks," I said softly, a polite smile gracing my lips, all the while hyperaware of being in the spotlight again. It was as if two sets of eyes were burning into me—one blue, one green.

I turned my head ever so slightly, catching sight of them. Boston, with those beach waves that made him look like he'd walked straight off some dreamy shore, and Reese, whose vibrant green eyes and tattoos seemed to promise adventure—and trouble. Both wore expressions I couldn't quite decipher. They were obviously aware of my free drink with the gentleman, and I was relishing it.

"New in town?" the kind stranger asked, attempting to recapture my attention.

"I guess you could say that," I replied absentmindedly, my thoughts elsewhere.

Even with my back to them, I could feel their disapproval. But I didn't need their approval. I just wanted to do my own thing—have fun on my own without needing either of them.

My third cocktail of the evening was making itself at home in my bloodstream when Willow finally sauntered up to the bar. "That line was ridiculous," she groaned, eyes sparkling with playful mischief that could only mean she needed a drink after said adventure.

"Willow, meet my friend, Brad!" I slurred out, gesturing to the man with a sloppy grin beside me.

"Ben, actually," he corrected with a chuckle, extending his hand towards Willow without missing a beat.

"Right, Ben!" I laughed, too tipsy to be embarrassed. Their hands clasped in a friendly shake. Willow's laugh mingled with ours, a sound that felt like home in Bayside.

My favorite song started to play through the crowded room, weaving its way into my veins. It was one of those irresistible songs that forced me to dance without hesitation. Willow shot me a grin while she waited by the bar for her drink. My feet were already two steps ahead, itching for the dance floor.

"Ben!" I called over the music, my voice laced with excitement. His eyes met mine, a mixture of amusement and hesitance flickering across his face. "Come on! You can't not dance to this!" I insisted, grabbing his hand.

He resisted for a fraction of a moment before his lips curled into a reluctant smile, and he let me pull him along.

I was in my element, bouncing and dancing as I sang along to the music. Ben's laughter mingled with the music as he watched me throw my hands in the air and move around him. Then, in a smooth motion, Ben spun me around, taking me by surprise. My hair fanned out before settling as he pulled me in close, our movements suddenly more intimate than I'd expected.

As I came to a stop, my gaze accidentally landed across the room, right toward Boston, Reese, and Parker. The three of them were standing around a pool table. Reese's cue stick hovered motionless over the green felt, his stance frozen mid-stroke. Boston leaned casually against the pool table, but there was nothing casual about the tension in his jaw or the concentration in his eyes. Parker, usually so laid back, was frowning, his eyes narrowing slightly as he watched me.

I couldn't decipher their silent accusations, but I felt them, sharp and unsettling. The last notes of the song played out and I seized the moment to retreat from their scrutiny, taking a long, steady sip of my drink.

A new song, one I didn't recognize, was turned up through the speakers, then. It acted as a siren call to the bartenders, though. A cheer cut through the air as every head turned in unison. The few girl bartenders who, moments before, were pouring drinks, dropped everything and rushed onto the bar.

"Come on, you two!" one of them shouted over the music, beckoning me and Willow with a finger and a grin.

We looked over at each other in excitement, accepting the challenge. Willow's laughter rang out, uninhibited and infectious as we hopped up onto the bar, our feet finding a spot between puddles of spilled drinks.

"Take a shot!" another bartender yelled, thrusting the neck of the tequila bottle toward us.

I grabbed the bottle first, fueled by the crowd cheering us on. The liquid scorched down my throat as I tilted my head back, then I passed it to Willow, who took her shot with a wink to the audience below. There we were, perched above the world, queens of the moment, stress dissolving with every pulsating beat of music.

I noticed Ben's laughter, his voice somehow audible over the chaos. "Now it's a show!" he called out, clapping his hands above his head. Willow's curls bounced as she matched my two-step with her own moves.

As we swayed, lost in our own little world, I caught sight of a familiar pair of piercing blue eyes. Boston was now at the bar, his arms resting on the counter, a muscle in his jaw ticking with intensity. Next to him, Reese's green eyes were narrowed, arms crossed over his chest as if he was about to burn the bar down.

"Are you going to take care of this, or should I?" I heard Reese snap at Boston. It was clear that neither of them appreciated the fun Willow and I were having. But their protectiveness was clashing with the wild night I was trying to have.

Before I could even process what was happening, Boston's voice carried over the music. "Chandler, get down."

I shook my head at him, not about to let them ruin my night—no one was going to pop this hot girl summer bubble. Certainly not Reese or Boston.

Then Parker appeared, his expression an odd mixture of amusement and annoyance. "Chandler, for fuck's sake, get off the bar." His gaze shifted to Willow and his tone lightened, filled with that familiar mischievous quality that always seemed to surface whenever she was around. "Willow, stay up there and take off the bra," he teased, eliciting a burst of laughter from her before she rolled her eyes dramatically. She stayed put, playing to the crowd.

The air shifted around us, thick with tension, as the divide between those on the ground and us on the bar grew more pronounced. I found myself torn between laughing the guys off with Willow and addressing the concern I could feel radiating from Boston and Reese.

"Come on, Chandler. You're too drunk. You're going to fall and hurt yourself," Boston added, softer now, as if remembering that his role had always been to look out for me, not scold.

My feet felt heavy as I considered my next move. Whatever I chose would tilt the delicate balance of our intertwined relationships —a dance far more complex than the one I performed on the bar.

Reese's patience snapped, the carefree facade he usually wore crumbling in an instant. "Fuck this," he muttered with an edge that tore through the bar. Before I could process his intent, strong hands gripped my thighs, and the world flipped upside down.

"Reese, put me down now!" My words tumbled out, slurred and ineffectual, as I dangled over his shoulder. I beat against the firm expanse of his back, but it was like trying to dent a brick wall.

My vision still struggled to right itself, but I caught sight of Ben —an inverted figure in my topsy-turvy view. He was scrambling, reaching out his outstretched hand, his features contorted with concern.

Boston's broad frame moved like a barrier between me and Ben. The golden retriever of my childhood memories, always so sweet-natured, now stood with a fierce determination to keep this other guy away. Boston's eyes were sharp, focused, and there was an edge to him that felt new, more hardened.

"Just let her go." Boston's warning was firm, yet his voice still held a familiar warmth, and I could tell he was trying to force a cold dismissal in his tone. I assumed that Boston and Parker would follow, but they didn't. They stayed put, still in heated conversation with Ben until I could no longer see them.

Reese's stride never faltered as we passed the sea of bodies in the bar, his grip on me unyielding. The tattoos tracing the contours of his arm muscles shifted with each determined step as he carried me effortlessly through the crowded bar.

He stepped out into the darkness of the back patio. The clamor of inside was instantly replaced by the quiet hum of the night. Reese finally set me down, and I could see upright again.

"Chandler, breathe," he said, his voice low and steady. His eyes held mine, fierce yet strangely protective, as if he'd just saved me from a burning building.

"I'm fine," I asserted, more forcefully than I felt. "You didn't have to carry me out of there like that." My attempt at sounding indignant was betrayed by a slight wobble in my stance, but I straightened up, determined not to show any weakness. "I can take care of myself."

Standing there, with the night air filling my lungs and Reese's eyes on me, I knew I had to be the one in control. This was about drawing lines, about asserting my independence from the bad boy who used to unravel me with just a look. The same boy who showed flashes of depth that few ever saw. And as our standoff continued in the silence, I realized that I wasn't just convincing Reese—I was also convincing myself.

Reese smiled with his signature cockiness making my blood simmer. It was the same grin that could make a girl's heart trip over itself, but right now, it only ignited a spark of defiance.

"Can you, though?" He tilted his head, amusement dancing in his eyes. "Because it seems like you can barely walk. And I think you have drunk vision, considering you were obviously flirting with that creep."

My jaw clenched against the heat rising in my cheeks—not from embarrassment, but from annoyance. "I do not have drunk goggles on," I snapped back, feet planted firmly despite the unevenness I felt.

Why did his opinion matter? Why did his words make me want to prove him wrong so badly? The questions circled in my mind like vultures. "And why do you care, Reese? You have no say in what I do." My voice grew louder, more forceful as I reclaimed the space his presence always seemed to shrink. "You're the one who broke up with me."

The words lingered, a reminder of a past we were still entangled in. Yet, beneath the layers of resentment and hurt, a flicker of the old connection we shared sparked reluctantly to life.

He clenched his jaw as he took a half step closer, the faint scent of his cologne wrapping around me like a memory I couldn't escape. "I didn't break up with you," his voice was low and rough with an emotion I couldn't name. "Chandler, there was a lot of shit going on. I couldn't even talk to you about the Boston situation. I didn't know how…"

He paused, raking a hand through his hair, frustrated. The gesture tugged at something deep inside me. "And then before he left town we finally talked. We had a conversation we should've had a long time ago." His eyes searched mine. "I saw him, Chandler. I saw how much he cares about you. I thought maybe it was a crush, but it's way more than that. I can't be the reason you two aren't together."

The words struck me cold and unexpected, like a sudden downpour. Those words drenched me in a reality I hadn't really expected. Anger flared hot in my chest, burning away the alcohol-induced haze. "You didn't give me any say," I breathed out, my voice shaking with a mixture of rage and hurt. "You made the decision for me."

Reese's expression flickered, regret flashing in his eyes before he masked it with that all too familiar stillness. But it was too late—I had seen the crack in his armor, the glimpse of the vulnerability he so rarely showed.

"Chan—" he started, but I cut him off.

"No, Reese. You don't get to decide what's best for me," I said firmly, finding strength in the clarity.

The words hung heavy between us, the truth of them settling around us like dust after a storm. And in that moment, standing face to face with him, I realized that no matter what came next, I was the one who would be making the choices for my heart.

Reese's shadow loomed over me, the streetlights casting a glow on his face. He took a deep breath, steeling himself for his next confession. "Look, Chandler," he said, his eyes locking onto mine, "if you and Boston decide you aren't meant to be... Then I'll be here waiting for you. I'd do whatever the fuck it took to make it up to you." He paused, his gaze unwavering. "But I'm not going to be the guy who stands in the fucking way."

I felt a surge of emotion—anger, confusion, and an undeniable flutter of hope that I immediately tried to squash. I stared back at him, my own resolve firming. "Well, maybe I don't want either of you," I retorted, my voice a mix of defiance and weariness.

That's when it happened. Reese smiled—the kind of smile that saw through every inch of me—one corner of his mouth lifting higher than the other, revealing a dimple that had always been my downfall. It was infuriating how he could shift the atmosphere and disarm me with one simple expression.

"Come on, Chandler," he whispered, his arrogance laced with a tenderness that almost made my heart skip a beat. "You and I both know that's not true."

Before I could respond, he changed the subject seamlessly. "Do you need a ride home?"

My pride flared, giving me the strength to refuse his offer. "No. I'll be fine," I said firmly, crossing my arms as a shield against his unsettling proximity.

"Okay," he conceded, pulling out his phone and typing a quick message. "Just texted Parker to make sure he's on his way out here." He pocketed the device and stepped back. "I'll see you around. And, hey, I can't wait to see how this summer plays out." He walked away with his hands in his pockets.

I realized that despite everything—the pep talks I gave myself, the confidence I thought I had, and my determined resolve to avoid him at all costs, Reese Carrington could still shake my world and set it back on its axis all at once. The force of his presence was like a tidal wave, overwhelming and impossible to resist. His words echoed in my mind, my heart racing from our interaction, making every ounce of my self-control want to crumble in an instant.

As he pulled open the door and walked back inside the bar, the set of his shoulders told a story of frustration. I'd always known about the storm brewing behind those vivid eyes—a storm that could either sweep me away or leave me shipwrecked. The cool exterior wall pressed against my back as I sank down, my knees weak from our intense exchange. I tangled my fingers in my hair, pulling at the strands like that would help me sort through my thoughts.

The rhythm of approaching heels cut through the haze of my thoughts. It was Caroline. I could tell because the shoes were bright pink. I tried to avoid eye contact and took a breath, bracing for whatever criticism she had come armed with.

"Chandler," her voice pierced the silence before I had even looked up, carrying a weight of disappointment.

Her heels clicked to a halt in front of me, and I forced myself to meet her eyes. She stood looking down at me, her expression etched with disapproval, another blow in my already exhausting, battered day. What more could she possibly have wanted from me?

"Caroline," I greeted warily, my voice reflecting my exhaustion.

She folded her arms, and sighed heavily. "You can't have them both, you know."

I swallowed hard, the knot in my stomach tightening. She was like a mirror reflecting the choices I'd been dodging back at me, the reality I wasn't ready to face: I was caught between two brothers, two hearts, and a choice I wasn't ready to make.

Her eyes softened just a fraction, but her words held firm. "You're going to have to pick one. You can't have both, and they won't be wrapped around your finger forever."

Those words, spoken with such finality, hung between us. It was then I saw it—the animosity flickering behind her stern stance. It wasn't just disappointment that colored her judgment, there was something else, a raw edge that seemed almost... personal.

"Neither of them deserve that," she added, her tone dipping into a rare display of empathy.

I remained crouched there, the chill from the wall seeping into my bones. Caroline towered above me with her harsh truths, waiting for my response. But what could I say when I knew deep down that she was right?

boston

I DUG my cleats into the dirt, the roar of the crowd rising like a beast behind me. Bases loaded, two outs, tied game—every single eye was on me, every ounce of hope targeted at me, at-bat.

Gripping the bat with white knuckles, I exhaled slowly, silencing all thoughts except for me and the pitcher. The world narrowed to this, to the stretch and pitch, to the spin of the ball hurling toward me. Time seemed to slow as I swung, feeling the crack of solid contact radiate through my entire body.

The ball soared. I didn't need to watch it land to know it was going far—the eruption from the stands told me everything. My teammates cheered as I glanced ahead to the runners ahead of me charging towards home plate, their paths clearing for me round the bases. Dust flew around me as I made the final sprint to home. I scrambled up, looked around, and was met with a moment I'd always dreamed of—the team was rushing out onto the field, surrounding me, shouting with excitement.

The guys piled on me, screaming and high-fiving. My first out-of-the-park home run—not just a home run, but a grand slam. An electric charge surged through my veins, a thrill that went beyond a personal goal. It was a childhood dream.

A lifelong dream of mine had come true and somehow Chandler still slipped through the adrenaline of the moment. I gazed at the sea of faces, searching for those bright hazel eyes, hoping to catch just a glimpse of her reaction and see her expression. Scanning the stands was a bust, though. There was too much excitement to find her, but I knew her well enough to know she was probably jumping up and down.

Parker slung his arm around my shoulders. "Knew it was going to happen this summer," he said, the corners of his mouth lifting in a wry smile with clear satisfaction in his eyes. "There's no coming back from that, man. Every major league team is gonna know your name now."

I just nodded, still half-dazed, the echo of the crowd's roar still lingering in my ears like a dream. We headed toward the dugout, the rest of the team trailing behind us, talking and laughing. And then Reese stepped forward, blocking my path with a stance that was all too familiar—confrontational, yet with a glint of something else in his eyes. Then his face broke into a smile.

"It kills me to admit it," he said, his voice not carrying his usual edge, "but that was pretty badass." There was a trace of respect, maybe even admiration, that I hadn't expected from him.

He reached out a fist, waiting for me to reach out, too, for the fist bump. But a memory from the other night resurfaced.

He had carried Chandler out of the bar, his arm secure around her waist. Watching them disappear was harsh, but I had no choice besides reluctant acceptance. It sucked—there was no better word for it—watching him take control, seeing how well he stepped into the role of protecting her at all costs. But deep down, beneath the discomfort, I knew his intentions were good. They shared a history that I wasn't a part of, one that I knew they probably hadn't completely shut the door on.

Chander alone would have to decide if she wanted to close that chapter.

Reese and I couldn't have been more different, but we both harbored an urge to protect Chandler. Maybe it was in our blood, or maybe it was simply who we were in relation to her—two people hopelessly drawn to who she was, how silly she could be when she let her guard down, her loyalty.

I knew I needed to give them space, to step back and let them have their moment. As much as I wanted to intervene, I couldn't. If she decided to be with me, I wanted her completely—without any lingering doubts or hesitation. So I stood there, watching from a distance, wanting to punch Ben in the face to keep my mind off whatever was happening between Chandler and Reese.

* * *

"Thanks, Reese," I said, returning his fist bump, bringing me back to the moment.

The crowd started to leave, and the team shuffled into packing up gear.

"Hey, let's celebrate at my house tonight!" Reese yelled. "A grand slam. We have to celebrate that shit."

Bailey, always over the top, started banging on the metal cage to get the team's attention. "Riley! Riley!" he chanted. The chant caught on, each team member joining in until my last name reverberated around the field.

"Riley! Riley!"

Coach clapped a sturdy hand on my back, guiding me out of the dugout. "You've got some fans who want to meet you," he said, his eyes crinkling with pride.

I shook hands with a line of men whose faces blurred together in my adrenaline-fueled haze—all except for one, Colin, whose firm handshake stood out from the others. "Impressive game," he said, his voice carrying an undertone of promise. He had to be someone important, no doubt. "You'll be hearing from me, kid."

"Thank you, sir," I replied, trying to seem engrossed in the moment. But the truth was that every few seconds my eyes darted to the stands, searching for a particular set of hazel eyes.

Where was Chandler? My heart sank a little with each glance that came up empty. I knew she had to be there, probably cheering louder than anyone else. If not for me, always for Parker. But she seemed to have vanished in the chaos. The stands were abandoned now, only a few popcorn buckets and drinks left behind.

I slung my baseball bag over my shoulder with a heavy sigh and made my way across the parking lot to where my truck waited under a spotlight from the dim glow of the overhead lights. And there she was, Chandler Hartford, leaning casually against the side of my truck as if she owned a piece of it, and, by extension, a piece of me.

"Grand slam, huh?" She said, light and teasing. "Couldn't have just hit a regular home run?"

I stopped in my tracks, a slow grin replacing my disappointment. I would do anything for this stubborn, complicated woman who had captured my heart from the first time she slipped that friendship bracelet on my wrist.

"Guess I just wanted to get your attention," I shot back, the words coming easier than expected.

She laughed, then, a sound that felt more like home than home plate itself. "You got my attention alright," she said with a softness in her eyes she hadn't shown much this summer. "But you're not off the hook. I need a word with you."

She wore a small smile. It was an expression I wasn't used to having directed at me. For once, she didn't seem upset.

"What did I do now?" I asked as I tossed my bag into the truck bed.

She put her hands on her hips, the stance familiar and somehow endearing. "You know," she started, an edge of curiosity softening her usual confrontational tone, "I always thought they were from Kristina." Her eyes searched mine, waiting for an explanation.

I turned back to her, leaning against the truck's side. "What was from Kristina?" I asked, trying to decipher what she was trying to tell me.

The evening breeze shuffled her hair as she looked up at me. She took a small step forward, closing some of the space I had put between us for so long.

"The roses you left for me after every performance this year," she said, her voice soft and unexpectedly vulnerable. "I thought they were from Kristina."

I stilled, processing her words. "What are you talking about?" How could she have found out?

"I got a call from my stage manager today," she explained, tucking a strand of hair behind her ear. "Told her I was on my way to a baseball game, and she said it was about time I gave that baseball boy the time of day. The one who left all the flowers. I know it was you, Boston."

I leaned back against the tailgate, arms folded as she stood with her hands on her hips.

I sighed, knowing she wasn't going to let this go unless I explained myself. "I still never miss a show. No matter how pissed I am at the world or how much I'm messing everything else up. I'll never miss you on stage, Chandler."

It was the truth. No matter what I was going through, no matter how broken and disconnected from the world I felt, I still couldn't bring myself to miss one of her damn shows. And I had tried.

Her expression softened for a fraction of a second before her resolve returned. "Boston, I don't know what to say," she said, a challenging glint in her eyes. "But don't think you're in my good graces just yet. You've been pushing me away all year. You have a lot more groveling to do."

I pushed off from the truck, stepping closer, the gravel beneath my shoes crunching softly. I wasn't holding back anymore. I knew I had a lot of work to do, to close every inch of distance my stubbornness had created between us. "For you, Chandler, I'd get down on my knees and beg if that's what you want." I meant every word.

Chandler reached up, her fingers brushing lightly against my cheek as she rose on tiptoes and pressed a soft kiss there. My world narrowed to the warmth of her lips on my skin, the sweet scent of her hair as it brushed against my face. She left a fire on my cheek that felt like it might burn straight through me.

"I'll keep that in mind." she said tenderly. "Thank you for the roses, Boston. I'll see you later tonight."

I took a deep breath, steadying myself—at the thought of actually having a shot with the girl I've always wanted. It wasn't just some far-off dream anymore—it felt real, like something I could actually reach out and grab. As I watched her walk away and I climbed into my truck, I was struck with sudden hope. Maybe she wasn't out of reach, as I'd always thought. Maybe this summer it would finally be the right time for us.

After we'd cleaned up, Parker and I made our way to Reese's crowded house party.

"Boston, I've been looking for you!" Caroline said just as I stepped inside. She came up beside me, pulling me in her direction by my arm. Then she leaned in close, toying with the hem of my shirt. "You were really impressive tonight."

"Thanks, Caroline. But the entire team was impressive." I was already getting tired of the attention. And if I was being honest, there was really only one person I wanted attention from.

"You're not acting like you missed me as much as I missed you," she pouted, her hand still lingering under the bottom of my shirt.

"Sorry, just exhausted from the game," I lied, trying my best to be polite and not let the disinterest take over. Caroline was beautiful, anyone would be lucky to get her attention. If I was being honest, I had no idea why something hadn't clicked between us. We had hooked up a few times last summer, and it was fun but I'd made it clear how I felt about her.

"Okay, Boston," she said, skepticism written all over her face. "I'll come find you later." I breathed out a sigh of relief, scanning the room for the familiar brunette that was consuming my thoughts.

I made my way around, exchanging brief nods and words with a few teammates, and eventually made my way back toward Parker.

"Really?" he asked the girl beside him, his voice filled with genuine surprise. "You don't think I have a shitty haircut?"

He was leaning against the kitchen counter. A girl whose name I didn't know was standing extremely close to him.

"No, I think it's a little douchey, but it suits you," she flirted back, her hand boldly skimming over Parker's arm.

Parker chuckled. "I really need to get a new haircut," he replied, ruffling his hair.

Then I noticed Willow. She was standing nearby, eyes narrowed, the grip on her red plastic cup tightening—the liquid inside sloshed dangerously close to spilling over the rim.

I stepped closer to her and blocked the view of Parker.

"Want to see what's going on outside?" I asked, hoping I could relieve her from the show.

"Yeah," she sighed, slumping her shoulders. "That girl's desperation is appalling."

"Lead the way," I said, gesturing toward the back door.

When we got outside, I spotted Chandler with a crowd near the patio sectional. Some people were sitting, others were standing, playing one of my least favorite games. Willow sat down next to Chandler.

"Chandler, truth or dare?" Caroline asked.

"Dare," Chandler responded, her hazel eyes gleaming with defiance.

Caroline considered her options before glancing at me. A tight grin spread across her lips. "Okay, I dare you to give Bailey a lap dance," she declared. A chorus of cheers and hollers erupted from the group.

Fuck. My heart stuttered in my chest. I swallowed, irritated but curious to see what she'd do. I knew her, and I knew she'd never back down from a dare.

She shook her head and laughed as she approached Bailey. Her confidence both impressed and unnerved me. I took a casual sip of my drink, the burn of the liquid barely registering as I fixed my gaze on Chandler. With every one of her deliberate steps towards Bailey, my hand tightened around my cup, knuckles whitening. A laugh escaped her lips as she settled onto his lap. It was the same sweet sound I'd heard a thousand times before, but tonight it grated against my nerves.

"Let's go girl," Bailey egged on. But his smile started to crumble when he bit his lip—a clear sign that he was more into this dare than he was letting on.

Something twisted in my stomach as I watched and, without thinking, I set my cup down with more force than necessary and walked over to them, placing a firm hand on Bailey's shoulder. "How about we not do this with Parker's little sister?" My voice was calm, but there was an edge to it I couldn't hide.

Bailey looked up, annoyance flickering across his features. "It's just a game, come on," he said dismissively, but he knew better than to argue. With a gentle tug, I helped Chandler off his lap.

Her eyes flared with indignation as she pulled me to a hidden area of the backyard, away from the prying eyes and laughter of the crowd. "Boston, what are you doing?" she demanded, hands on hips, the fire in her stance betraying how annoyed she really was.

"Me?" I echoed, unable to keep the frustration from seeping into my voice. "I'm looking out for you." She let out a scoff and turned to walk away, but not before firing back.

"Looking out for me? Fucking great. There you go, treating me like I'm just Parker's little sister. I'm not a child anymore, Boston. When are you going to realize that?"

I watched her turn to storm away. Her accusation was highly irritating because deep down I knew she was right, she wasn't a child anymore—I saw her as so much more. But admitting that felt like stepping off a cliff with no idea where the fuck I'd land.

"Fuck it." I snapped. I reached out and grabbed her wrist, halting her mid-step. She spun around, hazel eyes wide with surprise as she stumbled into my embrace. My grip tightened and I wrapped one hand around her waist—just enough to let her know I wasn't going anywhere. Not without resolving the tension that had been building between us. The world seemed to shrink and fade away, leaving only the small space between us, charged with years of unspoken truth and desire.

I lifted her chin gently, tilting her face up to mine. "If I thought of you as a child, would I kiss you like this?"

When my lips crashed against Chandler's, it wasn't just a kiss—it was a fucking declaration, a statement, everything I'd ever wanted it to be. I poured into it everything I'd kept locked away—every stolen glance, every lingering touch, every moment I'd spent picturing this. Her lips were like velvet against mine. There was no more holding back. Our tongues moved together seamlessly, our hearts pounding. There was no room for uncertainty or doubt—she needed to fucking know my desire. My hips pressed against hers as we backed against the ivy-covered fence.

A soft moan escaped her as she melted against me. Her hands found their way into my hair, pulling me closer and deeper into her. It was a revelation of desire and emotion that consumed us both, leaving us breathless. I wanted her to feel the way every inch of my body responded to her. I needed her to know that I could never see her like a little sister. After this moment she'd know exactly where I stood.

We broke apart, lips parted with reluctance. I rested my forehead against hers and looked down at her lips, ones I'd so often thought about, now slightly swollen and flushed a deeper shade of pink. I leaned back but lingered close enough to feel the heat radiating from her skin, to see her eyes flutter open, burning fiercely with desire.

"I don't see you like that," I whispered as I delicately traced my fingers down her arm, until they locked with hers.

I held her hand in mine for a moment then guided it down my body until it was pressed against my dick straining beneath my jeans —undeniable evidence of my thoughts. I could feel her pulse racing under my fingertips, see the rapid rise and fall of her chest. Her eyes glazed over as she realized what effect she had on me.

I released her hand, expecting her to step back, but she kept her hand exactly where I placed it. Her fingers began to trace small, intentional circles over my bulge. The unexpected boldness of her touch sent a rush of intense desire surging through my veins. I gripped the fence above her head to steady myself, my knuckles turning white. Every muscle in my body tensed, my hands trembled with the urge to lift her skirt and show her how badly I wanted her.

She smirked, her eyes glinting with trouble. "Boston," she teased, adding more pressure, her breath hot against my neck. "If I knew all I had to do was give Bailey a lap dance to get you to kiss me like that, I would have done it a long time ago."

"How about you don't ever do that again," I said, the words escaping through gritted teeth as I fought to keep my composure.

She cocked her head to the side, her eyes glinting with mischief. "Why? Because you think it would upset Parker?" She tilted her chin in a challenge.

I tightened my grip on her wrist, stopping the pleasure and torture she was inflicting with her hand. With a swift pull, I brought her against me. "No," I whispered, my hold firm but not rough. "Because I didn't like it."

She leaned back against the fence, a defiant look on her face. "What if you were the one I was giving it to?" She was trying to push the boundaries, but there was an innocence to her challenge that told me this was all uncharted territory for her. Still, I couldn't resist taking the bait. I bit my lip, fighting back a slight smile.

"Look," I started, voice low and steady despite the hurricane of emotions she stirred in me. "You can dance for me whenever you want." Leaning in closer, I whispered in her ear as I let the words slip out. "But when you do," I continued, my words deliberate, "you better be wearing less clothes... and no one," I emphasized, my tone dipping into something darker, more possessive, "no one will be watching us."

A sharp intake of breath was her only response. I could feel her quickening pulse where my fingers gripped her wrist. Her eyes softened just enough to let me know she was intrigued.

"Chandler!" A voice broke us out of the moment.

I released her, stepping back with a suddenness that left the space between us cold and gaping. She pivoted on her heel, the hem of her skirt swirling around her thighs, her expression a mix of mischief and amusement.

"Go on," I said, a half-smile on my face as I watched her leave.

She hesitated for a moment as she quickly fixed her hair, eyes still filled with that teasing challenge. She rounded the corner, leaving me alone with my thoughts.

I leaned against the fence, letting out a long breath. My head was spinning in the whirlwind of emotions she'd stirred up. I knew there was no going back. We'd crossed the line, and for the first time, I didn't care about the consequences.

chandler

"CHANDLER, YOU GOOD?" Willow asked, genuine worry in her eyes. I blinked, her concern pulling me out of the chaos of my thoughts.

"Um, can we sit down for a second?" My voice was barely a whisper, but she heard the urgency hidden within it.

"Sure, what's going on?" Willow's eyes were soft with empathy as she led me to a patio couch tucked in the corner of the garden.

I sank into the cushions with a sigh, the weight of the evening pressing down on me. I hadn't quite processed what just happened, but I needed her advice. "I'm struggling, Willow."

"Talk to me." She leaned in, sliding her phone into her back pocket, giving me her undivided attention.

"Reese told me he ended things last summer because he didn't want to be the reason Boston and I aren't together," I confessed. "And all year, all this time, it was Boston leaving me roses after every show. Here I was, thinking he was ignoring me..."

Willow's expression shifted from shock to intrigue as she leaned forward. "He did what? Boston did that? You sent me a snap saying that they were from Kristina!"

I nodded, focusing on the patterned throw pillow I was fidgeting with in my lap. "Yes, it was him... and on top of it all, he just kissed me. This summer has barely started, and it's already nothing like I planned. I was going to steer clear of both of them—they both hurt me. And now... I'm just... confused."

"Whoa." Willow's eyes widened. "Chandler, I get that this isn't the summer you had planned out in your head, but you can't control everything."

I looked up, my eyes meeting Willows, taking in her words.

"Life happens," Willow continued, her tone firm yet comforting. "You need to let the hurt go—let go of things you can't control. You can't let them have this kind of power over you anymore. Take your summer back. Do what makes you happy. It's okay if you end up exploring a connection with either of them—with both. It's okay if you decide not to be with either, but at least be civil with them. That way you can let go of the hurt and move forward."

I allowed myself a small smile, the weight lifting ever so slightly. Maybe Willow was right. Maybe it was time to reclaim the narrative of my own life, to face this unpredictable summer.

"You don't want to ruin this entire summer because you're upset at them and fighting to keep them at a distance when they're always going to be around. Do it for you, not for them." Willow's hand squeezed mine. "You can still have a hot girl summer." She winked.

A part of me wanted to resist, to tell her it wasn't that simple, but her positivity was hard to argue with.

"I guess I could do that," I murmured, considering the idea.

"You got this!" She beamed, her optimism infectious. "And who knows? Maybe you'll work it out and realize one of them really is for you. If not, there's always Bailey," she joked.

"Right," I chuckled with a hesitant smile.

"You're strong, Chan. Stronger than you know," Willow insisted. "Now, let's go show them how strong we are—let's go win on the beer pong table."

She was right. I needed to let go of some of the feelings I'd been holding in, to release their grip on me. Maybe it was okay to let

Boston in, and maybe I didn't have to be upset at Reese anymore. I needed to view the summer from an entirely new angle—this summer could be about healing, about opening doors, and seeing where that could take me.

"Chandler, come on! Focus!" Willow's voice snapped me out of my head as she gestured animatedly toward the cups on the other end of the beer pong table. She was all high energy and encouragement, her eyes wide with competitive fire.

I nodded, trying to appear invested, but my fingers fumbled awkwardly with the little white ball. It felt like the table stretched miles away, each red cup slowly floating in different directions.

"Sorry," I stuttered, dragging in a deep breath that did little to settle my thoughts.

With a flick of my wrist, more an act of going through the motions than any real attempt, I launched the ball. It soared before missing the mark once again. It bounced off a cup's rim, making it evident where the game was headed.

"Hey, Crew," I called over to the towering Blue Devil. "You're up." I placed the ball in his palm, which he accepted with a confused but eager grin.

"I got this," he winked, stepping into my place with the ease of someone who lived for competition.

With Crew there to pick up my slack, I snuck away from the game. The sounds of laughter and splashes were a soothing backdrop after the yelling that had surrounded the beer pong game. I found myself poolside, lowering onto one of the lounge chairs. I was people-watching when I caught sight of Caroline.

She had her hands on her hips, her head tilted back defiantly. She was delivering what I assumed was some sort of jab or harsh words to Reese. I knew exactly what it felt like to be under that scrutiny. She turned away to leave and my gaze caught his. I quickly averted my eyes, pretending to be absorbed in the pool lights, hoping Reese hadn't noticed me.

"Shit," I whispered under my breath. Out of the corner of my eye,

I saw him headed in my direction. I could feel his presence even before he spoke.

"Mind if I have a seat?" Reese asked, nodding toward the empty lounge chair beside me.

I slightly shrugged. "Your house. You can sit where you want."

He lowered himself on the lounge chair beside me, hands resting on his knees.

"Your conversation with Caroline seemed intense," I ventured. "What'd you do to get on her bad side?"

"It just happened naturally," he confessed.

"And I thought I was the only one she hated," I tucked a stray strand of hair behind my ear.

"No," he said with a slight smile. "There's plenty of us. I just happen to enjoy getting under her skin."

"You're sick," I laughed.

Reese raised an eyebrow with a smirk. "But I noticed you watching me over there. Was someone jealous?" he teased before relaxing back on the lounger.

"Jealous?" I managed a small laugh, though it sounded way too forced. "Not in the slightest."

He gave me a skeptical look before taking a sip of his drink. "Anyway," he said, shifting the topic, "I heard you've been getting a little wild tonight."

My heart skipped a beat. Panic fluttered in my chest. "What are you talking about?" My voice was steady, but inside I was wondering if he knew about Boston. About our reckless moment.

"Well, word on the street is you gave Bailey some kind of lap dance." Reese's tone was light and teasing.

"It was just a dare, Reese." I shrugged, not wanting to admit it. "But if you must know, I'm doing a hot girl summer," I said, borrowing Willow's phrase.

"Hot girl summer?" Reese snickered, amused. "What does that even mean? Sounds like an excuse to stir up trouble."

I bit my lip to suppress my embarrassment. "I don't know,

exactly. But for me it means focusing on me and doing what I want —avoiding catching feelings for anyone at all costs." I punctuated the sentence with a smile, a performance of confidence I didn't entirely feel—especially now, after that kiss with Boston.

Internally, I winced at my own words. It wasn't the catching feelings part I was truly trying to avoid, it was the inevitable ache that followed—the getting my feelings hurt part. Still, I kept that vulnerability tucked away, hidden beneath the poker face I was trying my best to keep on.

Reese leaned forward, resting his elbows on his knees, his green eyes locking onto mine with an intensity that made my heart skip. His playful smirk was still there, but there was something else—an edge of assurance.

"Trust me," he said, more genuine than I expected, "in my experience, you can't help when the feelings happen."

He flashed a quick dimple. It seemed genuine. And, despite my inner resolve, I couldn't help but wonder if he was right. If maybe feelings were impossible to hold back.

Willow's clearly fabricated coughing noises caught my attention, then. I turned and spotted her frantically waving me over to her.

"Uh, excuse me," I drawled to Reese, layering my voice with fake concern. "My friend seems to have caught a severe case of hairball."

Reese smiled and shot me a nod before resuming his poolside lounging.

"What's going on?" I asked as I reached Willow.

She bit her lip, arms unfolding to reveal a red stain the size of Texas on her white shirt. "I'm having an emergency," she shrieked.

"What happened, Will?"

"This—" she gestured to the stain. "I spilled my drink on my shirt. Crew and I are winning at beer pong, and we're up again in five minutes. I can't just leave."

I reached for Willow's hand. "Come on," I urged, tugging her toward the house.

"Where are we going?" She whined playfully, letting me guide her without resistance.

"Not far," I promised. We found the nearest bathroom and I shut the door, sealing us away from the party.

"Okay, trade me," I said, gesturing at the shirt.

Willow's eyes widened. "No, you can't wear this," she insisted, arms instinctively crossing over the giant blemish.

"I'm tired and ready to go home, I swear."

For a moment, she just stared, still resisting before she responded. "You're pretty great, you know that?"

"Oh, I know," I said before we quickly switched tops.

We walked out of the bathroom and immediately crossed paths with Boston.

"Whoa," he said, pausing mid-stride, "Are we wearing our drinks now?"

"As a matter of fact, we are," I retorted.

Willow's arms wrapped around me for a hug. "Are you sure you can get home okay?"

"Sure," I said, mustering a smile. "I'll be fine." The truth was that I needed solitude, needed to sort through the tangled web of emotions that had tied me up in knots. The whole summer was meant to be about me—focusing on work, staying away from men, and any other complications, but all I wanted was to dive deeper with Boston.

"Nah," Boston interrupted with a casual confidence that made my heart skip. "I got it. I'll get her back safely."

Willow glanced between Boston and me, a knowing look in her eyes. "Well, if you're sure..."

"Really, it's no trouble," I protested weakly, but even as I spoke, I could feel my resistance melting away.

"You're not walking alone," he said, his voice low and dismissive. "Plus," he added with a lopsided grin, "gives me an excuse to get out of here."

I managed a smile despite the fluttering in my chest. "Okay, then. Lead the way."

Willow shot me an exaggerated thumbs-up behind Boston's back as we headed toward the door. As he held it open for me, our fingers brushed fleetingly. I'd never been more aware of his slightest touch.

The laughter from Reese's party dissipated behind us as we stepped outside. The street was quiet as Boston walked beside me, hands casually tucked into his pockets.

"Thanks for the escape," he said, breaking the comfortable silence.

"Anytime," I replied, flashing him a slight smile.

We began our walk to Willow's, familiar butterflies stirring in my stomach—the same feeling from childhood games of hide-and-seek when I'd run breathlessly from him, hoping he'd find me. But now, under the streetlights, the fluttering felt different, more intense.

I stole a glance at him, trying to pinpoint everything about him that had changed. I was frustrated by his retreat from everyone this past year, including me. He hadn't responded to any of my messages, and I worried endlessly. But now, seeing him here, I realized that maybe it wasn't all bad. He had focused on himself, on baseball, on working out.

And it was... pretty hot, honestly. The way the fabric of his shirt strained across the muscles on his arm, hinting at the definition beneath, the veins standing out along his arms—strong and pronounced. He seemed so different in just a year—stronger, not just physically, but like he'd grown up. Maybe faster than he'd wanted to.

"You've been working out a little, huh?" I couldn't resist teasing because it was obvious.

"Something like that," he said with a shrug, as if it was nothing. As if all the hours of sweat and discipline didn't show in every new line on his body. "Gotta stay ahead if I want to make it anywhere."

I nodded. "Baseball or bodybuilding, Boston?" I teased.

"Maybe both. Just happy to provide you with some eye candy," he winked.

"Modesty suits you." I shook my head but secretly loved that he was showing hints of the playful Boston I was used to. It felt like old times, but also new and somehow completely different.

"Never been my strong suit," he admitted with a chuckle, the sound warm and familiar, sending shivers down my spine.

"No, it hasn't."

"I don't know, I guess working out just passed the time," he said with a casual smirk, the corners of his eyes crinkling in amusement.

"Passed the time?" I asked. "Most people play video games or binge-watch TV shows, but sure, turning into a Greek god works too."

"Hey, if you've got a better way to release some of this built-up tension, I'm all ears," he shot back, blue eyes sparkling with a challenge that sent another flutter through me.

"Knitting is very therapeutic," I joked, before breaking into a smile. "I have absolutely no idea what else could help release tension," I said sarcastically.

We continued toward Willow's house, the night air filled with our shared laughter and the unspoken recognition of something shifting between us—something new and a little bit scary; the unknown we were inching towards, one step at a time.

A softness settled over us as our laughter died down. But there was something else I needed to address—a concern that I'd wanted to talk to him about for a while.

I hesitated, then took a breath. "How are things with your mom?" My voice was softer now, tentative.

He glanced away, his jaw tightening just enough to betray a hint of the emotions he guarded so closely. "I mean, they're okay," he started, and let out a breath. "She didn't come to the first game, but she mentioned she might try for the others."

"Really?" I prodded gently, encouraging him to continue.

"Yeah," he sighed. "She called me the other day. Said she wants to reach out to Reese, see if he'll meet with her. So I guess we'll see how that goes." There was a hint of skepticism in his tone.

"Wow," I whispered. "That's a tough one."

Boston nodded, then gave a small shrug. "I don't blame him if he doesn't want to talk to her. Even though he and I have our differences, I think... I think she should have tried harder, you know?"

I reached out, my fingers brushing his forearm. He tensed under my touch before relaxing again.

"She's trying now, though. That's something," I said softly, meeting his gaze. There was more hurt behind those beautiful eyes than I'd realized.

"I guess." He let out a long sigh before continuing. "You know what the hardest part is? My mom hasn't asked me once how I'm doing. She just assumes that I'm okay."

"Assumes?" I echoed, my frown deepening. How could anyone assume that about Boston lately? His light had dimmed. It was obvious to anyone who cared enough to look.

"Yeah." He stopped walking, and turned to face me, the streetlight casting him in a glow that made his blue eyes sparkle. "It's like... she's so caught up in her own problems that she forgets I've got my own. Forgets I might need her."

"That's awful, Boston."

"It is what it is," he whispered. His vulnerability made my heart twist. "She's got bigger things to worry about than how I'm doing."

I wanted to tell him he wasn't alone, that he never would be, but I knew some assurances didn't need words—they were felt in the squeeze of a hand or the steadiness of a presence.

Reaching out, my fingers curled gently around his firm forearm, feeling the heat of his skin seeping into mine. I leaned into his side, resting my head against his bicep. "But I worried," I whispered. "Even when we weren't talking, I worried."

Boston's gaze slowly shifted, meeting mine with such intensity that a shiver ran down my spine despite our closeness. "I know," he admitted, his voice barely above a whisper, as if he was confiding a secret meant only for me. "Chandler, it wasn't you I was avoiding. It was everything—the world."

I tipped my head back to look at him fully, searching his face for any sign of the boy who used to be so full of light. "Why did you want to shut the world out?" I asked, my thumb absently stroking the prominent vein running along his arm.

"Sometimes," he said, "when bad things happen, you don't want to pull other people down into the darkness with you. It's easier to just... disappear for a while."

"Even from me?" The question came out faster than I intended, betraying the ache of being shut out.

"Especially from you," he said, his voice sharp. "You deserve better than to be dragged into this."

"How about you let me decide what I deserve?" I responded, pausing before continuing. "And don't even try to argue. You're not off the hook yet—you've still got a lot of making up to do," I said, trying to lighten the moment.

"Is that so?"

"Absolutely," I affirmed, crossing my arms for emphasis.

"Fair enough," he conceded, and as we reached Willow's front yard, he stopped and turned to me. He leaned in close, his breath warm against my cheek as he whispered, "Trust me, Chandler, I haven't even started yet."

The kiss he pressed to my cheek was gentle, fleeting, but it sent a shock of electricity through me. My heart was racing, both from his touch, and by what he meant with that statement. And suddenly the butterflies that had gone dormant began to stir once more, reminding me of the unfamiliar ground we were stepping into.

"I'm holding you to that," I managed to say despite the swirl of emotion. "Because I'm keeping score, Boston Riley. Tonight you earned one point."

Boston responded with a heart-melting smile. "One point? After tonight, that's all I get?" His eyes twinkled. I could tell he was on the brink of laughter.

"Rules are rules, Boston." I shrugged. "I don't make them."

"Oh, how convenient," he said, blue eyes sparkling with mischief. A moment later, he stepped back, hands tucked casually into his pockets as if the gravity between us wasn't shifting. "But let's not forget, I'm very competitive... and I'll do whatever it takes to win."

Stepping onto the porch, the wooden boards creaked under my weight and I paused to glance over my shoulder. "I can't wait to see what that entails."

"Chandler, wait up a sec." Boston's voice came out low and teasing. "I keep thinking about it."

"About what?" I asked.

"When I put your hands on me." He looked away, almost as if he was making sure no one else was around. "You surprised me."

His smirk was dimly lit by the glow of the porch light, casting shadows that danced across his sharp jaw. I couldn't help but mirror his expression, though the blush on my cheeks betrayed me.

"Yeah, guess I liked what I felt," I breathed out, the flirtation coming more naturally than I expected.

He nodded, smiling ever so slightly, a hint of mischief there. "You have no idea how good it could feel."

"Guess we'll have to see about that," I countered, feeling another wave of those rebellious butterflies.

"Uh huh," Boston nodded, his gaze never leaving mine. "Good night, Chandler."

With one last lingering look, I turned and went inside, shutting the door behind me.

boston

I PUSHED OPEN the door to the locker room, a blur of commotion and jumbled hair darting past me. The girl was throwing on a large shirt and sprinting out. Bailey smiled at me, smug as ever as he leaned against the lockers, his arm still outstretched from holding the door open for her escape.

"Cutting it close, aren't we?" I asked, eyeing him as I beelined to my locker. The echo of shoes tapping against the concrete floor signaled the rest of our teammates' arrival.

"Almost getting caught is part of the fun," Bailey replied, his lips twisting into a grin.

I shoved my bag into the locker. "Yeah, and coach kicking your ass would also be fun."

Our teammates began to file in, the locker room swelling with the sounds of locker doors slamming and muffled conversations. I scanned the room as it started to silence, catching Bailey and Reese exchanging barely-contained smirks. I followed their gaze to see Coach striding in, a pen in his hand, a bright orange thong dangling on the end.

I fought back a smile that I knew would piss off Coach. Around me, shoulders trembled and snickers were hastily smothered. Bailey's nonchalance stood out amongst the stifled amusement around him—he lounged back, arms crossed over his chest, trying his best to portray innocence.

Coach's glare swept across the room like a lighthouse beam, fierce and warning. "How many times do I have to tell you all this clubhouse is a gift," he barked, the thong swinging from the pen with each punctuating gesture. "If I catch any of you fooling around in the locker—," he paused for effect, "—room, you will be benched. And I'm not messing around this year."

Coach's eyes narrowed slightly as they landed on Bailey, but he continued undeterred.

"Try me," he added with a steely edge, "and all of you will take turns wearing this at practice." Coach shook the fluorescent under-garment one last time for emphasis before tossing it into a nearby trash can.

I risked another glance at Bailey, his expression now unreadable. When Coach finally walked out of the locker room, the rest of us erupted in uncontrollable laughter.

Coach didn't take it easy on us. We ran drill after drill. Bailey's little stunt had earned the whole team an afternoon of agony.

"Alright, hit the showers!" Coach bellowed, wiping his brow. "Don't forget, two hours from now, you're back here for Devils' Day Out. No excuses!"

Groans echoed around the field but Coach's glare silenced all complaints. "I don't want to hear it," he snapped. "Cry to your pillow, not to me. Now, get out of here!"

"Riley!" Coach yelled, catching me off guard. "You stay back. My office. Now."

I followed behind him to his office. He didn't say a word on the walk.

"Sit down," he said, pointing to a chair opposite his cluttered desk.

"Coach, if you think I had anything to d—"

"Would you just sit?" he cut me off.

I obeyed, sinking into the chair while he rummaged through the papers on his desk. Finally, he found what he was looking for and slid a packet across to me. "Don't say I never did anything for ya."

Confused, I picked up the packet. "What is it?"

"Open it and see for yourself."

The words Chicago Cubs were printed at the top of the first page, and my breath caught in my chest. Plane tickets, itinerary—it was all there. A dream, laid out in front of me.

"Chicago... They want me to visit?" I stammered, my voice barely above a whisper.

"You'd be perfect for their organization," Coach said with a nod. "They're one of the best, and they're interested in you for the draft."

"Coach, this is..." a wave of disbelief crashed over me, and I slowly sank back into the chair.

"Enjoy the moment, kid. You've earned it," Coach encouraged, leaning back in his chair with satisfaction. "Only downside is that you'll miss the Bayside Ball, but duty calls."

"Thanks, Coach."

I looked down at the envelope again and Chandler's face flashed in my mind. I hadn't realized until that moment how I felt about it— I wouldn't have the chance to ask her to the ball, to finally have her on my arm. Did I really have to miss that?

"Now get outta here." Coach gestured toward the door.

I lingered long enough to avoid the rush for the showers, then got in and out and changed quickly. As I was walking out of the locker rooms I heard a high-pitched voice.

"Hey, Boston!"

I turned to Caroline, twirling a strand of blonde hair around her finger.

"Caroline," I acknowledged with a nod, ready to make my escape.

She pouted playfully, stepping forward. "Haven't seen much of you yet this summer. Was hoping you'd be giving me more attention."

Her tone was flirty. Caroline was hard to ignore—girls like her usually were—and if this was last summer, she would have had my attention.

"Sorry, it's been busy," I shrugged, thinking that 'busy' was an understatement. Between practices and the complicated Chandler situation, there wasn't much room for anything—or anyone—else. "I've had a—"

"Lot going on? I know." She cut across me with a dismissive wave of her hand. "But you're here now, and since you're part of the team, you're part of all team activities."

"Right," I agreed, unsure where she was going. But I knew better than to argue—especially knowing how pissed off Coach already was. "Devil's Day Out, huh?"

"Exactly," she confirmed with a smile that suggested she was pleased to have captured my attention, even if only for a moment. "And I need your help."

I let out a resigned sigh. "Okay, what do you need?"

Her expression softened, and she rewarded me with a pleased smile. She handed me a pile of small envelopes and then a pile of large ones.

"Here. These need to go inside this." She tapped a finger on the large manila envelopes. "And don't peek."

"Wouldn't dream of it," I whispered, wondering what the hell I was doing this for. Taking a seat in the chair nearby, I started stuffing envelopes, the paper shuffling softly with each motion.

"Thanks, Boston. You're a lifesaver," she squealed.

"No biggie," I said with a half-smile, wondering if Chandler would be roped into this event too. "But, um," I paused my envelope stuffing. "Why are you doing all this anyway?"

Caroline halted mid-step, turned back to me, and sighed. For a moment, she looked almost vulnerable. "My mom," she began, her voice tightening. "She's convinced I'll mess up being the president and won't do the job as well as she did." A shadow crossed her face as she added, "So I have to prove I can not only handle this, but outdo her."

"Got it. Moms... they're great, aren't they?" I tried to keep the tone light, but something about her disappointment felt familiar.

"Right?" Caroline chuckled, shaking her head. "Right. I get it. They come with the family package, but there should also be a therapist thrown in there somewhere."

When she let her guard down like that, Caroline wasn't so bad. We continued to work on her project, slipping into a comfortable silence. Soon, the room began to fill up with teammates and committee members. I caught sight of Chandler and Willow toward the back, heads together in quiet conversation.

"Coach kicked our ass today." Parker slid into the seat beside me, his eyes scanning the growing crowd.

"When does he not kick our ass?" I asked, raising an eyebrow.

Suddenly, a piercing whistle cut through the noise, and the room fell silent. Caroline stood at the front, confidence radiating off her. With a flick of her wrist, she commanded attention like a pro.

"Alright, everyone!" She lifted her chin and shoulders. "Each player teams up with a committee member. Inside your packet, you'll find envelopes—each one is numbered."

Curiosity rippled through the room as Caroline continued. "You must complete each task listed inside, and you need to submit photo proof in the group chat. First team who submits all photos and followed directions wins," she said, pausing for everyone to process the instructions.

"Let's make this Devils' Day Out one for the history books," she concluded, a spark of determination lighting her eyes. The excitement and chatter in the crowd rose again.

"Five minutes," Caroline announced, checking her watch. "Then we open our envelopes and may the best team win!"

I glanced around, hoping I could get Chandler's attention and that she'd partner with me, but I also wondered what kind of tasks were inside the envelopes. I knew this was going to be more than a game—we were all competitive, and the committee took anything Blue Devils related very seriously.

Reese's voice cut through the buzz as he pushed off from the wall and stepped into the circle that had formed around Caroline. "And winner gets what?" he asked, suspiciously.

Caroline's smile broadened. "Great question. I've talked with Coach and the winners get a room upgrade next week for the away tournament," she declared with emphasis. "Both members on the winning team get their own suite." A collective cheer rose, and I understood the excitement. Last year I had to share a tiny hotel room with Parker, and we were practically on top of each other.

A designated committee member began passing out the envelopes as Caroline continued to speak. "Willow," she gestured toward her, "will create a group chat and add everyone." The crowd shifted, moving closer to grab their envelopes.

"First one completed must have all photos in," Caroline added, "and type 'Blue Devils' once completed. We will review all photos at the end of the day and make sure the winner has completed each task. Any questions?"

I turned toward Chandler, but before I could get her attention, a firm grip grabbed my arm.

"Boston, you're with me." Caroline's tone left no room for argument, her fingers squeezing assertively just above my elbow.

"Uh, sure, Caroline," I managed, taken back by her sudden claim on me.

I shot Chandler an apologetic look hoping my expression conveyed to her that I'd have rather been her teammate. Chandler's smile softened, understanding and forgiving as always.

Parker stood up before he said, "So, which of you ladies wants to have me all to themselves today?"

"Ew, not I," Chandler quipped, a grimace on her face.

Willow stepped forward. "I'll oblige, but just so we're clear, I am very competitive. We win or we don't do it at all."

Parker's grin was instant. "Lead the way," he said before they disappeared into the crowd.

"Come on, we've got to strategize," Caroline tugged at my sleeve impatiently, her eyes filled with competitive fire. I let her pull me away, but not before casting a lingering glance back over my shoulder.

Reese had his arm casually draped around Chandler's shoulders. My stomach tightened. I knew that meant they were partners. They would have to spend the day together. After last night, I couldn't stand the thought. I know Reese said he was stepping back, but could I really trust him? Last year, he'd used her to get to me. What if he was planning to do it again?

"Okay, you drive. I'll keep track of the envelopes," Caroline instructed with an assertive nod that snapped me out of my thoughts about Chandler and Reese.

"Sure," I replied, shaking my head slightly to refocus on the task at hand. As much as I tried, thoughts of Chandler getting into Reese's truck, her laughter mingling with his, kept intruding.

I walked over to Caroline's side of the car and opened the door for her before making my way around to the driver's side.

"Thanks," Caroline said as she settled into the passenger seat. She wasted no time pulling out the first envelope from the stack she was cradling.

Curiosity got the better of me. "Don't you already know what's inside?"

She tore open the seal and peeked inside with a smirk. "As a matter of fact, I don't. Some of the committee members helped organize this part. Keeps it interesting."

"I see," I said, turning the key and stealing one last glance toward Reese's truck. I tightened my grip on the steering wheel, forcing myself to look away. Today was about winning the prize, nothing else.

"Ready?" Caroline's excitement brought my attention back to her and whatever we were about to take on. We had a mission, and I needed to focus on that... and only that.

"I guess so. What does it say?" I asked, glancing over at Caroline as she pulled a folded piece of paper from the envelope, a playful smirk on her lips.

"It says to write your partner's name and something others might not know about them on one of these sheets of paper," Caroline read aloud, her eyes scanning the instructions. "And then hold it up in front of their favorite view in Bayside."

"Sounds simple enough," I shrugged, trying to muster some enthusiasm. "Where's your favorite view?"

"That's easy," she replied, tucking a stray lock of hair behind her ear. "Go straight, and I'll tell you when to take a left."

I nodded and then shifted the truck back into park just before we left the lot. "Actually, since we're here, we should probably do mine first."

"Okay," she said, looking intrigued. "What's your favorite view?"

"Right here." I pointed toward the ballfield.

"Here?" Caroline's voice was surprised, but she quickly put on a smile. She scribbled something down on the small paper and stepped out to take a photo, leaving me alone with my thoughts for a moment.

When she got back into the car, I couldn't help but ask. "What did you write?"

Caroline just winked, placing her phone down. "Oh, you'll find out."

The engine hummed softly as we cruised down the main street of Bayside, but inside my mind was adrift. I couldn't shake off thoughts of Chandler. I knew her favorite view would be the lake. She always had to see it as soon as she got to Bayside, and then again before she left.

"Stop right here!" Caroline's voice pulled me back to the present, and I hit the brakes, in the middle of a busy street.

"Here?" I asked, looking through the windshield at the row of storefronts. "Your favorite view is this street downtown?"

She snickered. "No. Get out of the car, silly."

Stepping onto the sidewalk, I followed her finger as she pointed with enthusiasm to a massive painting across a brick wall. It was a vividly-colored mural, the word Bayside in large letters in the middle.

"Look at this," she said. "This painting has everything from Bayside in it. There's the baseball field, there's the lake..." her voice trailed off as she gestured toward the familiar landmarks depicted on the mural.

"Even Mrs. Patsy's pet pig," I chimed in, laughing as I spotted the little guy peeking through some bushes. The whole town, captured in swirls of paint—it was unexpectedly really cool.

"Exactly!" Caroline beamed, pleased with my reaction.

I took the piece of paper, scribbling down her name with the words, "going to run the world someday" on the paper. I could see her not just being the president of the Blue Devils' committee, I could easily see her bossing around the staff in the White House. Holding it up, I snapped a photo with the mural in the background.

"Okay, on three we'll send our photos in the chat together," she said, her eyes twinkling with excitement. "Ready? One, two..." she counted as we sent in our photos.

We pressed send simultaneously, and within seconds, our phones buzzed with incoming notifications from the group chat. I couldn't help but let out a laugh as I scrolled through the string of photos and notes on them.

Reese's photo for Chandler was of course a picture of the lake.

Chandler gets overly excited about seeing heart-shaped rocks - Reese

I smiled. I could picture her, eyes lighting up as she found one that made her squeal.

Chandler sent a snapshot of the same part of the lake, taken from Reese's boat. The sight turned my stomach.

Reese has an annual Disney membership ... for himself - Chandler

Willow is feisty but sleeps with a nightlight - Parker

Parker is kinda cute but cries at Christmas movies - Willow

The thread continued with hilarious facts. Bailey had apparently hooked up with two roommates, who were both on the cheerleading squad.

And then I saw it—the note Caroline wrote about me. I blinked at my phone screen, unable to speak for a second.

Boston is great with his tongue - Caroline

I turned to face Caroline, seething with anger. "Why the fuck would you write that?" I asked, struggling to keep my voice level.

She laughed as if it was no big deal. "It was supposed to be funny, Boston," she said, her tone dismissive, as though my irritation was nothing but an overreaction.

"Really, Caroline?" I clenched my jaw.

"Come on, lighten up," she said, still smiling, still not getting it. "This day is just about having fun."

But it wasn't funny—not to me. Messages from the group chat started rolling in as I glanced back at my phone.

CREW

BOSTON, MY BOY!!!!

PARKER

Show off. I got cries at Christmas movies.
Who the fuck doesn't cry at Christmas
movies?

BAILEY

Pointers, now! Drop em' in the chat.

REESE

We all know Bailey doesn't know what the
fuck he's doing with his tongue.

I put my phone back in my pocket. "Caroline, you can't just—" I started, but she cut me off with a wave of her hand.

"Relax, Boston. It's just your teammates and the committee members who saw it. They're my best friends on the cheer team," she said dismissively. "Plus Willow and Chandler." Her eyes flicked to mine, looking for a reaction. "Is that why you're upset? Chandler?" she asked, her voice suddenly taking on an edge. "Didn't she hook up with Reese last summer? Why do you even care?"

The mention of Chandler's past with him pissed me off, but I pushed the thought aside. "That's not the point."

"Please," Caroline scoffed. "Boston, everyone knows we hooked up last summer. And let's be honest, we'll probably hook up again this summer." She gave me a look that was meant to be enticing. "It's not a big deal."

I took a deep breath, feeling the weight of her words—completely over the entire thing. "Caroline," I said, lowering my voice, hoping she understood I meant every word I was about to speak. "It's not going to happen. Ever again."

She folded her arms across her chest.

"Yes, we hooked up last summer," I continued, "but I made it clear before anything happened that it wasn't going to go anywhere. And it isn't."

Her eyes, once playful, flashed with anger then. "Fine," she spat, turning on her heel and leaving me standing there. "I'll meet you at the truck."

Relief and unease coursed through me. What the hell was going through Chandler's mind? I knew she'd see that note. Knowing how stubborn she was, I wasn't going to be surprised if this one incident made her hate me all over again.

chandler

"WHAT THE FUCK," I blurted out, looking at my phone screen, jaw on the floor.

Reese, leaning against his sleek black truck, arched an eyebrow in response. "What?"

"Did you see what Caroline wrote about Boston?" I said, my eyes scanning my glaringly bright phone screen once more.

I turned the screen around and he squinted at the words before his lips curved into a smirk. "Oh shit, that a fucking boy. Maybe we are related after all," Reese snickered, and shook his head.

I scowled, unamused by his unnecessary support. "It's not funny, Reese. Why would she say that?"

"Chill, Chandler. She's probably just messing with him." Reese shrugged.

"No, I'm sure she's not." I pressed my lips together, trying to suppress the unsettling images flooding my mind. The thought of Boston hooking up with her, of him going down on her... I went queasy. It wasn't just disgust swirling in my stomach—it was a searing heat, a rage threatening to boil over. "Why is she so horrible?"

"That's just Caroline," he shrugged. "Trust me, she and I have never gotten along. She's hated me for as far back as I can remember, and anytime I get the chance to piss her off, I don't hesitate."

"I wish I enjoyed being on her bad side," I said.

Reese leaned against the open door of his truck, arms folded, watching me with an expression that was half mockery, half genuine curiosity. "So, you wanna quit? Or should we keep going?" The corners of his mouth twitched, and I could tell he was barely holding back a full-on grin.

"Quit?" I spat, yanking my gaze from the infuriating message to meet his challenging stare. "Not in this lifetime, Carrington." Climbing into the passenger seat, I crossed my arms over my chest. "We're still playing. And now we're winning."

His smile broke free, lighting up those electric green eyes as he shut the truck door after me and climbed into the driver's seat. I stubbornly turned my attention outside, watching the scenery blur by as Reese pulled out onto the road.

"So, are you going to open the next envelope to tell me where we're going, or am I just going to drive around until you get over the fit you're throwing?" Reese asked.

"Fit? I don't throw fits," I retorted without looking at him, staring out the window. "Strategic displays of displeasure, maybe, but not fits."

"Ah, of course, how could I mistake the two?" he snickered, casting a sidelong glance at me. "Strategically display the next envelope, then?"

"Fine." My response was short, but I was grateful for the distraction. Anything to pull my thoughts away from Caroline and Boston and the nauseating images that were flashing through my mind.

I reached for the envelope and tore it open, sending a shower of paper fragments into my lap. "Let's see what this round brings." I unfolded the note, not giving Reese the satisfaction of seeing me ruffled.

"Swap a clothing item to wear while grabbing a slice at the best pizza place in town," I read aloud. This was going to be interesting.

"Okay, so what are we swapping?" Reese asked in amusement.

I glanced around the truck's interior and spotted his gym bag. "What do you have that's clean?"

"Um," he began, as he kept his eyes on the road but reached in the backseat and rummaged through a bag, pulling out a jersey. "I have this."

I eyed it skeptically. "No, I'm not wearing your jersey. What else do you have?"

"Hm..." Reese looked down, then pointed to the shirt he was wearing. "This? But it's got my last name on it too."

"Holy balls, you really are conceited." I sighed. "Who only has shirts with their last name on it?"

He flashed a grin, all confidence and charm. "I came straight from baseball, what do you expect?"

"Right." I pondered for a moment, biting my lip. "Can I have your shorts?"

"Sure," Reese said with a devilish grin. "But I don't have anything on underneath them."

"Reese!" I exclaimed, half exasperated, half amused. "Why aren't you wearing anything underneath?"

"Again," he replied with a lazy shrug, his eyes locked with mine, "came from practice, just showered."

"Convenient," I whispered under my breath, already plotting the quickest way to win this round of the game. "Give me the damn jersey," I said, slapping my palm against my forehead in despair. Reese tossed it over with a teasing glint in his eye.

"What's in it for me?" he asked, his smirk growing wider. "Your panties?"

"No way in hell, Carrington." I rolled my eyes, glancing down at what I was wearing to figure out what I could offer him. "You can have my socks."

"Chandler, I'm not wearing your smelly ass socks," he said playfully.

"Reese, my socks don't smell bad!" I protested, though I couldn't help but laugh at the absurdity of the situation.

"Still, I'm not wearing them." He shrugged.

With a huff, I searched myself for an alternative. An idea popped into my head. I slipped my hand beneath my shirt and slid off my tank top, flinging it at him. "Here."

He caught the piece of cloth, holding it up and eyeing it suspiciously. "How the hell am I supposed to wear this?"

"I don't know, Reese. You're a big boy, figure it out," I teased, knowing full well that the stretchy fabric stood no chance against his broad shoulders.

We parked near the pizza place and Reese, without hesitation, peeled his shirt off. I stole a glance—okay, maybe more than just a glance—at his defined muscles and the way his tanned skin seemed to glow even in the shade of his truck. But I quickly turned away, focusing on anything else.

As soon as we burst through the Derald's Pizza doors, Parker and Willow dashed out, grinning like they'd just robbed a bank. Their swapped attire was impossible to miss: Willow was drowning in Parker's Blue Devils shirt, looking surprisingly fierce. The shirt he was wearing, on the other hand said, "A Little Bit Dramatic" across the front.

"Nice shirt, drama queen!" Reese yelled at Parker, a smirk on his face.

Parker spun around mid-stride with his middle finger raised. "You're literally in my sister's purple tank top, Carrington. See you at the finish line!"

I couldn't help but snicker at them, but the competitive fire in me flared. I latched onto Reese's arm, tugging him forward. "Hurry up—they're beating us!"

"We'll catch them," Reese said, but he was already making his way to the counter. I stood on tiptoes to watch over the crowd as Reese ordered. The lady behind the register caught sight of him and did a double take, her lips quivering.

"Can I get two slices? Any kind—whatever is quickest, please. The lady gets feisty when she's hungry," he said, winking at her.

She nodded, pressing her hand to her mouth, shoulders shaking from suppressed giggles. "Coming right up," she managed to say without bursting into outright laughter.

"Chandler, stop staring. You're not helping my street cred here," Reese teased without looking back at me.

"Your street cred went out the window the moment you put on my tank top," I retorted, but my heart fluttered at the sight of him— so out of place, yet somehow owning the moment entirely.

I was cut off mid-sentence as a collective gasp echoed through the restaurant, all heads turning toward the entrance. Bailey walked in wearing nothing but bright pink polka dot underwear. He strode up to the counter, confidence not faltering for even a second, despite the shocked and amused faces. A moment later, his partner walked in behind him. The smiley face boxers she was wearing actually looked cute on her.

"Wow," I muttered, momentarily forgetting our own clothes swap. Reese turned to see what the commotion was about and let out a low whistle.

"Bailey never disappoints. Had to lose the shirt to get the full effect," Reese said, laughing.

"Guess we've found someone who enjoys the spotlight even more than you do," I teased.

"Okay, let's hurry and take this picture," he said, grabbing the paper plates and turning to me with an impish grin. "Ready?" Reese asked, his arm brushing against mine as he lifted his slice for the photo.

"Smile," I said, and we both leaned in close as I turned and made sure the Carrington name was visible. "Got it," I declared, checking the photo before nodding in satisfaction. "Let's go"

I grabbed Reese's arm, urgency pumping through my veins as we bolted out of the pizza place. The group chat was blowing up with updates from the others. My gaze immediately landed on the photo of Caroline wearing one of Boston's batting gloves while he sported her bright pink headband. My smile wavered for a second, wondering if my own photo in Reese's jersey might stir up annoyance in Boston. But I shrugged it off—Caroline's tongue comment in the chat had set the bar. "Hey, we've gotta wrap up the last task before sundown," Reese said, casting a glance toward the horizon where the sun was starting to dip low, painting the sky in hues of orange and pink.

"Right," I agreed, feeling the weight of the day.

"What's the last one?" he asked.

"Alright, it says we need to go to this address," I handed him the slip of paper, "and then, there's a twist."

"Doesn't surprise me." He shrugged, accepting the challenge with a grin as he started the engine.

"Once we get there, we have to... tell each other something no one else knows. Then, we take a selfie and submit it. Apparently, we're staying for some 'Devils' Day Out' celebration and the winner announcement."

"Something no one else knows?" he echoed as he rubbed his chin in thought.

As we approached the address near the lake, the scenery shifted into something unexpectedly serene. Reese pulled up to a spot that seemed too beautiful to have gone unnoticed before. A long stretch of sand was dotted with pergolas, twinkling lights hanging above casting a warm glow over tables topped with flickering candles.

"Wow..." I murmured, stepping out of the truck. The earthy scent of the lake mingled pleasantly with the crisp evening air.

Reese joined me, and together we stood taking in the view. "Not what I expected from Caroline's twisted game," I said.

"It's... pretty cool." I caught his eye, and for a moment, we shared an unspoken acknowledgment of the day's madness culminating into this final moment.

"Shall we?" I gestured to the water's edge, where we'd likely find the best angle for our selfie.

"Let's do it," Reese agreed, and we made our way closer to the lake, ready to reveal our secrets and capture the moment—a snapshot of vulnerability against a gorgeous backdrop.

"Okay, you go first," I prompted as we approached the lake, the sand shifting beneath our feet. The day had been long and eventful and though it had been orchestrated by Caroline, the final setting was calm and beautiful.

Reese paused, his gaze lingering on the shimmering lake before turning to me. "I want to let her in."

"Who?" I asked, curiosity piqued.

"My real mom," he said, his tone bittersweet. "I'm thinking about meeting with her." I'd expected his secret to be superficial, some confession about baseball. Not something so important and vulnerable.

But then again, Reese has always been full of surprises, he always kept me guessing.

"You should," I encouraged, touched by his vulnerability. "I know she did something awful, but she's a good person."

"Something awful?" His eyes locked on mine. "Do you know what it's like not having your mom around? When everyone else does? Every milestone, every game... She was never there." His voice cracked, revealing a pain so raw, so deep—I could feel how hurt he was.

I reached for his arm, my fingers brushing against the fabric of his sleeve. "I can't even imagine. I'm sorry. But you've missed so much time together already—maybe there's a future where you don't have to miss time with her anymore."

"Maybe," he conceded, with a doubtful shrug. "But anyway, that's something no one else knows. Your turn."

I hesitated, my thoughts swirling. "I want to be an actress," I began, echoing a dream I'd held close for so long.

"Nope, that doesn't count," Reese cut in, a half-smile playing on his lips. "Everyone knows that. Go again."

"Okay," I said, steeling myself. "I'm terrified. Because of you." I let the words spill out without thinking.

"Me?" He frowned, his eyebrows raised in confusion. "Terrified of what?"

"Last summer... you really hurt me," I hesitantly admitted, biting my nail. "And I don't want that to happen again. I'm scared to jump into anything because I don't want anyone to have that power over me."

Reese's expression softened, the lines of his face relaxing as if he truly did understand the weight of my words. He halted mid-step, his gaze locking onto mine, a severity in his eyes that I'd rarely seen. The wind picked up, sending a stray lock of hair into my face. His hand moved almost instinctively, tucking the strand behind my ear.

"Chandler, I'm sorry," he said. "I never wanted to hurt you. Believe me, if I had a choice, we'd still be together."

My chest went tight, but I pushed past it. "You do have a choice, Reese."

He shook his head slowly, disappointment crossing his features. "No, Chandler, I don't." His whisper carried a heavy weight that tugged at the very air between us.

"What does that mean?" My heart raced. I needed to understand.

"I've been a shitty older brother to Boston my whole life. I could have done things so differently..." he paused, looking out over the lake, his expression shadowed by twilight. "We could have worked through this together, but no, I had to be a dick. I took out all the pain from my mom on him. And he loves you. I can't take that from him too."

I held my breath for a moment as I processed his words. "But—"

"Chandler," he cut in, his gaze intense, "I know what we had, but I think there's always been something between you two. Look how mad you got about Caroline. Don't worry about getting hurt, and don't let it hold you back." He paused, breathed, then continued. "And like I said, if that doesn't work out, come find me." He winked.

"When did you get so wise?" I smirked. It was hard to hear, but he was right. I owed it to myself, and to the younger version of me who would faint at the thought of Boston's attention, to know there was a chance to explore whatever may be between us. Even if I wasn't prepared for it this summer, I needed to figure out what had always lingered between us.

I stood there, thinking about his words, the silence between us stretching out. Despite everything, I saw a Reese that few others did —the thoughtful, kind man beneath his cocky exterior.

"Okay, we did the task," I said, mustering a smile to lighten the moment. "Let's take the selfie."

Together, we angled the phone, capturing our faces against the backdrop of the lake. With a click, the moment was captured, and I sent the photo off into the chat.

We turned back toward the lake. Darkness had settled fully now, punctuated only by the twinkling lights along the shore. More people had gathered, their laughter and chatter growing louder as we walked towards the party. I was suddenly acutely aware of the oversized jersey hanging around me. Reese's jersey—I had been so caught up in the game that I'd forgotten to take it off. I couldn't help but wonder what Boston would think about me wearing someone else's jersey—Reese's jersey.

boston

CAROLINE and I completed the last stupid task, and I headed toward the lake where everyone was gathered. I couldn't even remember what we talked about, I couldn't focus. I was looking for Chandler. A few people patted me on the back as I passed, their acknowledgments barely registering as I looked around for her.

It didn't take long to find her. But then it hit me—she was still wearing his jersey. My skin was tingling with heat and I was suddenly growling without realizing it. I wanted to rip that jersey off her, to show her who she really belonged to. She was sitting at a table with a few others when she noticed me approaching.

I ran a hand through my hair. "Can we talk?" It was more a demand than a question.

"Sure," she said, rising from her seat.

"Why do you still have that on?" I asked, unable to hide the annoyance. "The game is over, Chandler."

She turned to face me fully, the jersey hanging loosely off one shoulder. "It was just a game, Boston. It doesn't mean anything."

"It does to me," I said, my jaw set firm.

Her hazel eyes caught mine, a hint of defiance sparking in them. "Are you jealous?" she asked, crossing her arms.

"Yes," I whispered, shoving my hands into the pockets of my jeans. "Yes, Chandler. Is that what you want to hear? I'm jealous."

She tilted her head slightly, letting out a soft laugh. "Boston, you have no room to talk. What about Caroline's message about you today?"

"I'm sorry you had to see that," I said, finally breaking the brief silence. "I don't know why she did that."

She stopped walking and turned to face me. "I do," she said softly. "She likes you, Boston. I get why she likes you."

She wasn't just saying words, there was something behind them—something that told me exactly what I needed to know. It felt like a door cracked open, like she was finally starting to let me in.

Taking a deep breath, I reached out and gently lifted her chin, tilting it so that her eyes met mine. "That doesn't matter. I want you."

She inhaled sharply, and for a moment there was nothing else but us.

A smile touched her lips. "Even when I wear his jersey?" A glint of humor returned to her eyes, challenging me.

I leaned in closer and growled in her ear. "I want to rip that damn jersey off you."

Her gasp was soft. "Why?"

"Because you're mine. You always have been," I said, nipping at the delicate skin below her ear. My hand slid under the hem of the jersey, drifting to the small of her back. "Not his. Mine."

She melted into me, her eyes fluttering shut as our lips hovered close, almost brushing against each other.

"WE WON! WE WON!" The shout ripped through our bubble, and we both turned toward the sound. Willow was jumping ecstatically beside Parker.

"Wha—?" Chandler's mouth hung open, her earlier resolve forgotten.

Some of the other committee members nearby were shaking

their heads with smiles as they finished double-checking that the photos submitted to the group chat had followed the rules.

"Come on," I said, motioning toward the commotion. "Let's go congratulate them."

We started to make our way back, me leading Chandler in the darkness. Laughter and cheers grew louder, but then there was a sharp, sudden crash. Chandler screamed.

I spun around to find Chandler on the rocky ground, one hand gripping her ankle. Tears welled in her hazel eyes.

I dropped to my knees beside her. "What just happened?"

Her lips pressed together in a thin line before she managed to speak. "I think... I just rolled my ankle on a rock."

"Let me see." My fingers brushed against her skin softly, feeling for swelling as she drew in a shaky breath.

I'd known injuries over the years playing baseball, had sprained everything possible. "Does this hurt?"

"Sort of." She winced as she tried to move it.

Exhaling a heavy breath, I slid one arm under her knees, the other around her back. "Okay, come here," I said, hoisting her up into my arms.

"Hey! What's going on?" Willow's voice carried over the party noise as I walked toward the high-fiving crowd, Chandler in my arms.

"Someone took a little tumble," I explained, shifting her weight so they could see her ankle.

Parker looked over, his brow creasing with concern. "What happened?"

"I'm fine," Chandler called out. "I think I just twisted my ankle."

"Trip on a heart-shaped rock?" Parker couldn't help himself, a teasing smirk playing on his lips.

"Shut up, Parker," she shot back.

"Sorry, sis," he said, the smirk fading as he caught her glare.

"I'm gonna take her home, get her some ice," I called out to Parker and Willow.

"Boston, I can get home by myself," Chandler protested, her independence flaring even in discomfort.

"How? Are you going to hobble there?" I raised an eyebrow at her stubbornness.

"Fine." Her cheeks flushed, either from embarrassment or annoyance—I couldn't tell which. But it didn't matter. Right now all that mattered was getting her home safely.

"Hey, congrats on winning," she said, nodding toward Willow and Parker who were still riding a high from their victory.

"Thanks!" Willow beamed, her eyes already glittering with plans. "I'm going to take the longest bubble bath and enjoy every last second of that suite next week!"

"Can't argue with that," Chandler said with a smile. "You deserve it, Willow. And hey, Parker, congrats on your win too."

Parker grinned, his arm slung around Willow's shoulder. "Uh huh, just make sure you get home safe, Chan."

Willow glanced at me, her expression softening. "Boston, take good care of her, okay? I'll be there later to check on her."

"Will do," I assured her, adjusting Chandler slightly to ease the pressure on her ankle.

Reese leaned casually against the wooden beams of the pergola, as he glanced over at us. "Everything cool over here?" he called out.

"All good." She was fine with me, and I didn't need his help.

Reese flashed a wink, his smirk suggesting he saw right through my façade.

I hoisted Chandler's weight against my side as I carefully made my way to the truck. I helped her up and she laid her ankle gently across the dashboard. It already looked swollen.

"Comfortable?" I asked, starting the engine with a glance towards her.

"As can be," she said, offering a small smile that didn't quite reach her eyes.

When we arrived a few minutes later, I parked as close to the door as possible, killed the ignition, and scooped Chandler into my arms before she could protest.

"Really, Boston, you don't have to carry me," she murmured with a mix of appreciation and stubborn independence.

"Chandler," I replied, leaving no room for arguments as I nudged the door open with my shoulder. "Just relax, okay? I got you."

Once inside, I carefully placed her on the couch, elevating her foot with a pillow. Then my gaze shifted to the jersey she was still wearing. It had been irritating me since the moment I saw it draped over her.

"Before you get too comfortable," I glared at the jersey, "can you take that off now, please?"

She rolled her eyes. "Men and their egos," she teased, attempting to push up from the couch with a grimace.

"Hey, easy there." I stepped forward, placing a hand on her shoulder to stop her efforts. "I got it."

Chandler sighed. "I just need to go to the bathroom. My pajamas are hanging in there."

"Alright," I conceded, scooping her up into my arms as her fingers gripped my shirt. Her closeness was intoxicating, but I focused on the task at hand.

"Thanks, Boston," she said, softly. "I can take it from here."

With her ankle now the center of my attention, I made my way to the kitchen in search of Advil, water, and an ice pack. I found everything fairly easily, then set the items on the nightstand next to her bed. Crossing back to the bathroom, I leaned against the wall in the hallway. The sound of fabric rustling and drawers opening filtered through the door. After a few minutes that felt much longer, she emerged. The sight of her took my breath away.

She stood there in striped pajamas with short shorts that hugged her in all the right ways. Dark hair spread over her shoulders, framing her face like she was some kind of bedtime goddess. It was just pajamas, but damn she made them look good.

"Are you happy now?" she asked, pointing down to her pajama shirt.

"Ecstatic," I said sarcastically, but the sight of her without his jersey eased the tightness in my chest. "Stripes suit you," I said, offering my arm.

"Shut up," she laughed, taking the support and hobbling alongside me to her bedroom.

I helped her onto the bed before hoisting her ankle onto a pillow, then gently tucking the covers around her.

"Seriously, Boston, you don't have to do all of this."

"You're talking to someone who has sprained everything capable of being sprained." I gently placed the ice pack on her swollen ankle.

"Ouch!" she winced, then softened. "Thanks, though. For everything."

"Hey, I still have making up to do," I said, with an easy smile. "Does this gain me any points?"

"I think you're at about two points now."

"I'll work on that," I said with a playful wink. "But for now, try to get some rest."

"I'll try," she muttered, a blush creeping onto her cheeks. She settled into the pillows, looking cozy and warm. "Night, Boston."

"Try not to roll off the bed and break something else," I said, half joking as I leaned in to press a kiss on her cheek.

"Ha-ha, very funny."

I backed toward the door and flicked off the light. Chandler's room glowed softly from the streetlight shining through the curtains. "Good night," I said as I pulled the door closed behind me.

I left through the front door and shut it behind me then slid into the leather seat of my truck. I ran a hand through my hair as I let out a long sigh. Today was one of those days that seemed to go on forever, especially with Caroline testing the limits of my patience. With a turn of the key, the engine rumbled, shaking off the silence of the quiet street.

My hand hovered over the gear stick just as my phone buzzed in my pocket. Chandler's name flashed on the screen.

CHANDLER

Is it true?

ME

Is what true?

CHANDLER

You know. What she said… Caroline.

I killed the engine, taking in the silence of the quiet street again. I couldn't leave like this—not without making sure Caroline's stupid comment didn't get to her head. I swung the door open and made my way back inside the house.

My knuckles tapped softly against her bedroom door. "Yes?" she squeaked.

I inched the door open, revealing her sitting up on her bed. There was an unmistakable look of surprise on her face, as if she wished she could disappear inside the depths of her comforter.

"I thought you left already," Chandler murmured, almost pulling the comforter up to cover her eyes.

"Almost did," I admitted, leaning against the doorway. "I need you to know... She doesn't mean anything to me, okay? What she thinks doesn't matter."

"Okay," she said, lacking conviction. It was clear there was more weight to her thoughts, worries that even my reassurance couldn't reach.

She drew a breath, her words tumbling out hesitantly. "Caroline, she's popular, she has all this experience and I haven't even..."

I crossed the room, the distance between us closing with each step until I settled onto the bed beside her. The mattress dipped under my weight.

"You haven't even what?" I asked, searching her face.

Chandler's hands shot up from under the blankets, covering her face. Her voice was muffled but her embarrassment was palpable. "Boston, I'm just not that experienced, and you have this history with her... and probably lots of other girls."

I hesitated for a moment, then let out a small laugh. My hand reached out, gently pulling her hands away from her face. "Chandler, you have no idea how cute it is that you're acting jealous right now."

She blinked, confusion mixing with the red tinge of embarrassment on her cheeks. "What?"

"Seriously," I continued, not being able to keep the smirk off my face. "In some weird way, I think it's hot because it means you like me enough to be jealous."

"Shut up," Chandler scoffed, her hazel eyes darting away from mine. "It's not hot." She fidgeted with the hem of her blanket, creating little ripples in the fabric. "And now it's even more embarrassing that you know I've never... done that before."

"It's not embarrassing," I said softly, catching her gaze and holding it.

Her expression faltered, vulnerability flickering across her features. "It isn't?"

"No," I confirmed, brushing a strand of her hair behind her ear. "It would be so fucking hot to do something with you no one else has."

Her eyes flicked up to meet mine, surprise etched into every line of her beautiful face.

"What?" she asked, hopeful. "You think it'd be hot to do that... with me?" A blush crept over her cheeks, her question hanging between us like a delicate secret.

I couldn't help but smile at the innocence and earnestness in those bright hazel eyes. Leaning closer I whispered, "Chandler, I'd do anything you wanted me to. You just have to ask."

She glanced up at me through thick lashes, a hesitant smile playing on her lips. "How would someone ask for that? I wouldn't even know..." she trailed off, fingers still fidgeting with the fabric.

"Just be honest with me," I said softly. "Tell me what you want."

She opened her mouth, then closed it, clearly uncertain. The look she gave me next was vulnerable, but I could see her trying to muster the courage to tell me what was going on in that head of hers.

"Okay," she whispered. "I guess I'm curious to try it." Her words tumbled out in a rush of breath.

"You guess?" I asked. I paused, choosing my words carefully. "I'm not going to do anything with you if you aren't sure. It's okay if you're not ready. There's no reason to rush it."

She nodded slowly, absorbing my words but then her eyes sparked with determination, stopping me mid-breath. "Boston, I want to try it," she said decisively. She bit her lip, a small, nervous gesture of hers that drove me wild.

"Try what exactly?" I asked, even though I knew what she meant. I needed to hear her say it, clearly, without any lingering doubt.

She drew in a sharp breath, her hazel eyes fixed on mine. "I want you to..." her voice trailed off for just a second before she found her courage again. "...Go down on me."

A smile broke across my face, for the strength it took her to finally say it. "All you had to do was ask," I said softly. My thumb grazed her cheek, tracing the line of her jaw gently as I pulled her toward me.

"Are you sure?" I whispered against her lips, needing that final confirmation.

"Yes," Chandler breathed out. "I'm sure."

With a confident nod, I traced my thumb along her lower lip, reveling in her softness and warmth. I pressed my lips to hers, the kiss growing from tentative to hungry as we found a rhythm belonging to just us. She tasted so good, so sweet, like the cranberry drink she'd had earlier.

"Is your ankle alright?" I asked, gently laying her back on the bed.

She nodded then grasped the hem of my shirt and pulled it over my head, tossing it to the floor. Her glossy eyes roamed over my abs approvingly.

I leaned over her, pressing kisses on her neck, nibbling and sucking the sensitive skin. My lips pressed against her fluttering pulse, a delicate beat that urged me on. My mouth grazed her collarbone and she made a small sound of pleasure. I'd found a sensitive spot, and my own desire soared.

"Keep making those noises for me," I said, my breath hot against her throat. Her moans and sharp inhales would tell me everything I needed to know. The way her breath caught, a sign to linger; her quiet moans would urge me on. And it wasn't just about understanding what she liked and what she needed. Knowing her body's language, the way she reacted to me without having to say it—it was about the connection between us. Both of us knew there was nothing else like it.

My fingers trailed over her silky pajama shirt, deftly undoing each tiny button with one hand. My lips followed as I worked my way down, savoring her soft skin against my mouth. When I reached her breasts, I grazed my thumb over one nipple. A soft gasp escaped her lips, and I responded, flicking my tongue over her peaks before drawing one into my mouth, then the other. Her flesh between my teeth was intoxicating. Her hands roamed my body, gripping my back, pulling me closer as she moaned softly.

"Do you want me to keep going?" I whispered, tracing a line of fire down her abdomen, stopping where her hips curved.

She moaned in response, a simple affirmative "mhm" that vibrated through me, fueling me.

With tantalizing slowness, I peeled her wickedly short bottoms away, revealing her panties, drenched. I groaned, I couldn't take it anymore. My mouth was watering at the sight of her, my thoughts racing with what it would feel like to slide myself deep inside her. Her eyes were still wide with desire and she sank her teeth into her bottom lip as she watched me shift myself between her legs.

"You're so wet," I grumbled, licking my lips, captivated by the sight of her. "So fucking hot."

I traced the edge of her soaked panties with my fingers, teasing her sensitive skin. Her hips arched involuntarily, begging for more. My dick was rock hard, straining against my pants as I complied, pressing a soft kiss against her clit still hidden beneath the wet fabric of her panties. She let out a low moan, squirming.

I slowly slid them down her legs, finally giving me a clear view of her, glistening. My heart pounded in my chest, my own breath growing thick. I couldn't resist sliding my hand down, running my fingers through her wetness. She gasped at my touch as I circled my thumb around her clit, teasing her relentlessly.

"You're perfect," I whispered, as I lifted her good ankle and placed it over my shoulder.

I lower my head, my tongue tracing a path along her inner thigh with open mouth kisses. She moaned as I inched closer to her center, my breath hot against her. I teased her with my tongue, flicking it gently against her clit before taking it into my mouth and sucking.

"Oh god, yes," she gasped.

"Fuck, you taste so good," I whispered against her skin before slowly licking her from top to bottom.

I continued to kiss and suck, starting slow and gentle before building the intensity. I couldn't help it, I wanted to devour her. She let out breathy moans as she bucked her hips against my mouth. Her body trembled beneath me.

"What do you need?" I breathed out.

"More," she moaned, squirming.

"You want my hands?"

"Yes," she begged.

I slowly slid a finger inside her, feeling her warmth and wetness envelop me. Her tight walls clenched around me and I groaned in response, waves of need surging through me. She pushed herself further onto my hand, gasping and arching her back. My own body was screaming, my throbbing dick begging to be freed, but I pushed the thoughts aside. I continued working her with my finger, licking up every last drop of her with my tongue as she moaned, her eyes rolling back in pleasure.

"Look up at me," I instructed. "I want to see how much you want this."

She obeyed, her gaze locking onto mine as I teased and tormented her with my fingers and tongue. Her pupils dilated with lust, her breath came in shallow pants as she pressed her hips against me.

"Boston," she panted out, "That feels—so good."

I slipped another finger inside her.

"Fuck!" she squealed.

"You okay?" I asked, gently pumping once, twice.

"Yes. Don't stop," she urged.

She was so tight. She clenched around my fingers and I curled them upward, searching for the spot I knew would send her over the edge.

"Oh shit," she cried out.

"That's my girl," I coaxed.

Her body tensed as I sucked and licked her swollen clit, my tongue moving in time with my fingers. Her hands gripped the sheets as she moaned in pleasure, growing louder as I intensified the pressure and depth.

I could feel her body responding to my every movement. Her hips rocking and grinding against my face threatened to undo me. Tension was building in her body. I knew she was close, and I was determined to send her over the edge—to give her everything she deserved, every bit of pleasure she'd hoped this would be.

"Keep talking to me, pretty girl."

"Boston, please, don't stop."

My name tucked between her soft moans was the sexiest sound I had ever heard.

"I think... I'm going to..." she panted, digging her nails into my back.

"That's it. Come for me, Chandler."

I could feel her fluttering and pulsing around my fingers as she came, her body shaking in waves of ecstasy as she threw her head back, moaning and gasping. I slowed my movements, drawing out her orgasm for as long as I could. She collapsed back onto the bed, her body limp and spent, a satisfied smile playing across her lips.

"Are you alright?" I asked, desperate to hear her voice.

"More than alright," she managed, the words tumbling out on a broken sigh as she reached for me, guiding me back in close.

"You're so beautiful," I breathed, planting a kiss on her lips.

Her hand trailed down my chest, fingertips tracing the lines of my muscles before reaching the waistband of my shorts.

Her touch sent a jolt of desire straight through me, and I found my body responding with an urgency that could barely resist her. But as her fingers trailed lower, I captured her hand, lifting it to my lips and pressing tender kisses along her wrist.

"Not tonight," I whispered.

"You don't want me to touch you?"

"I am dying for you to touch me. You have no idea... but you're not just some girl to me. You're more than that, and tonight needs to be about you. I need you to know, no matter what happens," I said, the depth of my honesty surprising even me, "with me, you'll always come first—even if you hate it."

Then I pulled her close, our bodies pressed together as I held her.

Her lips curved into a small smile. "Always putting me first, just like when we were kids," she reminisced. "The first day we met, you didn't even know me and you gave me your jar of fireflies."

I smiled at the memory. "Couldn't stand seeing you upset—even back then," I confessed. "Plus, couldn't let Parker think he had you beat."

"He was so mad. I don't even know how you collected that many," Chandler giggled, then her laughter faded into a contemplative sigh. She laid her head back down and looked away for a moment, lost in thought before bringing her eyes back to me with a hint of mischief. "So about Caroline," she said, and my heart sank. "She was definitely telling the truth."

I let out a breathy laugh. "You drive me crazy."

She drove me crazy, but she made me feel alive. There was nothing I could compare it to. The rush of being on field, the adrenaline of the game—none of it compared to this. None of it compared to her.

chandler

MY HAND SWEPT across the cool, empty sheets, feeling for Boston. Disappointed, I looked around the room until I spotted a tray on the dresser with breakfast—bacon, eggs, and toast looking more perfect than I could have managed. There, propped against a glass of orange juice, was a note.

Practice early, didn't want to wake you. P.S. You snore, but it's cute. -B

I couldn't help the laugh that escaped me. "I do not snore," I said quietly to myself.

I pulled the tray onto my lap as I sat on my bed. I replayed last night with each bite, a smile lingering on my lips until realization dawned. Willow.

Willow must have seen Boston—or heard him—this morning. What is she thinking right now?

I stepped out of my room, the morning sun casting a soft glow across the hallway. I blinked away the remnants of sleep and found

Willow entrenched in a fortress of paperwork. She glanced up at me, her eyes twinkling with mischief.

"Well, look who it is," she drawled, arching an eyebrow. "How's your ankle?"

"Feeling so much better today. Just needed a little rest," I replied.

"Good, good. And you wanna tell me why a super hot six-foot-five Blue Devil was doing our dishes this morning?"

My cheeks flushed. "He... uh, he may have made me breakfast," I muttered, tucking a strand of hair behind my ear.

Willow's smirk deepened. "Oh, breakfast? Is that what we're calling it?" The corners of her mouth danced upwards in amusement, as if she knew good and well there was more to the story than I was willing to admit.

I tried to change the subject, nodding towards the sea of binders and papers she was working on. "What are you doing with all of this?" I asked, hoping to divert her attention from the details of my night.

She shrugged nonchalantly, though her eyes remained bright with curiosity. "Oh, you know, more organizing for the committee."

I leaned against the door frame, watching her shuffle through some forms. "You're sure doing a lot for them this summer, Will."

"I know," she sighed, a determined glint in her eye. "If I want to get a job on the coaching staff, first step is impressing my dad, which means being an outstanding committee member. So I have to do whatever it takes."

"Alright, pass me a stack," I said, reaching for a chunk of the paperwork that littered the living room floor. Plopping down cross-legged beside her, I began to sort through the binders.

"Okay, details, please!" Willow leaned in, anticipation wafting from her in waves.

"Willow," I chastised gently, but couldn't hold back a grin, "ladies don't kiss and tell."

"Who says anything about talking?" she shot back playfully. "Can ladies blink? Blink twice if you hooked up."

Suppressing a laugh, I smirked and blinked twice.

Willow squealed, clapping her hands together. "I knew it! But what kind of hookup? You didn't go all the way—I know you would have told me immediately."

"Your confidence in our friendship is touching," I teased before her next words stopped me.

"Wait a minute..." she narrowed her eyes in suspicion. "Did Caroline's message inspire something? Blink twice if it did."

Rolling my eyes for effect, I blinked twice again with a mix of giddiness and embarrassment.

"OMG! Was she right?" Willow's voice hit a pitch that could shatter glass.

"Shh!" I hissed, even as I snickered. "She was so right!"

We erupted into laughter, the sound filling the room and bouncing off the walls. Our giggles subsided as we continued flipping through the pages.

I wasn't sure how much time had passed by the time the last of the binders snapped shut with a definitive thud. Willow pushed back her chair, stretching her arms above her head.

"Alright, girly," she said with a mischievous twinkle in her eye. "Let's get ready. We have a committee meeting to attend."

I groaned theatrically, tossing a binder on top of the pile. "Oh great, that means an hour of Caroline talking, followed by bathroom duty."

Willow giggled. "She's been on one this summer—but don't let her get to you."

"I'll do my best," I replied, rolling my eyes for emphasis.

We parted, going into our rooms to get ready for the day before making our way to the Blue Devils' clubhouse.

When we arrived, Caroline was pacing the front of the room, clipboard clutched tight in her grip as she scribbled notes. The other committee members were seated in a semi-circle, their attention split between idle chatter and Caroline.

"Let's take a seat in the back," Willow whispered, nodding towards the unclaimed chairs.

"Deal," I agreed, as we settled in.

"Okay," Caroline began, tapping her pen against the clipboard to get the room's attention. "This week we have a big game against the Comets, and this weekend is the big away tournament. We always bring home the 'W', so I assume we'll do the same this year. We'll have a dinner prepared for the players before the Comets game. We will also be booking the rooms—two players per room, two committee members per room—and we need to put an itinerary together for the tournament—planning all meals and any work on orders sent from the coaching staff, so let's get on it."

"Sounds thrilling," I drawled, giving Willow a knowing smirk, the sarcasm clear only to her.

"Shh," she chastised playfully. "I say we push for Italian."

"Alright, I think that covers the essentials," Caroline concluded, silencing the whispers of side conversations. There was a pause as she scanned the room, stopping on Willow and me at the back before a small smile tugged at the corner of her lips. "Oh, and before we begin, congratulations to Willow for winning the Devils' Day Out prize."

A ripple of polite applause that barely counted as clapping fluttered through the room and Willow smiled proudly. "Thank you, thank you," she chimed. "And I must say, I'm especially delighted because I'll be sharing the suite with Chandler."

"Can't wait," I said, returning her smile with one of my own.

"Let's get it going, the work won't do itself." Caroline clapped once before making her way to a desk, clipboard still clutched firmly under her arm.

I leaned closer to Willow, our shoulders brushing lightly. "So, what's this weekend's tournament about?"

"It's the annual pitch invitational. We hosted it last year, but this year it's a couple hours away," she whispered back, her excitement palpable. "It's much more exciting when we get to travel. Run around the hotel, get into some trouble."

"Trouble is the last thing I need," I responded, but a hotel suite with robes and an oversized bathtub didn't sound too bad.

Willow leaned in, the mischievous twinkle never leaving her eyes. "Speaking of trouble," she began, teasingly tucking a strand of her curly blonde hair behind her ear. "It's dollar beer night at Gin & Jerry's tonight. The team usually goes. Feel up to it? Or did you have too wild of a night last night?" Her smile was infectious, the corners of her mouth curling up in anticipation.

I laughed lightly, rolling my eyes. "I think I can manage that," I said. The thought of another night out with the team—and one person in particular—made me a little more excited than I cared to admit.

"Am I interrupting something?" The question popped our bubble. Caroline stood there, eyebrows arched, looking at us impatiently.

We both flashed our best attempt at genuine smiles. "Not at all," Willow said.

"Good." Caroline didn't seem convinced, but she pressed on regardless. "You two are in charge of laundry duty. You need to wash, iron, and hang the away jerseys in each boy's game outfit bag." Her tone left no room for argument—an order, not a request.

"Isn't there a team manager for this kind of stuff?" Willow's bubbly personality never wavered, even as she was questioning the fairness of the task.

"Nope, maybe when you're on the coaching staff one day, you can see about figuring that out," Caroline retorted, giving a sly smirk.

"Maybe I will," Willow shot back, undeterred by the challenge.

The washing machines hummed a rhythm in the background as Willow and I tackled laundry duty. Steam from the iron mingled with the scent of detergent as we pressed each jersey completely wrinkle-free, since, according to Caroline, wrinkles would tarnish the team's image on game day.

"Hey, Will," I ventured hesitantly, breaking the silence. "Question."

"Answer," she quipped without missing a beat, her eyes never leaving the shirt she was ironing.

I took a deep breath, the words tumbling out almost of their own accord. "What was your first time like?"

Willow paused, the iron hovering above the fabric as a smile played upon her lips. "Eh, the typical story. Prom night." She carefully placed the iron down and hung the jersey with practiced ease. "My boyfriend and I had been together three years, and then we went to different colleges after that."

"Did you both decide it was going to happen that night? Did you have to convince him?"

"Umm, yeah, we both agreed, but it was a disaster. There should be at least one member of the party who knows what they're doing. That bear could not find the cave, if you know what I mean." A knowing look was in her eyes. "Why? Are you thinking about it?"

I nodded, pressing my lips together as I passed her another jersey to iron, thinking about how I might see it happening for myself. What that night might look like—who I'd want it to be with.

"I mean, yeah," I began, the hum of the washing machines filling the silence. "I'm in my second year of college, and basically the only one who hasn't had sex." I fidgeted with the hem of another jersey, a blush creeping onto my cheeks. "I could see it being with Boston. I trust him, and we've known each other forever."

"I love that for you," Willow mused, her lips curling into an impish grin. "If you're ready. I'd just talk to him about it."

"That's the problem," I sighed, imagining how long it would take me to persuade Boston that I was ready. "Since he's known me my whole life, and because he's Parker's best friend, he's so protective. I feel like he'd never believe me."

"Okay, I have an idea." Willow's eyes sparkled with mischief, and suddenly I was all ears.

"What?"

She leaned in closer, as if sharing a secret. "What kind of under-wear are you wearing right now?"

"Umm, black lacey ones?" I replied, unsure where this was headed.

"Perfect. Take them off. Right now."

"Are you serious?" My voice pitched high with disbelief.

"Dead serious. Do it, right now," she urged, nodding towards the privacy of our corner in the laundry room.

With a nervous laugh, I complied, pulling my oversized t-shirt down to cover me as best as it could. I shimmied out of my shorts, and I let my underwear slide down to the floor before stepping out of them. Quickly, I redressed in just the shorts, the absence of my underwear feeling a bit bizarre.

"Okay, what now?" I whispered, still half convinced we were about to be caught in the most absurd act of our entire friendship.

"See that outfit bag over there? The one with number 29 on it?" Willow pointed to Boston's gear, hanging on the team rack nearby.

"Y—yes?"

"Put them inside the bag so he finds them. Then, send him a text on the first day of the tournament—before they get to the locker room. Tell him that you left him a present in his locker, and you want 'it' to happen this weekend." She paused, her expression serious but her eyes dancing. "I'm telling you, no man can resist a cute pair of panties. And this weekend will be the perfect time. Anytime we go out of town we all end up room swapping. There will be a way to get you two together without anyone knowing."

I stared at her. The audacity of her plan was ridiculous, crazy—absolutely unlike me, yet... There was a part of me that wanted to entertain it because for one, I had already taken off my underwear, and two, Willow was so excited about it, I couldn't possibly back out.

"Here goes nothing," I whispered, more to myself than Willow. With a tiny act of rebellion that sent adrenaline coursing through my veins, I unzipped Boston's game attire bag, slipped the black lace inside, and zipped it back up. It was done. A tiny thrill shot through me thinking about Boston, about what he'd think when he found them.

Later that night, Willow and I carved a path through a sea of bodies, the dim glow of neon signs washing over the crowded Gin and Jerry's. The smell of spilled beer and raucous laughter filled the air, pulling me further into the night. We found ourselves a spot at the bar, elbows resting on the sticky surface, waiting for the bartender who was a flurry of motion at the far end.

"Think he'll notice us before we turn thirty?" Willow quipped, her blonde hair sparkling beneath the overhead lights.

"Maybe if you show more cleavage," I joked, still focused on the busy bartender.

Reese slid in casually beside us, leaning against the bar as we waited.

"Ladies," Reese said, voice smooth as silk. "Looking good tonight."

The clink of glasses drew our attention as the bartender slid two tall drinks in front of us. Willow and I exchanged a glance, both knowing we hadn't ordered them. Two Jack and Cokes—a choice neither of us would normally select.

"Compliments of the gentlemen in the back," the bartender said with a conspiratorial wink, nodding toward a dimly lit area of the crowded bar.

We leaned back, craning our necks and shifting our bodies, but we couldn't make out the faces of our anonymous admirers.

"Is this part of your plan?" Reese interrupted, amused.

I turned to find him leaning casually against the bar, his green eyes glinting mischievously.

"Why yes, it is!" I replied confidently. "Hot girl summer, open for business."

Willow chuckled beside me, as she nodded in agreement. We raised the glasses, ready to toast to our unexpected fortune.

"Sorry about that," the bartender interrupted, his hand closing over mine to still the ascent of my drink. "The guys who sent these said they were meant for the other two girls over there." He gestured apologetically to a pair of women chatting animatedly on our left.

Reese's smirk widened, the corners of his mouth playing at that familiar edge of arrogance and allure as he picked up a frosted beer bottle another bartender had slid to him. "So much for a hot girl summer," he quipped, the words laced with that carefree taunt that always seemed to find its way under my skin.

He laughed as he dropped a twenty dollar bill on the counter then stepped away toward the pool table, the dim lights casting his tattoos in an amber glow.

"Lovely," I murmured to myself, cheeks warming with a mix of embarrassment and irritation. "And how did he get a drink before us?" I asked Willow.

"Baseball perks," Willow said, rolling her eyes. "They know their orders and they hardly wait."

"Must be nice," I said with a touch of envy.

"Still," Willow continued with a huff, "that bartender is a jerk. He could have at least let us keep the drinks he already gave to us."

"Agreed," I nodded, wishing Reese hadn't just witnessed the mix-up.

After what felt like an eternity of being ignored, we got our drinks. Then we made our way over to the pool tables where the real action was.

The click and clatter of billiard balls filled the air, mixing with the music pulsing through the bar. My gaze landed on Boston mid-shot. His focus was intense, his athletic form bending gracefully over the table. Then his piercing blue eyes caught mine, and time seemed to slow as he shot me a wink, hit the ball, and sank it into the corner pocket.

"Looks like someone's happy to see you," Willow teased, nudging me with her elbow.

"Or maybe he's just proud of his shot," I deflected, feeling a blush creep up my cheeks.

"Right," Willow drawled, clearly not buying it. "Because Boston winks at everyone when he plays pool."

"Shut up," I retorted, taking a sip of my drink to hide my smile. Boston had always been my crush growing up. It was comforting when he was around—but lately I was feeling new, different things about him.

We leaned against the high table near the pool area, watching the game unfold. Boston was clearly in his element, surrounded by teammates. And yet, his glances kept finding their way back to me, each one sending a thrill down my spine.

"Go talk to him," Willow nudged, her tone laced with encouragement.

"Okay, okay," I said, taking a deep breath and steadying myself for the encounter. With each step closer to where he stood, the sounds of clinking glasses and boisterous laughter seemed to fade into the background.

Boston stepped away from the pool table to set his pool stick back, his look of concentration giving way to a warm smile as he noticed my approach.

"Hey," I said, hoping my voice didn't betray the nervous flutter in my stomach. "Thanks for breakfast this morning."

"It was nothing," Boston replied with a shrug. "Had to make sure you started the day off right."

"So thoughtful," I commented, my heart rate picking up at the proximity. "So, Willow caught you, huh?"

"Yeah, I was so quiet, too." He smiled, running a hand through his wavy hair. "I was slipping the last pot away when her door opened up. Just gave her a smile and said I was on my way out."

"Smooth," I teased, a playful smirk tugging at my lips.

"Always," he retorted. "Getting caught was worth it. I haven't been able to stop thinking about last night. Practice was almost impossible to get through."

I inched a bit closer to him, feeling the heat from his gaze.

"Which parts were you thinking about?" I asked, with a smile. "Please do share."

Boston's eyes darkened, a playful yet cautious smirk forming on his lips. "Don't make me say it," he warned, biting his lip. "Your brother's right over there."

I leaned in, my shoulder brushing against his arm. "What? You don't think he'd approve?"

Boston's eyes flickered toward where Parker stood nearby, surrounded by teammates, before they rested back on me. A half-smile curved his lips, a familiar playful glint lighting up his icy blue eyes. He spoke so quietly I could barely catch the words over the conversations and music playing. "Probably not."

Then, as if moved by an impulse hidden beneath his casual stance, he reached out ever so slightly. His pinky trailed over mine before they locked—intertwined for a brief moment, a gentle touch that sent a surge of heat through my body. It was our own private exchange, hidden from the view of others, but it spoke volumes.

He paused, a shadow of seriousness crossing his face. "But I should probably talk to him soon... let him know how I'm feeling about you." His voice was steady, but I caught the slightest glimpse of something deeper, possibly apprehension—or maybe hope.

My breath hitched, and for a moment the noise of the bar faded into a distant murmur. That small gesture, the brush of his skin against mine, had sparked a tiny flutter in my chest. It was cute, it was thrilling, and it was reassuring. He had just confessed to having feelings for me, strong enough feelings to make him want to have a conversation with Parker.

"Hey, Chan, is flannel still in?" Parker asked, interrupting our conversation, his towering frame suddenly casting a shadow over me.

I looked up, smirking. "No, Parker, not for you," I joked, knowing full well that it looked fine on him.

"Damnit," he sighed, defeated. Before I could further indulge in

Parker's attire, Willow and Bailey approached with their own agenda.

146

boston

"MOVE OVER, it's my turn to pick the song!" Bailey exclaimed.

"Too slow!" Willow said, darting towards the machine, her finger jabbing the button triumphantly. "Ha!"

"Ugh, you're lucky you're hot," Bailey grumbled, though the grin on his face gave away his attempt at any real annoyance.

"Please," Willow shot back, "feel free to keep the compliments coming."

Bailey leaned in, his voice dropping to a conspiratorial whisper. "And that ass... How are you not seeing anyone? Is it because you're the coach's daughter?" His words, though teasing, carried a hint of genuine curiosity.

"Because I'm not scared to go there," he added with a lopsided smirk, as if challenging both Willow and himself.

Willow let out a laugh, her response diffusing the moment into something light and flirtatious again. "You should be," she warned him, her tone still airy but with an edge of sincerity.

"Scared?" Bailey scoffed, raising an eyebrow. "For you, honey, I'd break so many rules."

I glanced at Parker, who seemed momentarily clouded by the

interaction unfolding before him. His eyes were fixed on Bailey, his jaw twitched noticeably. It was subtle, almost imperceptible, but I saw it—the flicker of discomfort, maybe even jealousy.

"Hey, I'm just gonna go close out my tab," I announced, making a beeline for the bar, stepping away from this awkward interaction.

I had just finished paying when I spotted her. With one last nod to the bartender, I turned, only to catch a glimpse of Chandler slipping into the bathroom out of the corner of my eye. I made a quick decision and veered off course, treading silently down the dimly lit bathroom hallway.

I leaned casually against the wall, patiently waiting for her. Finally, the door creaked open and she emerged looking beautiful as ever in that dress—oh, that dress, clinging to her in all the right places.

"You really had to wear that dress, didn't you?" The words escaped me before I could reel them back.

Chandler's cheeks flushed pink. Her eyes sparkled with mischief as she tilted her head. "Oh, this old thing?"

In a fluid motion, I bridged the gap between us, my hand slipping into hers and pulling her close. A shiver passed through her as I leaned in, the dim light casting shadows that danced across her face.

"You're killing me, you know," I whispered, thumb grazing her cheek with a touch meant to memorize every contour, "looking this beautiful tonight."

Her lips parted slightly, a soft exhale escaping as her eyes searched mine. The blush on her cheeks darkened. Then, without another thought, I captured her lips with mine, as I pressed her against the wall. Our tongues explored tentatively at first, then more boldly, as if we both were starved for each other.

She moaned softly into my kiss as she slipped her fingers beneath the hem of my shirt, trailing tantalizingly slowly over the ridges of my abs, igniting a fire on my skin. My muscles contracted instinctively, a shudder rippling through me and threatening to unravel all of my painfully built up self-control.

"Chandler," I breathed out, pulling back just enough to rest my forehead against hers. "I can only hold back for so long."

"Why are you holding back?" Her fingers trailed over the button of my jeans, her gaze locked onto mine with an intensity that forced the truth out of me.

"I need to have a conversation with my best friend," I confessed, the weight of his potential disapproval weighing heavy in my thoughts.

Her lips curved into a wistful smile, her kindness that I adored shining through still. "I get it," she whispered back, understanding.

Our moment was shattered by footsteps approaching. With one last glance, we reluctantly broke apart, stepping away from each other just as a few others pushed their path to the bathroom.

Pushing through the crowd, I made my way back to the bar where I last saw Parker. The thumping of my heart matched the pounding bass from the speakers. I was doing everything I could to breathe and calm down the rush of adrenaline flowing through my veins. Two thoughts were running through my mind as I inched closer—how much I cared about Chandler, and how Parker, my best friend, would feel about it.

I scanned the dimly lit room for his familiar face. I found him slumped over in a booth, engaged in what seemed like an important conversation with... a passed out drunk?

"Man, listen," Parker slurred, a glassy look in his eyes as he poked the snoring figure beside him. "I know I'm that guy who always makes people laugh, but I have problems too, you know?"

The drunk man let out a loud snore, and Parker nodded sagely, "You know, all the hook-ups lately... They've been fun. But at what age do you find someone meaningful? Someone who you can laugh with after all the sex?"

The man shifted, his arm flopping off the table before he let out a groan—a sound that might've been mistaken for agreement.

"I know, first world problems, right?" Parker chuckled. "You're probably thinking, this stupid handsome guy, complaining about all the women in his life."

Suppressing a laugh, I approached the booth. "Um, Parker, you do know that man is passed out, right?"

Parker blinked up at me, his lips spreading into a wide grin. "Boston! Meet my new friend," he gestured toward the unconscious person.

"Okay, buddy, we need to get you out of here. Come on." I slid Parker's arm over my shoulder, realizing tonight would not be the night for our little heart-to-heart.

As we staggered toward the exit, Chandler caught my eye. Her gaze was filled with concern, and she swiftly moved to our side. "What's going on?"

"He's had too much to drink," I explained, trying to maneuver Parker's uncoordinated steps.

"Okay, thanks for taking care of him." She gave me a knowing look—one that said she understood there would be no conversation with Parker tonight. Then she walked back to Willow.

"Holy fuck, Boston," Parker suddenly exclaimed, loud enough to turn a few heads. "Have you always had muscles like this? I'm impressed. Good fucking job."

I shook my head, fighting a half-smile as I helped him into my truck.

My phone vibrated in my pocket just as I started the engine. I fished it out as Parker mumbled something incoherent beside me.

CHANDLER

Thanks again for taking care of Parker

ME

Always

CHANDLER

Was hoping we'd get to hang a little more

ME

Tomorrow after the game?

CHANDLER

Okay, doing what?

ME

Me taking you on a date...

CHANDLER

And where would we be going?

ME

Just be ready pretty girl

The next day was a blur of adrenaline and sweat. We'd just barely won the game, and Coach was pissed—and pissed might've been an understatement.

"Ten runs!" Coach roared, his voice echoing off the walls. "We should've been up by at least ten runs! This slacking off ends now, or we can kiss the tournament goodbye!"

He grabbed his clipboard and hurled it against a locker with a resounding crash. We all fell silent, waiting to see what he would do next.

"Get it together," he snapped before walking off, leaving us in silence.

Steam from the showers mingled with exhaustion as I twisted open my locker. The cold metal door swung open, and I began to stash my gear away, my mind replaying the shit show of a game. The clank of the closing door revealed Reese, leaning casually against the locker next to mine, a look on his face that told me he was contemplating something.

"That game wasn't pretty, huh?" he said, breaking the silence.

I shook my head, tossing my damp towel into the laundry hamper nearby. "Nah, but we'll pull through this weekend."

He paused, shifting his weight. "Saw she was at the game tonight."

I knew that "she" meant my mom—our mom. "Yeah, she's trying to make it to more games," I replied, attempting to play it off. I secretly hated when she missed any games at all.

"Feels too little too late," Reese muttered, almost to himself.

"Maybe hear her out?" I suggested. "Decide for yourself, instead of believing only what your dad says."

His jaw clenched, disbelief flashing in his eyes. I braced for some comment, a low blow, but instead, he sighed. "All in due time, I guess." Pushing off from the locker, he slung his bag over his shoulder.

"Pretty sure she's waiting outside," I called after him.

He paused, then without turning back he threw the words. "Nah, I'm good," and he disappeared around the corner.

The locker room emptied, and I followed, heading for my truck. She was there, by her car. Her smile widened as I approached.

"Hunny, you were great!" She wrapped me in an embrace.

"Thanks, Mom. Glad you could make it."

"Me too," she said, pulling back. "I love seeing you play, but that game was too close for comfort."

I noticed her gaze drifting past my shoulder, searching. I knew exactly who she was searching for. "Mom, I don't think he's ready to talk yet."

She nodded, a touch of sadness in her eyes. "Oh, I know. Not rushing it. I'll be here when he's ready."

"Are you doing okay back at home? Remembering to eat?" I asked.

"Oh, you know me, I do just fine," she said, but the look in her eyes told me that she probably relied on takeout more than she should. I was used to being the parent most of the time, but there was only so much I could do from Bayside—and it would do me no good to worry about it.

"Alright, well, I gotta get outta here. Got somewhere to be," I sighed.

"Okay, hunny. See you at the next game," she responded, giving me another hug before stepping into her car and driving away.

As the taillights faded into the distance, I took a deep breath, ready to shift the night's focus—to Chandler.

I made a quick stop to grab a few things and then navigated towards Willow's. The thought of seeing her drove all other thoughts out of my mind.

She was sitting on the porch steps, a damn goddess in white. Her bright hazel eyes caught mine, and even from a distance, I could see a smirk on her face.

"Hey," I called out as I stepped out of the truck. "You see my date anywhere around here?"

"Sorry she wasn't able to make it," she laughed, standing up. "You had her stressing during that game."

"So I keep hearing," I grinned, closing the gap between us. I reached for her hand, feeling the warmth of her skin against mine. "But damn," I looked her up and down. "You look... stunning in that dress."

"Thank you. You look good too, Boston, but what kind of date are we going on if you're wearing that?" She eyed my casual attire—a cutoff shirt, backward hat, and jeans.

"Girl, you've never been on a date with me. Hop in," I replied with a wink, leading her toward the truck.

It was a short drive, filled with easy banter and comfort that comes from knowing someone your whole life.

As we veered off the main road, the landscape opened up to reveal an isolated spot where the world seemed to hold its breath. We could see the lake, a serene mirror reflecting the sky, and the trees stood silent all around us. The sun was dipping below the horizon just as we pulled in.

"Is this where we're going?" Chandler said, barely containing her excitement as she peered out into the stillness that surrounded us.

"Give me a sec," I said, hopping out of the driver's seat and making my way to the back. I opened the tailgate and laid out the thick blankets I'd brought, trying my best to create a cloud of coziness. I flipped a switch and the twinkle lights strung up around the truck bed burst to life, casting everything in a warm, starry glow.

Fancy restaurants weren't my thing, but creating a special moment for her—that I could do.

I opened the passenger door and reached for Chandler, guiding her gently from the truck until she was safely on the ground.

Chandler's gasp filled the space between us when she saw it. Her hands flew to her mouth, eyes sparkling bright. "This is beautiful... This setup... This place..."

"Nah, you haven't seen anything yet—wait till the stars come out," I said. I knew how incredible it was from sitting there so many times before, thinking, reflecting, and letting it bring me peace.

She turned to me, her smile wide and full of wonder. "I can't wait."

She hopped into the truck bed with ease, immediately making herself comfortable in the cushions and blankets, but then curiosity must have gotten the better of her as she started rifling through the cooler.

"Is there anything you didn't think of?" she teased. "You're making all my other dates look like hot garbage right now."

"Can we please not talk about all your other dates?" I joked.

As she settled in, I leaned against the truck, watching her with a half-smile on my face. She didn't know it, but when I pictured my future, I saw her. Yes, baseball was there, too—it always would be. But more than that, I saw us lying in the bed of my truck under the stars, lost in a place where everything else faded away. If we'd had a terrible day, if we could hardly handle the shit we were going through—none of it would matter If we could have moments like this.

"Turkey sandwiches? And is that... cheesecake?" Chandler's squeal of delight pulled me out of my thoughts. Her excitement buzzed like the twinkle lights surrounding us, illuminating her in a soft, warm glow.

"Because they're your favorites," I said, watching her face light up as she unwrapped a sandwich with care.

"Best date ever," she cheered before taking a bite, and I couldn't help but laugh at her pure joy over a simple turkey sandwich.

"Wait until you try the cheesecake—it's from Maria's," I added. The sun had dipped lower, painting the sky in hues of orange and pink, a backdrop I would never get tired of.

As beautiful as the sunset was, it was only the beginning. Darkness crept in slowly, the vibrant colors fading from the sky. I watched, almost holding my breath, for the moment when she saw the stars.

"Look, Boston!" Her face lit up with wonder as they began to reveal themselves one by one until the entire sky was filled with twinkling lights.

"Amazing, isn't it?" I whispered, taking it all in. She nestled into me, her head resting against my chest as I put an arm around her.

"Beautiful," she responded, her gaze fixed on the sky. I watched her, mesmerized more by the reflection of the stars in her eyes than the sky itself. She was a part of this universe, but here with me, she grounded me in a way nothing else ever had.

I whispered in her ear. "They've got nothing on you."

Her eyes met mine, wide with surprise, and I felt the truth of my words resonate deep within me. I had been to this spot countless times before, but the view of her—her gentle kindness, her unwavering loyalty, the quiet strength in her questioning gaze—was so much more powerful than any starlit sky.

"Thank you," she said softly.

We sat there, surrounded by the tranquility of the night as time seemed to stand still. It was just us, the stars, and the quiet beating of our hearts.

"Chandler," I began, my voice barely above a whisper. "I'm sorry. For not stepping up last summer, for keeping you at a distance this year."

She shifted slightly, tilting her head to meet my gaze. "Boston, I never gave up on you," she said, confidently. "You're strong enough to get through anything. The real you... you light up a room just by being there. You make all of us smile, make us better. I knew that the real you was still in there. We all need that Boston—I needed that Boston again."

The reflection of the night sky danced in her eyes, but all I could see was her belief in me—unwavering and sincere, even if I didn't believe I deserved it. "What if I'm not that Boston anymore?"

Chandler took my hand, her grip firm. "It's not something you can or can't be, Boston. It's just who you are—you, at your core." She squeezed my hand. "And I know you'll find him again."

I looked down at our intertwined fingers, feeling the strength that always seemed to emanate from her. Her confidence in me was both a comfort and a challenge, and despite my doubts, I knew that she was the reason I was slowly making my way out of the darkness.

"Trust me," she added, as she kissed me on the cheek. Her hazel eyes were reflecting the soft glow of the twinkle lights around us. "Although," she confessed, a flicker of uncertainty crossed her features, "I might see you a bit differently than everyone else—I did sort of have a crush on you growing up."

"Don't know how I missed something like that."

She fiddled with the ends of her wavy hair, a bashful smile playing on her lips. "Guess you were too busy worrying about baseball. Nothing new there," she teased.

I couldn't help but smile. "Facts," I conceded, leaning in slightly. "And what about now? Do you still have a crush on me?"

Chandler bit her lip, an impish glint sparking her gaze. "I guess you'll have to wait and see," she retorted.

I took her hand in mine, locking my fingers around hers. As if sensing the heaviness of the moment, she turned her attention back to the stars, breaking the brief silence with a dreamy tone.

"Know what I wanna be?" she mused, tracing a finger across the constellations.

"What?"

"A star," she declared with a wistful sigh.

I couldn't help but snicker. "I think you're aiming for the wrong kind of star."

She nudged me playfully. "You know what I mean. I want my own Hollywood star. To be an icon of my time, like Jennifer Aniston."

"You'll do it," I said, genuinely. "Be the big star. Spread your wings, pretty girl. And no matter what, I'll always be your biggest fan."

Her smile widened as she continued on about her Hollywood star, and I smiled at the dream of hers. When she had been quiet for a while, tucked into my side, I cleared my throat.

"Alright, so I know I've got a lot to make up for. Last time we tallied points, you had me at a measly two. Where did this date get me?"

Chandler tilted her head back to look at me, her eyes glinting with mischief. "Hmm, let's see," she pretended to ponder, tapping a finger against her lips. "I'm thinking... a solid five."

"Five?" I feigned indignation, clutching my chest as if struck. "Only five?"

Her laughter rang out, clear and bright against the backdrop of the night sky. "Well, it might just be a new record for you, Boston Riley."

We snickered together, our shared laughs mingling with the soft rustle of leaves around us. The conversation flowed effortlessly from there, each topic more engaging than the last. We watched the stars, lost in the beauty of the night. The stars paled in comparison to the girl in my arms, whose presence made my heart feel fuller than I ever thought possible.

"Come here," I whispered after our laughter had trailed off into the night. Chandler turned her gaze toward me, a question in her bright eyes. I propped myself up on one elbow and closed the distance between us. Our lips met in a gentle kiss, soft at first, then gradually deepening as the world faded into nothingness around us. Our tongues met, exploring each other with a passionate curiosity. I felt her body respond to every touch, pressing against me as if seeking warmth.

Eventually the kiss slowed, and we parted, foreheads pressed together, breathing each other's air. I wrapped my arms around her, pulling her close. At that moment I found myself thinking that if the stars would align just long enough to give me her heart and nothing else, then I'd be absolutely okay with that.

chandler

WITH EIGHT BAGS BETWEEN US, Willow and I had definitely overpacked. She heaved her floral suitcases into the storage compartment while I wedged mine beside it.

Caroline was crossing off names on her clipboard as each person entered the bus.

"Oh, looky!" Willow said, peppy as ever. "Your boy is in the back," she said with a wide grin as she nudged me toward him.

Boston was sprawled out in the last row. I couldn't see his face, but his wavy hair caught the sunlight streaming through the tinted bus windows, and we both knew it could only be him.

"There she is," Boston said, as I got closer, only loud enough for me to hear. "Was hoping you'd sit with me. You want the window seat?"

"Sure," I managed, cheeks burning. He stood up to let me slide in, our fingers brushing in a silent hello that sent tiny shockwaves up my arm.

The rest of the team started piling onto the bus, laughter and chatter filling the space. Then, as always, Parker made his grand entrance.

"Damn, we have to be crammed on this bus?" he complained

theatrically. "I was hoping since I'm so important I'd get the whole tour bus sitch. Have my own bed and bath."

Laughter erupted, and in a collective effort, napkins, which had been left in the cup holders, flew through the air, crumpled and aimed for Parker.

"Alright, alright," he chuckled, ducking as he claimed his throne a few rows ahead of us.

As the last few stragglers made their way onto the bus, I scanned for any sign of Reese. Crew and Bailey had already found their seats, stirring up some kind of conversation with the coaches near them, while Caroline continued to tick off names with precision. But there was no Reese. Then, just before the doors closed, he stepped inside and slid into a seat up front.

"And we're off," Boston whispered, as he lifted up his hood and leaned back in his seat.

The bus started its departure, making its way out of the Blue Devils' parking lot. Boston shifted slightly in his seat, uncrossed his arms and sneakily slid his hand over until it found mine, fingers intertwining. I adored the intensity of his touch, the way his strong hand felt wrapped around mine.

"You doing okay?" he murmured, his thumb tracing circles on the back of my hand, hidden from view.

"Fine," I breathed out, relishing the electric connection between us.

"Alright, folks," Bailey's voice cut through the murmurs of drowsy athletes and half-hearted conversations. He stood up, a grin plastered across his face as if he were about to present the greatest gift on earth. "We need votes. Which home run dance should I do this weekend?"

With that, Bailey commenced in a little jig, his knees bumping against the seats by him. His feet shuffled awkwardly in the confined space.

"Or option number two!" Bailey called out, moving straight into another dance without missing a beat. The second dance was nearly identical to the first—same awkward shuffles, same wild arm movements—but no one cared.

"Bailey, you're a clown!" someone shouted from the middle of the bus.

"Both dances were the same, you idiot," Parker added, snickering.

Then Reese calmly said over the chatter, "Bailey, you never even make it to first base. Why the fuck would you have a home run dance?"

Laughter erupted throughout the bus, the sound mingling with the crinkling of more flying napkins. Just as the laughter reached its peak, Coach quickly shut it down. "Bailey! Have a seat or you can walk the rest of the way!"

He peered over his laptop, his eyes fixed on Bailey. The warning was clear and carried the weight of consequences that none of us doubted he would enforce.

"Okay, okay, I'm sitting down," Bailey relented with a dramatic sigh, plopping back into his seat which made way for a fresh wave of giggles and snickers. He threw a mocking salute towards Coach Levy.

"Never a dull moment with him, huh?" I whispered to Boston, shaking my head but unable to suppress my own smile.

"He keeps things interesting," Boston replied, his gaze lingering on me for a second longer than necessary. Then his hand inched toward my seat until his fingers grazed the hem of my shorts. His hand slipped further, a soft caress against my inner thigh that set my pulse racing.

"I'm glad you're here," he said softly, barely a whisper.

"Me too," I murmured, giving him a slight smile.

Both of us were lost in a bubble of flirtatious secrecy as the scenery outside blurred past us. The thrill of our hidden exchanges behind the watchful eyes of our friends was intoxicating, the risk of getting caught only adding fuel to the fire igniting within me.

After a while, the hum of the bus's engine and the rhythmic sway of the journey had a soothing effect. I fought to keep my eyelids open.

I couldn't resist Boston's warmth, and before I knew it, my head had found its way to his shoulder, fitting perfectly against him. I was drifting, floating on the edge of consciousness when the bus came to a gentle halt, stirring me. My eyes snapped open, and I instinctively pulled away from Boston's embrace, straightening up.

My eyes drifted around, unfocused and hazy.

"We're here," Boston signaled with a nod toward the front.

"Did anyone see me fall asleep on your shoulder?" I asked, a little worried, as I scanned the seats ahead of us for my brother.

"Relax," Boston assured me, reaching out to squeeze my hand discreetly. "I stayed awake. No one looked back. Except Willow, once."

"Thank goodness," I sighed, relief washing over me.

"Your secret's safe," he grinned, that mischievous twinkle in his eye.

We all piled out, squinting in the bright sunlight, our limbs grateful for the freedom after the long ride. Caroline, clipboard clutched like a lifeline, was already marching toward the hotel lobby with purposeful strides.

"Make sure you've got everything," she called over her shoulder, assuming someone would be carrying in her luggage.

"I got it," Boston said gently, reaching for my bags before I had the chance to hoist them out.

"But I can—"

"Don't even try it," he teased, effortlessly lifting my luggage as if it weighed nothing as he brought them inside and set them on a luggage cart.

Willow was playing queen bee. I smiled as I watched Parker and Bailey split her bags between them, their faces resigned but good-natured. No one wanted to upset the coach's daughter.

We filed into the lobby. Caroline stood at the center,

commanding attention as she began distributing the keys like precious tokens.

"Okay, listen up! Parker and Reese, you're together," she announced, handing them their cards. "Boston and Bailey, Willow and Chandler." She paused, then continued. "Devils' Day Out winners get the upgrades. That means suites for Willow and Parker, and whoever's paired with them." Then Caroline continued to hand out the rest of the room keys.

"That's the kind of service I've been looking for!" Parker exclaimed, throwing a victorious fist in the air.

"Absolutely no room switching," Caroline added sternly, her eyes sweeping over us as if daring anyone to challenge her.

Boston locked eyes with me, and gave me a nod as he headed to his room. He disappeared toward the elevators with Parker and a few others.

"Chandler, don't worry, I'm on it," Willow promised, pulling me aside by the elbow and into a corner of the lobby. Her eyes sparkled with mischief, her voice low and conspiratorial.

"On what?" I asked, watching as she typed something on her phone.

"You rooming with Boston," she whispered, flashing her phone screen at me. "Just sent Bailey a text. He's rooming with me now."

I blinked at her. "Willow, is Bailey going to think... you know, that you want to hook up?"

She snorted, flipping her hair over her shoulder. "Oh, trust me, absolutely not. Bailey's harmless. I can handle him."

Before I could protest, Bailey interrupted us, sliding a card into my hand with a sly wink. "I'm not gonna ask, and I know nothing," he muttered under his breath, a grin teasing at his lips.

"So babydoll, am I getting lucky tonight?" he joked, nudging Willow with his elbow.

Willow rolled her eyes dramatically. "If by 'lucky' you mean sleeping on the couch and as far away from me as possible, then absolutely," she retorted, her tone dripping with sweetness.

Bailey narrowed his eyes. "Wait, you won the suite? Why do I have to sleep on the couch?"

"Bailey, don't you know anything about women? The minute I open my suitcase, one bed will be buried under a mountain of clothes!" Willow retorted.

"Ah man, how did I sign up for this?" Bailey groaned, but laughter quickly followed.

I hesitated outside Boston's door, clutching the swapped key card. Instead of swiping it, I knocked, heart pounding. The door swung open to reveal his blue eyes lighting up with surprise.

"Willow and Bailey are playing matchmaker," I blurted out as he leaned against the doorway. "Bailey switched our cards."

Boston's eyebrows shot up, and for a split second, doubt clouded his features. "And you're okay with that?" he asked, tilting his head slightly, a lopsided grin forming on his lips.

With a small shrug, I said, "I can make him switch me back if—"

"Are you kidding me?" Boston cut me off. "You're the only person I want to room with. If you're okay with it, then get in here, girl."

Relief washed over me, and I pushed the cart into the room, my cheeks flushed with a mixture of excitement and nerves.

As I looked around the hotel room, I paused in surprise. "Oh, I thought this was supposed to be a double room," I said.

"Yeah, the couch pulls out into a bed." Boston shifted his head toward the couch.

I started unpacking as Boston retrieved his bags, my gaze fell upon the dreaded uniform bag—the one that held more than just sports gear. Willow's crazy idea suddenly felt like a ticking time bomb.

"Damn zipper always sticks," Boston said, totally unaware of my inner turmoil as he tugged at the bag.

"Let me help you with—" I started, but it was too late.

The bag ripped open and my lace underwear slipped out, fluttering to the floor.

I froze, mouth wide open, unable to form words or move. My brain screamed at me to do something—anything—but my body refused to cooperate. It may have been the most humiliating moment of my life. Universe- 3, Me- 0.

Boston paused, looking from the delicate fabric on the floor then back to me, a confused expression spreading across his face. There was a silent moment where we were both frozen in place, unable to move.

"Uh, Chandler..." he began, a hint of red creeping up his neck.

"Um." The only word I could force out, the only word my brain would allow me to form.

Boston's voice cracked with a mix of horror and confusion as his piercing blue eyes met mine, "I know that looks bad but I promise I have no idea whose those are. I haven't been with anyone this summer."

His words spilled out in a rush, a desperate attempt to clear the misunderstanding before it bloomed into something worse. There was an earnestness in his gaze, a vulnerability that I rarely saw in the confident athlete who lived next door.

For a moment, I tried to maintain my facial expressions, to keep up the pretense that this was all some terrible mistake. But as I watched him stand there, so genuinely distressed over my panties on the floor, my seriousness crumbled. I couldn't hold back the amusement tugging at the corners of my mouth.

"Okay, I have a confession," I said, the words tumbling from my lips as I sat down on the edge of the bed, trying to gather the courage that seemed to scatter like leaves in the wind.

Boston's brow furrowed slightly, his concern giving way to curiosity. "What?"

"They're mine," I admitted shyly, heat rising to my cheeks under his intrigued stare.

"Okay, go on." His tone was gentle, inviting me to explain the madness of finding my lingerie in his uniform bag.

Sucking in a breath, I let out a little laugh to ease my nerves. "Well, I think... I was trying to surprise you with them, hoping you'd like them." The last part came out in a near whisper.

There was a pause—a heartbeat or two—before the atmosphere in the room shifted. Something in Boston's stance softened, and the echo of my confession hung in the air, charged with unspoken possibility.

Boston picked up the delicate fabric, his expression morphing from shock to something else. A roguish grin played across his lips as he held them up, a lightness in his eyes. "Fuck," he sighed. "These are sexy."

He tossed the underwear back into the bag. "I can work with this," he added, his gaze locking onto mine with an intensity that sent shivers down my spine. "I'm keeping them for good luck."

Before I could protest or even muster a coherent thought, Boston was standing before me, close enough for me to feel warmth radiating from his body. His hand reached up, tucking a stray lock of hair behind my ear with a tenderness that contrasted with the playful glint in his blue eyes.

He leaned in, and I could almost taste the proximity of what promised to be a kiss that would surely sweep me off my feet—

A sharp knock at the door shattered the moment. My heart leapt into my throat, and Boston paused, his gaze snapping toward the source of the interruption.

"Coach wants us at practice in 10," came Parker's muffled voice from the other side. The urgency in his tone was unmistakable, a reminder of the reality waiting just beyond these four walls.

"Meet you in the lobby!" Boston called out, reluctantly. He turned back to me and in one swift, fluid movement, his lips brushed against mine—a fleeting but electrifying contact that promised more.

"I'll see you for dinner later," he whispered, before he grabbed his bags and left the room.

As the door clicked shut, I collapsed onto the bed, heart pounding against my ribcage. I let out a shaky breath, melting into the mattress as the remnants of his quick kiss tingled on my lips, the anticipation of dinner—and whatever else might unfold this weekend—setting my thoughts ablaze.

boston

"HEY, let's take a quick look at the field before practice," Parker said. I nodded without hesitation.

"Sure thing, man," I replied, hastily shoving my equipment into my locker. I hung the uniform bag on the rack, then trailed after Parker. The field was as inviting as ever, the bleachers were updated —the dugouts were nice. We couldn't complain. When we returned to the locker room, the atmosphere had shifted. The door swung open and panic coursed through my veins. Some of the staff were busy at work, pulling uniforms from their bags and hanging jerseys neatly in each player's locker. My teammates lounged around, the usual pre-practice locker-room talk filling the air, but all I could focus on was the potential disaster unfolding.

"Damn it," I whispered under my breath, scanning the room frantically. Had my bag been unpacked yet? And more importantly, where were Chandler's panties—the ones she'd trusted me with?

My heart raced. The idea of them being discovered here, in the sanctity of the guys' locker room, was enough to send me into full-blown crisis mode. It would be more than just embarrassing—it would be catastrophic.

"Everything cool?" Parker nudged me, his brow furrowed in concern.

"Uh, yeah," I lied, eyes darting around, wondering if they'd sorted out my jersey yet.

Parker clapped me on the shoulder, unaware of my internal mayhem.

When I reached my locker, I peered inside, trying to calm myself. The one item I was desperate to see was absent. Not in the bag, not draped over the jerseys, not on the floor. My stomach twisted with anxiety wondering where the fuck they were.

But then a hush fell over the room. I glanced up and saw Coach standing in the entryway, anger written all over his face. In his hand dangled Chandler's lacy underwear.

"Would anyone care to explain this to me?" His voice boomed, cutting through the stillness. "The locker room was spotless earlier. Now there's women's undergarments on the floor."

Light chatter passed through the team, faint snickers coming from the back rows. I sank onto the bench, my head falling into my hands.

"Doing this at our home facility is low, but here? While we're away? It's appalling," Coach continued, his gaze sweeping over us, searching for the person responsible. "You should all be ashamed."

He jabbed the air with the panties, Chandler's panties, and my face burned with mortification.

"Anyone want to step up? Who's to blame for this?" His challenge seemed to echo endlessly off the walls.

"Coach, I—" my voice cracked.

"Speak up!" Coach demanded, his eyes narrowing in on me.

"Uh, I was just—"

"Was what?" he pressed, clearly unimpressed by my stammering.

Bailey, who'd sat silently next to me, was watching me closely, probably catching on. I was on the verge of owning up to it when he shifted forward with a sheepish look.

"Coach, sorry," Bailey interjected, speaking up despite the glare piercing from Coach. "They must've just... fallen out of my bag. They're a lucky charm from my girl."

The room held its breath, waiting for Coach's reaction. His face turned a shade darker, the vein on his temple standing out as he processed Bailey's confession.

"Is that so?" Coach's words came out wrapped in ice. "Well, congratulations, Bailey. You're fucking wearing them to practice." He tossed the underwear at Bailey, who caught them awkwardly. "I warned you all about messing around. Now clear out!"

I watched, helpless. My fingers twitched with the overwhelming urge to snatch them away from his hands. But I couldn't move. I was frozen.

With a disgusted wave of his hand, he dismissed us. "Thanks to your little stunt, you'll be running drills for the next two hours—or until I decide I'm no longer pissed."

Bailey slipped the underwear over his shorts. Parker was holding in a laugh, a playful grin on his face. He pulled a piece of the fabric between his fingers and stretched it until it snapped back. "You're a fool, but those are some sexy ass panties."

I cringed as laughter erupted around us. Bailey scrambled to adjust the lacy garment back up.

"Whoever those belong to has good taste," Parker continued, not realizing he'd just touched his sister's underwear. He winked at Bailey before he said. "I'm sure they look hot on whoever they belong to—but definitely not you, my guy."

Groans and whispers rippled through the team as we began to file out, but Bailey hung back, leaning close to me.

"From the look on your face, I'm guessing these have something to do with your roommate this weekend. You fucking owe me," he whispered, barely audible in the shuffling of feet and clanging of lockers. "And her brother just said her panties were sexy," he whispered, the words seething through his clenched teeth.

"Bailey, you don't—" I started to protest, but the words died in my throat. Parker was ahead of me, his presence a reminder that I couldn't exactly explain or own up to them being his sister's.

"Let's just get this over with," he grumbled. This would have been hilarious under any other circumstance—but not knowing they were Chandler's panties.

We trudged out onto the field, ready to get our torture of a practice over with.

"Hey, Bailey! Looking good, man. I think thongs are more your thing!" One of the outfielders jeered.

"Seriously, dude?" I shot back, throwing him a glare. "He's been grilled enough."

"Chill out, guys," Parker chimed in while mid-run, an edge in his tone that said he wasn't in the mood for games—none of us were happy about running drills.

The sun was high, casting the field in a harsh glare. But it wasn't the brightness that had me squinting—it was the sight of Chandler and Willow standing by the fence, frozen like deer caught in headlights.

"Shit," I sighed, jogging over to them and praying they hadn't seen what I thought they had. But one look at Chandler's face told me that she knew.

"You wanna tell me why Bailey is wearing my underwear?" Chandler said through gritted teeth. Confusion and pure horror ran across her face as she pointed toward Bailey, who was now hopping awkwardly from one foot to the other, trying to adjust the lacey garment without drawing more attention.

"Yeah... about that," I stammered, running a hand through my hair. "Coach found them and made Bailey wear them as a lesson." I paused, giving her an apologetic look. "I'm really sorry. I had no idea they were going to take our jerseys out."

Chandler's cheeks turned a shade of pink, but before she could respond, Willow buckled over in laughter, pointing at Bailey who was attempting to sprint down the baseline with as much dignity as one could muster in his situation.

"Woohoo! Go, Bailey! That's how you put on a show!" Willow hooted, whistling loudly enough to wake the dead. Her laughter was infectious, and despite the mortification hanging thick in the air, Chandler couldn't help but let out a laugh too.

"Willow!" Chandler hissed, trying to hide the smile on her face. She crossed her arms, shaking her head at the absurdity of it all.

"Sorry, Chandler," Willow said, trying to contain her laughter. "This went horribly wrong."

"I have to get back before coach makes us run even more," I said, gesturing toward my teammates.

"See you later," Chandler replied, still visibly shaken but with a smirk beginning to form. "Try to get it back, okay?" As she pointed her gaze at Bailey.

"Will do," I smiled, throwing her a wink before rejoining the team, thankful she wasn't angry.

After a long and exhausting practice, we showered then headed to the conference room for the team dinner, our bodies aching and minds scattered. I spotted Chandler immediately, hair up in a messy bun, cheeks flushed, a look of utter exhaustion on her face. She looked so beautiful, even worn down from the day's events.

"Hey, Boston!" Parker called out, waving me over to join him at the bar with a couple of our teammates.

"One sec," I said over my shoulder, already making my way to the buffet line. "I'll meet you guys at the table."

I grabbed a plate and filled it with all of Chandler's favorites—chicken alfredo, garlic bread, and a Caesar salad. I even snagged a large glass of water with a wedge of lemon, knowing she'd need it.

Just as she finished setting aside some boxes, I pulled her away. "Hey," I said, clearing my throat to get her attention.

She looked up, genuine surprise and gratitude in her eyes. "Boston, you made me a plate?"

"Least I could do after that... interesting practice," I smirked, nodding towards an empty table nearby.

"Yeah, thanks for that by the way," she said, rolling her eyes good-naturedly as I pulled out a chair for her.

"Lesson learned." I winked, taking a seat across from her. "So, how was your day?"

My fingers gently reached under the table skirt, moving slowly and subtly to avoid drawing attention. I caressed her ankle, slipped off her shoe, and lifted her foot between my legs to massage it.

Chandler took a bite of the chicken alfredo, her eyes closing in appreciation. "It was fine. Caroline had us running around doing things that didn't even make sense, but hey, our shift is over now."

"That's a relief," I sighed, before continuing. "Listen, I um... I wanted to talk to you about something."

She set her fork down, her expression shifting to concern. "Is everything okay?"

"Yeah, it's fine," I said, trying to sound casual. "About tonight. We don't have to share a bed. I'm happy to sleep on the pullout. It's really no big deal."

"I know, and you're not sleeping on the pullout, Boston," she said softly, her eyes meeting mine.

I could sense the exhaustion in her every movement, but she still managed a grateful smile as she took another bite of food. Parker walked up behind her with his own plate, joking about today.

"Well, I'm always down to see women in lingerie," he chuckled. "But Bailey, today? That was a new experience."

Chandler and I exchanged knowing glances, suppressing our laughter. It was our little secret, and I was prepared to take that secret to the grave.

The rest of the team and committee members filed into the room, and Coach stood up. "I expect us to win tomorrow, there is no other option. You know what to do, so we need to get it done," he boomed, his steely gaze sweeping over the room.

Willow couldn't help but tease her father. "Oh, Dad. A man of many words."

The room erupted in laughter, easing the tension somewhat. The rest of the meal flew by in a blur of laughter. Chandler had a smile on her face most of dinner, and I couldn't help but marvel at how far we'd come. I couldn't wait to get her alone, to hold her in my arms and forget about the world outside our hotel room.

As dinner wound down, I stood up, helping her to her feet. "Ready to make our escape?" I winked, a mischievous glint in my eye.

She blushed, but her eyes sparkled with an answering fire. "I thought you'd never ask."

She slipped away first and waited around the corner, then I slipped out after her.

In the room, Chandler excused herself to shower, while I turned down the lights and turned on the hotel radio. She emerged from the bathroom with wet hair and wearing one of my oversized shirts. It took my breath away.

"You look," I stammered, words failing me. She smelled like coconut and sunshine, and all I wanted to do was pull her into my arms and never let go.

"Thanks," she blushed. "I borrowed one of your shirts, hope you don't mind."

"Mind?" I grinned, stealing a glance at the way the fabric hugged her curves. "I've always wanted to see you in my clothes."

She laughed and I couldn't keep my hands off her a moment longer.

I pulled her into my arms, her damp hair brushing against my cheek. "And I've wanted to do this all day."

I drew near and her lips parted, inviting me in and I eagerly obliged. The sweetness of her tongue danced with mine as the kiss deepened, our hands roaming each other's bodies. Her fingers raked through my hair, pulling me closer, as if she couldn't get enough. As we kissed a burning desire grew within me, an insatiable hunger that threatened to consume me whole.

I pulled away for a moment, trying to regain my composure. "Chandler," I whispered, "we can stop if you want to."

But she shook her head, her eyes burning with desire. "No," she said, softly, "I don't want to."

"I'm trying to be a gentleman," I said between kisses, doing my best to hold back from the urges threatening to overtake me. But she was having none of it. She pulled me back in, her lips crushing mine with a fierce intensity that took my breath away.

"Don't be a gentleman tonight," she murmured between kisses. "Keep going."

All my restraint melted away. I surrendered to the heat that coursed through my veins, the burning need that consumed me. I ran my hands over her body feeling the soft curves of her hips, the firmness of her breasts. She moaned as I touched her, her body responding to mine.

I could feel myself growing harder with every touch, every kiss. She reached down and traced circles through my pants, her fingers and nails teasing me, driving me wild with desire. I groaned, the pleasure almost too much to bear.

"You're killing me," I whispered into her ear.

She laughed softly, a low, sexy sound that made my cock jump. "Good," she whispered. "I like seeing you squirm."

And with that, I gave in. I pushed her back onto the bed, my body covering hers. She wrapped her legs around me, pulling me closer, grinding herself against my hard cock, searching for the friction we both desperately needed.

I knew I needed to hold back and take it slow with her, so I carefully rolled us onto our sides, making her lock eyes with me.

"Tell me what you want," I rasped, my palms journeying upwards, until they found their destination. My hands cupped her breasts, each one fitting perfectly in my large hands. I teased her nipples with my thumbs, feeling them harden under my touch. She gasped, her nails digging into my back as she pressed her hips against mine.

"Touch me," she begged, panting.

Reacting to her, my hand glided down her body, tracing the

curves of her hips before slipping beneath the edge of her panties. Heat radiated off her, and I knew she was wet and ready for me. I slid a finger inside her, feeling her clench around me, and she let out a low moan.

"Oh god, yes," she gasped, her hips bucking against my hand. I added another finger, pumping in and out of her while my thumb circled her clit.

"Fuck, you're so wet," I groaned against the shell of her ear, as my dick twitched in my shorts.

"Please, keep going," she panted, her hands gripping my shoulders.

I upped the pace, my fingers moving faster inside her. Her muscles tightened around me, and I knew she was close. I leaned down to capture her nipple in my mouth, sucking and biting gently. Her face flushed with pleasure, her lips parted.

"Mmm, Boston," she moaned.

I watched her as she hesitated slightly, and I carefully studied her face, trying to decipher her thoughts. Then she leaned in and whispered, "Let me do this." My breathing faltered as she trailed her fingers under my waistband. Her hand trembled slightly as she grasped me, then wrapped her fingers gently around my hard length.

"Holy fuck," I let out the moment she touched me.

My eyes rolled back when she freed me from my shorts. The sensation of her skin against mine was almost too much to bear. I slowed the pace of my fingers on her, becoming utterly distracted by the way she was taking control. I bit my lip, trying to regain my composure, but it was no use. My body was completely at her mercy. She began to move her hand up and down, her fingers tightening around me with each stroke, and I had to remind myself to keep my hands working her.

She was getting more confident with each passing moment, her movements becoming more sure and deliberate. I could feel myself getting closer and closer to the edge, but I didn't want it to end. I wanted to savor every moment of this exquisite torture.

I continued to explore the depths of her, my fingers curling and uncurling within her.

"Oh... fuck," she moaned, and it sent shivers down my spine. I could feel her inner walls clenching around me, begging for more as I quickened my pace. My mouth found hers once again in a passionate kiss, our tongues dancing together in a rhythm that mirrored the movements of my hand.

Her fingers stroked and teased my length, every delicate touch, every firm squeeze sending waves of pleasure coursing through my body.

"Shit, that's it," I groaned as she picked up her pace, her hand sliding up and down my shaft.

I could feel her getting closer as she let out a gasp. I moved my hand faster, curling my fingers inside her in just the right way to make her cry out in ecstasy. She threw her head back, her body writhing beneath me as she came undone.

"Oh fuck, oh fuck, oh fuck," she chanted, her body trembling as she came.

"That's it, pretty girl. You look so good when you come for me."

I continued to move my hand, drawing out her orgasm as long as I could. When she finally went still, I pulled my hand away, licking her off my fingers.

"You taste so fucking good," I whispered, my voice husky with desire. My own orgasm was building, and I knew I wasn't going to last much longer.

I continued to thrust into Chandler's hand, the intensity almost unbearable. I warned her through gritted teeth. "Fuck, Chandler, I'm going to come." She looked at me, eyes sparkling with desire and mischief.

"You're so big," she whispered, her hand moving faster. "I love the way you feel."

That was all it took. With a final thrust, I exploded, my come spilling onto her hand and her stomach. She kept stroking me until I was completely spent.

When the last tremors of my orgasm subsided, I looked down at her with a slight smirk. "Do you want to taste what you did to me?"

She nodded, her eyes fixed on the mess I had made on her stomach.

I slowly trailed my fingers through the come. Then I brought my fingers to Chandler's mouth. She opened eagerly, her tongue darting out to lick the come from my fingers.

"Mmm," she moaned softly as she sucked them clean, her eyes never leaving mine.

"Holy fucking shit," I breathed, collapsing onto the bed next to her. "You're going to kill me."

Chandler let out a small laugh. "This would be a fun way to go."

The moonlight streamed through the curtains, casting a gentle glow over the room as I held her in my arms, almost drifting off to sleep.

"You've gotta be at a solid 10 points by now," Chandler yawned.

"Only ten?" I asked, trying to sound disappointed. "Thought I'd be in the hundreds."

"Someone had high hopes for himself," she teased.

I leaned in closer to her ear. "After that performance tonight, I might have to start keeping score for you too."

"Is that so?" she laughed. "Well, then I'd better step up my game."

"Nah. You're doing just fine," I whispered, closing the gap between us with a soft kiss on her lips.

"Goodnight," she murmured, already halfway to dreams.

With one arm around her and her hand resting lightly over my heart, we drifted into sleep.

chandler

"CHANDLER, grab the silver ones over there," Caroline said, her hands gesturing toward a stack of shiny trophies on the edge of the table. "We need to get these sorted before the first games wrap up."

"Got it," I replied, my fingers closing around the cool metal as I began to distribute them into neat rows designated for each tier winner.

Willow slid in next to me, a mischievous glint in her eyes. "So, how was your night last night?" she asked with a knowing wink.

"Good," I said, feeling my cheeks warm under her expectant stare.

"Did you finally, you know, give away that V-card?"

I exhaled a laugh, shaking my head. "No, not yet. I told you, Will. I doubt he believes I'm ready."

"Since our underwear plan didn't work out so well, what if you try Plan B?" she prodded, neatly placing a trophy on the table.

"Which is?" I found myself genuinely curious, even as I lined up another award.

"Talk to him. Tell him how you're feeling."

I sighed, the weight of her suggestion settling in my chest. "I guess I could do that."

"Chandler, just tell him." She paused before continuing. "Guys are never the best at reading your mind—trust me."

"It's just..." I hesitated, my hand hovering over a smaller trophy—probably a participation one. "I didn't plan on my summer being this way. The more I'm around him, the harder it gets to stay strong and keep my feelings about him buried."

"Feelings are tough," Willow murmured, her attention drifting across the field. I followed her line of sight to where Parker was rallying his teammates with a clap on their backs and an infectious grin. "Sometimes no matter what we do... we just can't ignore them."

"Hey, speaking of feelings," I nudged her gently, my curiosity getting the better of me, "you doing okay with all that?" I tilted my head toward my brother. "I mean, after last summer and everything."

Willow's gaze lingered on Parker for a fraction too long before she snapped back to the present, forcing brightness into her smile. "Oh, yeah, don't worry about me. He doesn't seem like the type to settle down, and we're great as friends." She busied herself with another trophy.

"You sure?" I pressed, not entirely convinced but willing to let it slide until she was ready to talk about it. She was right, he wasn't the type to settle down but maybe the right girl just hadn't come along yet.

"Positive," she confirmed, though her voice wavered just enough to make me wonder if she did have feelings for Parker. "Anyway," Willow suddenly perked up, her eyes sparking with mischief, "you know who isn't such a great friend? Bailey!"

"Bailey?" I echoed, quirking an eyebrow in amusement. "What did he do now?"

"His snoring is so loud, Chandler. Like a freight train barreling through the room." She rolled her eyes dramatically. "So, I kept pressing the recliner button on the sofa he's sleeping on. When it would close, he would fall on the ground and it would wake him up."

"Wait, seriously?" I snickered.

"Every time," she nodded with glee. "He kept cussing at the couch, like it had a grudge against him!" She let out a loud genuine snicker, lightening the momentary shadow that had crossed her features earlier. "I laughed myself back to sleep each time. Comedy gold, I tell you."

"Remind me never to fall asleep around you," I teased, unable to hold in our laughter as we turned back to the trophies.

After we finished our work, we got to settle in and relax as we watched the games.

"Come on, Blue Devils!" I yelled. They had won the first game, and now the second was teetering on the edge of intensity.

Reese was on second base, ready to run, his eyes fixed on the pitcher. Boston was next up to bat, his bat resting casually over his shoulder as he eyed the mound.

"He's got this," Willow whispered, as if she could predict the outcome of the play.

The pitcher wound up, releasing the ball with a flick of his wrist. It bounced off the plate, skidding away before the catcher scooped it up, prompting the umpire's loud call. "Ball!"

"Stay focused, Boston," I said to myself.

The pitcher grinned, clearly plotting, before he tossed out a changeup. But Boston wasn't fooled. At the very last moment, he swung. The crack of the bat meeting the ball sliced through the cheers, sending a line drive into the outfield, just out of the center fielder's desperate dive.

"Go, Reese!" we screamed. The stands erupted as Reese dashed from second, rounding third and charging home, while Boston took his place on second.

We were all on our feet then, our cheers rising as the scoreboard ticked up a run in our favor. Parker stepped up to the plate, his confidence palpable even from the bleachers.

"Come on, Parker!" My cheer tore from my throat, vibrant and hopeful.

The pitcher, still recovering from Boston's hit, threw another pitch. Parker connected with it solidly, and we watched, holding our collective breath as it soared toward the third baseman. Boston stays planted on second, not taking the chance. The ball bounced a few times through the dirt before the third baseman snatched it up and hurled it to first.

"Run!" I screamed, as if my voice could help Parker get to the base faster.

Parker's foot hit the bag a mere millisecond before the ball smacked into the first baseman's glove, and I released the breath I hadn't realized I'd been holding.

"Safe!" yelled the umpire.

"Thank God," I exhaled, feeling the tension drain away from my shoulders.

The next batter stepped up and got on base, driving Boston past third and in to score. After a pitching change, the other team got out of the inning with a double play, but the damage had been done.

"We got this!" I yelled as the teams switched. Our team was a wall—they let one batter on base, but gave them no chance after that. No runs scored, and since we were already ahead, we wouldn't have to bat again in the bottom of the ninth.

"Out! That's the game!" The final call rang out, and the field was suddenly a blur of motion. Players rushed onto the diamond, high-fiving and cheering.

"Great game!" I shouted, jumping up and down the bleachers. All I wanted was to find Boston, but Parker was closest, and I threw my arms around him first.

"Amazing job, Park!"

"Thanks, sis!" he beamed, ruffling my hair.

Then Boston was there, turning from another congratulatory embrace. I caught his eye, and something passed between us—a current, a spark.

"Congrats! You killed it," I said, my voice somehow both loud and intimate.

"Thank you," Boston replied. And then, to my surprise, he swept me up into a spin. His strength was effortless, his laughter genuine, and for a moment, the world whirled away until he set me back on my feet, my heart racing for reasons beyond excitement from the game.

The rest of the Blue Devils merged on the field after the postgame handshake. Amidst the chaos, I locked eyes with Reese, who was wiping sweat from his brow with a nonchalance that only he could pull off after such a heated game. "Nice moves out there," I called out to him.

Reese shot back his infamous smirk playing at the corners of his mouth before he sent a wink in my direction.

Crew and Bailey jumped in the air and bumped bodies. Bailey, of course never one to be unnoticed, thrusted his fist into the air as he strutted past us, shouting triumphantly, "Fuck yeah! We're going out tonight and celebrating that shit!" His enthusiasm was contagious, spreading quickly through the team.

I couldn't help but laugh at Bailey's antics, sharing a look with Reese that said we were both in for whatever wild plans were unfolding. But then my attention was caught by a tender moment unfolding at the edge of the field. Willow wrapped her arms around her dad in a heartfelt embrace. He, a stern man throughout the tournament, softened under her touch, his face breaking into a genuine smile—one I hadn't seen once this weekend.

A couple hours later, Willow and I were getting ready for the night in her suite.

"I love the lighting in this bathroom," Willow said, her hands a whirlwind of motion as she pulled items out of her bathroom bag.

"I know, it's such a nice suite," I said, looking around at how much more room she had compared to the regular rooms.

"Okay, so the guys are still downstairs," she said, laying out an array of cosmetics on her vanity. "They're probably stuffing their faces with that third round of appetizers and making their way to the lobby bar."

"Sounds about right," I laughed.

"Which gives us ample time to transform into goddesses," Willow continued, picking up a mascara wand and gesturing for me to sit down.

"Or at least attempt to," I quipped, taking a seat and watching her work her magic.

"Hey, no self-deprecation on my watch," Willow scolded lightly, her hand steady as she worked on my lashes. "You're going to knock it out of the park—have them all stunned."

"Thanks, Will," I whispered, thankful for her unwavering confidence.

"Speaking of knocking it out of the park," Willow segued, a grin spreading across her lips, "I told my dad to have the center fielder stay more toward left field anytime number 3 on the other team went to bat."

"And?" I prompted, my curiosity piqued as I opened my eyes to see her beaming.

"He said I was spot on," she exclaimed. "He said I was his kid after all. They got him out every time."

"Seriously, Will," I said, leaning back as she finally set the mascara wand aside, "you're going to be the best coach ever. You know that, right?"

"Oh, I know. It's just getting other people to see that," she said, tilting her head.

"Trust me," I reassured, giving her a warm smile, "they will."

"Anyway," she shifted gears, delving into the depths of her suitcase. "I have the perfect outfit for you tonight. If you're planning to lose that V-card, you need to look hot." With a huge grin, she pulled out a black minidress, with a daring stomach cutout.

"Willow, I can't pull that off," I protested, eyeing the dress like it was cursed.

"Oh, girl, you can and you will," she insisted, her tone leaving no room for argument as she shoved the garment into my hands.

Hesitantly, I held up the small piece of fabric, stretching it slightly. "Alright, let's see how this goes," I said, hesitantly.

Stepping off the elevator into the lobby, the chatter around the bar hushed as all eyes turned our way. Clutching Willow's arm, I fought the urge to hide behind her confidence.

Boston's blue gaze found me. His reaction was a silent gasp, his hand pausing mid-air before his glass dropped down onto the bar with a loud clunk. He shifted, his posture altering subtly as if the sight of me had surprised him. A warm flush bloomed across my cheeks.

"Chandler, go back to the room," Parker interrupted our silent moment.

I turned toward my brother, giving him a glare. "Why?"

"You forgot to put your clothes on," he teased, never missing an opportunity to embarrass me.

"Shut up, Parker," I retorted, rolling my eyes.

"Looking good, Willow," he added, nodding at her.

"Why, thank you," Willow beamed, accepting the compliment with a flair that only she could pull off.

"We got everyone?" Bailey asked, looking around the lobby.

"Yeah," Parker added. "Reese and a few others are already at the bar."

"Then let's go," Bailey encouraged, pointing toward the exit.

The group's laughter faded into the background buzz of the lobby and we made our way outside. The night air greeted us as we crossed the street on our way to the bar nearby.

Boston held back just enough so that we lagged behind the others.

"Hi," I managed, suddenly aware of the space between us.

"You look fucking amazing," he bit his lip, sending a shiver down my spine despite the warm evening.

"Thank you," I whispered, surprised at how his simple words could make my heart race. As we walked, our hands brushed occasionally—a simple touch, yet subtle enough to be our secret exchange.

boston

AS WE APPROACHED THE BAR, the music's bass bounced through the walls. It was a country bar with smashed peanuts on the ground, and the crowd was filled with cowboy hats.

"Should've known it'd be crowded on game night," Parker commented, his eyes scanning over the sea of bodies packed in the dimly lit space.

Weaving through the crowd, we made a beeline for the bar where the bartender was already pouring shots. We shouted our orders and waited, shoulder to shoulder, packed uncomfortably tight against the other patrons.

"Let's grab that booth before someone else does," Willow suggested, pointing toward the back where Reese and a couple of other guys had claimed space.

"Good call," Chandler agreed, taking the lead as we navigated through the crowd, drinks in hand.

Willow and Chandler slid onto the cushioned seats, settling into the booth. The rest of us stood around the perimeter talking about the game, but then we were interrupted.

"Hey, isn't that the pitcher from today's game?" A high-pitched voice pierced through the noise, turning heads as a trio of girls approached. They were overly excited and confident—a little too confident.

"Oh my gosh, it is!" another squealed, her gaze locking onto Reese.

One of the girls slid next to him, making her presence known. "I couldn't take my eyes off you when you pitched today," she purred, her admiration was evident. "Literally, the hottest pitcher I have ever seen."

"Is that so?" Reese replied, taking a casual sip of his drink. "Happy to keep the game entertaining for you."

The girl basked in his attention, oblivious to his sarcastic remark.

"Shortstop's more my speed," said the girl who had positioned herself beside me and Reese, leaning in closer than necessary. As she did, I noticed Chandler and Willow look up in my direction.

"Whoa, check out the muscles on this one," the third girl cooed, her fingers dancing over Parker's forearm with an audacity that left him blinking in surprise.

"Hey now," Parker chuckled, stepping back with a good-natured grin, "hands off the goods, ladies. This merchandise isn't for sampling."

The girls, undeterred, continued, giggling amongst themselves and attempting to flirt with us. The girl who had practically crawled on top of Reese was the most forward. "That little dinosaur tat on your wrist is adorable!" she squealed.

"I need to use the bathroom." Reese excused himself, escaping quickly.

"Great game," the girl next to me beamed as she inched closer.

"Thanks," I replied, trying to keep the conversation light, all the while noting Chandler's subtle shift. Her drink clinked onto the table, and her posture straightened.

"Must take a lot of practice to hit like that," the girl continued, her gaze locked onto mine with an intensity that was hard to ignore. "You make it look so easy."

"Uh, yeah, lots of practice," I said, glancing back at Chandler whose eyes were now fixed on her hands, an obvious sign of discomfort.

"Hey, Parker!" I called out, hoping to redirect the attention, but I caught a different sort of distress unfolding. The girl next to him was practically draped over his shoulders, admiring him a little too closely.

"Wow, I just can't get over these muscles. Guess you'd have to have a good arm to be a catcher," she cooed, her hand boldly sliding across his bicep again.

The look he shot Willow then was deadly. His mouth formed a silent "help," and Willow let out a loud snicker.

"Sorry, honey," Willow finally chirped, standing up with a playful roll of her eyes. "I need to steal this one for a dance."

The girl huffed, obviously put out, but relinquished her grip as Willow tugged at Parker's hand. She guided him away from the booth and toward the dance floor where others were swaying to "Save a Horse, Ride a Cowboy".

"The way you grab the ball and launch it at the first baseman is so impressive," the girl beside me flirted. "I mean, you're just impressive."

Before the words fully registered, Chandler's presence cut through the conversation. She slid between us, her hand finding its way to my stomach, holding me assertively.

"Sorry," she interjected smoothly, giving the girl a tight smile. "I'd like to dance with my boyfriend."

The girl shot Chandler a glare but said nothing. Chandler, meanwhile, took my hand and led me toward the dance floor. We maneuvered our way to an unclaimed space against one of the dark walls at the back, away from prying eyes but still surrounded by others dancing.

Chandler wrapped her arms around my neck, and I drew her closer by the waist. Leaning in, I whispered just loud enough for her to hear over the music. "It's so sexy when you're jealous."

"Maybe I wasn't jealous," Chandler retorted, her breath warm against my ear. "Maybe I just thought I was saving you."

"Uh-huh." I grinned, knowing the truth.

Bodies moved all around us, creating an intimate bubble in the crowded room. As we moved together, my fingers traced patterns across her lower back, sending a shiver that I felt even through the fabric of her dress. Leaning closer, I whispered, "You in that dress... it's making me think things I probably shouldn't."

The corners of her lips curled up into a shy blush, yet she continued to match my rhythm step for step, our bodies syncing to Morgan Wallen's "Cowgirls." The heat between us was building with every sway. Chandler's body moved against mine in a way that was both teasing and insistent, pressing into me, inviting my hands to explore her.

As the bass reverberated through our bodies, she spun around and pressed her ass against me, a motion that had me biting back a groan. It was a slow, sensual grind that had us both breathing heavily. I could feel myself growing harder by the second. I kept my hands firmly on her hips—it was all I could do to keep myself in check. The dim lights cast a seductive glow over her features as she looked back at me, a sly smile playing on her lips.

"Chandler," I breathed out, my voice a ragged whisper as my palms roamed over the contours of her body. "Every inch of you is so sexy."

My hands drifted down her body, then up the hem of her dress, teasing her soft thighs. She took my hands and slid them to her ass, pulling me closer still. I involuntarily tightened my grip in response. The sensations were almost too much. My mind raced with thoughts of what I wanted to do to her.

She must have sensed my desire, because she began to grind against me more insistently, her movements becoming more deliberate and sensual. I almost couldn't resist running my hands beneath the fabric of her dress sliding against my skin. I wanted to tease and torture her the same as she was doing to me, but I held back.

I leaned in, my chin brushing against her smooth cheek as I found the delicate shell of her ear. I nipped at it gently. "You have no idea what you're doing to me," I murmured.

Her laugh was low, seductive. "I'm just dancing," she teased, as she continued to move against me.

I groaned in response, my fingers tightening even further as I cupped her ass, pulling her harder against me. She let out a moan of pleasure, her body trembling as she grinded against my growing bulge.

I wanted to rip her dress off and take her right there on the dance floor. Instead, I continued running my hands over every inch of her body that I could reach, exploring the curves and valleys of her form.

The heat between us felt like it could have burned the place down, and as she turned to face me again, our eyes locked, and I saw the desire in her eyes, and it mirrored my own.

I swept her off her feet, then, hooking her leg around my waist as I lifted her effortlessly. She gasped, her body pressed against mine, heat radiating through our clothes as I held her, I lowered her back down slowly, my hands gliding up her body, relishing every inch of her soft skin along the way. I could feel her nipples hardening through her thin dress, and I knew she was just as turned on as I was.

"Oh my gosh, look at them!" Chandler exclaimed, eyes wide. I turned to look at what she'd spotted, what had pulled us out of the moment. "Willow has Parker line dancing! We have to go see!"

I couldn't help but smile at her enthusiasm. I rearranged myself, trying to hide my erection before I let her tug me forward, weaving through the crowd that had gathered around Willow and Parker. As we made our way closer, I grabbed my beer from the table where I'd left it.

"Look at him go!" Chandler beamed, leaning back against the edge of the booth. Her amusement lit up her eyes. Those eyes were alive with the kind of warmth that drew people to her, a natural magnetism that made her the center of any room she entered.

Willow's laughter rang out above the music as she guided Parker through the dance steps, her arm locked in his. She moved with easy grace, her blonde hair swaying with each step. Parker gave it his all, trying his best to be a good sport despite his two left feet.

His foot caught on hers, and he stumbled backward, barely catching himself before taking a tumble. Chandler laughed so hard she cried.

"Love that goofy grin on his face when he's with her," I said once I caught my breath, watching as Parker shook off his near-fall with another burst of laughter.

Chandler let out a long sigh. "I know. They'd be such a cute couple." Her gaze lingered on the pair, soft and thoughtful.

Parker swaggered back to the booth, a grin still plastered on his face as he reclaimed his drink, condensation beading down the glass. Willow trailed behind him, her cheeks flushed with laughter.

"Man, if I wasn't balls-deep into baseball, I think I'd make a fine cowboy," Parker said, tilting his beer back to drink.

I cocked an eyebrow and smirked. "Really? You do realize cowboys do more than just look pretty. There's actual work involved."

He snickered, leaning back against the booth. "Who said anything about work? I'm talking about riding my horse shirtless, maybe sporting nothing but a cowboy hat, rounding up all the ladies."

"Because that's exactly what being a cowboy is," I shot back, sarcastically.

chandler

"I LOVE COMING BACK WITH YOU," Boston said, putting his arm around me as we entered the hotel room. The door clicked shut behind us, sealing us in our private sanctuary for the evening.

"I have to admit, this little getaway has been pretty fun." I said, trying to hide my nerves. I twisted the lock and took a deep breath, still facing the door.

My heart raced, the reality of the situation sinking in. Tonight, I could lose my virginity to my brother's best friend—someone who'd always been a constant presence in my life, but never in this way. This was Boston, the boy who had been the epitome of my childhood dreams—the reason my younger self believed in love. There was no hesitation in my mind; there was no one better than him.

Boston's shadow fell over the dimly lit room as his hand reached to draw the curtains closed with a gentle swish.

"Come here." His voice was gentle, and I could practically feel his blue eyes on my back.

When I closed the space between us he cupped my chin, tilting my head to meet his gaze. "You're always the most beautiful girl in any room," he whispered, "but tonight you took my breath away."

"Really? I didn't think I could pull this dress off." The response escaped my lips before I could catch it, despite the sincerity in his expression.

"You pulled it off a little too well." The affirmation was soft but fierce, and then, without another moment wasted, he leaned in.

His lips crashed into mine. When our lips met, all my nervous thoughts were swept away. It was a kiss wrapped in years of hidden desire. Our tongues danced together to the same rhythm only we knew. His taste was intoxicating. My fingers curled into his hair, tugging him closer while his hands roamed my back, tracing the delicate outlines of my dress.

His hands moved to my waist, pulling me into him as the kiss grew more intense. My own hands found their way up his chest, tracing the contours of his muscles beneath his shirt. The sensation of his heart pounding in time with mine sent a thrill through my veins.

I moaned, arching my back into his touch. He responded by lifting me effortlessly in the air. My legs instinctively wrapped around his waist. In one fluid motion, he lowered us onto the bed, our lips never parting.

I straddled him as we kissed with a hunger that had been simmering just below the surface for years. Boston's hands roamed my body, leaving a trail of goosebumps. The heat between my legs was building, my core aching for him. I grinded my hips against him, our tongues moving together.

"Boston," I breathed, lost in the heat of the moment, "I want you. I'm ready."

Boston pulled back slightly, searching my face with foggy eyes. "Ready for what?"

I took a deep breath, feeling a mix of excitement and nerves. "I want you to be my first," I confessed, looking up at him through my lashes.

Boston's eyes narrowed slightly, as he tilted his head. "Tonight?"

I nodded. "Yes, now."

"Why?" he asked, his hand came up to cradle my cheek, his thumb gently rubbing away the tension there.

"Because I want to do this with you, and I know I'm ready," I admitted, feeling confident in my decision.

His touch was tender, the action protective. "That's not something you should rush," he said gently. "There will be other weekends—just because we're here doesn't mean it has to happen now."

"I know it doesn't have to happen now, but I want it to." A wave of frustration hit, mixing with a sharp pang of rejection. I dropped my arms from around him. "It's fine if you don't."

Before I could turn fully away, his grip tightened on my arm, pulling me back against his solid frame, refusing to let me turn away. "I really fucking want to," he said, surrendering. "Only if you're sure."

"I'm sure," I affirmed.

He kissed me again, and this time, there was no turning back. I pulled away from the kiss as I reached for the hem of my dress, and then lifted it over my head before I tossed it on the floor—exposing the black lingerie beneath.

"Holy fuck," he breathed out, half-curse, half-prayer. He bit his lip—an unconscious gesture that sent waves of desire crashing through me. "You're perfect," he breathed, his blue eyes filled with need as they roamed over my body.

He kissed my neck and collarbone, his breath hot against my skin, before he lifted me and flipped me around. I relished the softness of the cool sheets against my skin as he gently guided me down on the bed.

His right hand worked to unhook my bra before taking one of my nipples into his mouth, swirling his tongue around it and teasing it with his teeth. He trailed soft, lingering kisses down my body until he reached my stomach. I let out a gasp as he parted my legs and his lips moved to my inner thighs making me tremble in excitement.

"That feels so good," I purr, arching my back and running my hands through his hair.

When he finally reached my clit, he teased me with his tongue, flicking lightly before sucking and licking with more intensity. I was squirming beneath him, my hands gripping the sheets.

"Boston," I begged, "I want you inside me."

He looked up at me with a smirk and reached for his wallet, then slowly slid on a condom.

"I'll do my best to get you through any pain," he said, tentatively. "But tell me if you need to stop."

"Okay," I whispered.

He pressed his broad tip against my slick entrance, teasing me with a hint of what was to come. My body responded instinctively, arching towards him and trying to take him in, but he held back.

"Are you ready?" he asked, searching my face.

"Yes." My breath shivered in anticipation.

He pushed inside, carefully, taking his time and moving agonizingly slowly. I gasped at the sensations, a mix of pleasure and pain. He reached for my hand and pinned it to the bed. His fingers slid between mine in a tight grip, in a promise—he was there to comfort me through this. His touch made me feel calm and alive all at once.

"Are you okay?" he asked, pausing in concern.

"Yes, keep going," I whispered, breathlessly.

"Is this what you want?" he breathed, spreading my legs slightly wider.

"Yes... I feel so full," I moaned, my voice barely above a whisper.

He grinned down at me, his eyes dark with desire. "I'm not all the way in yet."

I wrapped my legs around him tight as he slowly pushed himself deeper, my body continuing to stretch. I could feel every inch of him, the thickness of his shaft, the pulsing veins that ran along his length.

"Damn, you're so tight," he groaned before starting to move— slowly at first, as if savoring every inch of me. With each thrust, he picked up the pace, driving deeper and deeper inside me. The sensation was overwhelming.

"Fuck," I moaned, closing my eyes as my nails dug into his back.

"Eyes on me, pretty girl," he demanded, his voice rough with desire.

I complied, and he began playing with my clit, teasing and rubbing it in circles with his thumb. The combination of his fingers and his cock was almost too much to bear. He was hitting all the right spots, and I felt a heat building inside me that I had never felt before.

"Chandler, I've wanted this for so long," he murmured. The grasp of his hand on mine remained firm and unwavering as he kept it pinned.

"I know," I breathed out. "Me too."

I could feel my orgasm building, and just when I thought I couldn't take it anymore, he angled his hips, hitting a spot that sent me over the edge.

He whispered in my ear, "Come for me, Chandler. I want to feel you come on my dick."

He continued to thrust at just the right angle, like he knew exactly how to keep me on the cliff of pleasure.

"I'm... I'm..." I moaned, not able to form the words.

"That's my girl," he said, panting.

I screamed in ecstasy as my body convulsed around him. He continued to thrust at just the right pace. He wasn't done yet, though. I could feel him swelling inside me, and the thought of him coming undone sent another wave of pleasure crashing over me.

"Oh god, yes—Boston." I dug my nails into his back, urging him on as he rocked his hips into me. He kept going, bringing me to another orgasm until I was a panting, sweating mess.

"Oh fuck," he gritted through clenched teeth, his body tense and shuddering with his release. I lay there, spent and satisfied, feeling the aftershocks of pleasure coursing through my body. It was my first time, but it was perfect—because of him, the gorgeous boy I trusted, who always made me feel safe and protected.

Lying there, our breath seemed loud in the quiet of the room. I turned my head to watch Boston's chest rise and fall, his eyes closed as if he was savoring the moment just as much as I was. A lingering sense of disbelief had me whispering, "I didn't expect it to be like that."

Boston's eyelids lifted, revealing those icy blue eyes that always seemed to make me melt. A chuckle escaped him. "What did you expect it to be like?" he asked, his voice low and slightly hoarse.

I bit my lip, feeling suddenly shy. "I don't know... I've heard horror stories from my friends about their first time."

"Horror stories?" His lips curved into a smile, and he propped himself up on one elbow, gazing down at me with an affectionate curiosity. "Maybe they weren't with the right person."

My cheeks flushed with heat as I managed a playful retort, "Or maybe they just didn't have a Boston to set the bar so high."

His smile deepened, and something tender flickered across his features. "Well, tonight was a first for me too."

Curiosity piqued, I tilted my head, brushing a lock of hair behind my ear. "How?"

He leaned in, his breath tickling my skin. "Being with you, Chandler, it's different. It's unlike anything else."

The corners of his lips tilted upward in a smile that reached his eyes, lighting them up in a way that made my heart skip a beat. He had been out of reach my whole life, but there he was, in front of me, giving me a look that said I was the only one who mattered.

"Being with you is so much better than any stupid hook-up I've ever had," he continued, his voice dropping to a husky whisper that sent shivers down my spine. "You're not just some girl, Chandler. You're you. And I care so much about you... that changes everything."

I snuggled closer to him, feeling a warmth that had nothing to do with the tangled sheets or our bare skin. It was the warmth of being seen, of being cherished for who I was rather than the image I presented to the world.

"Thank you for tonight," I murmured, pressing a soft kiss against his chest, feeling the steady beat of his heart. It was a thank you for the way he took care of me, for the honesty, and for seeing me as someone worth caring about.

Boston tightened his embrace and held me close. As I closed my eyes, for the first time in a while I let myself embrace some of the feelings I was having for him. It was a risk, but with Boston, it felt like a risk worth taking.

boston

"THANKS FOR THE COFFEE," she tried to speak with the toothbrush still in her mouth, emerging from the hotel bathroom with a frothy grin.

"Only the best for you, gorgeous," I called out, leaning against the door frame.

"Ugh, do we have to leave? Can't we just—I don't know—live here forever?" She gestured at the cramped but cozy room, half-joking, but there was a wishful tone behind her words.

I smiled, walking over to hand her the cup. "You're going to be a big star one day. You've got many hotel rooms ahead of you to enjoy."

She spat out the toothpaste and rinsed her mouth before accepting the coffee with a grateful smile. "You really believe I'll make it, huh?"

"Always your biggest fan," I said.

As we started shoving clothes into our bags, I glanced at Chandler. "So, how many points did I score this weekend?"

Chandler zipped up her suitcase and sat on the bed, a smirk playing on her lips. "Keeping my cards close to my chest for now, thank you very much."

"Alright then, I'll just have to keep working at it," I replied with a wink.

"I wouldn't expect anything less," she said, her eyes sparkling.

"Hey," Chandler added, as she slung her purse over her shoulder, "I'm gonna swing by Willow's room. I'll meet you at the buses?"

"Sounds good," I nodded toward her half-closed suitcase. "Leave your bags. I'll take them all down."

"Thanks," she said, stepping closer. "You're the best, you know that?"

She leaned in and pressed a quick kiss to my lips. As she pulled back, my hand instinctively reached out to graze her arm, wanting to hold on to her for just a second longer.

"See you soon," she whispered, her breath warm against my skin.

"See you," I echoed.

With one last look, Chandler grabbed her coffee and slipped out of the room, leaving behind the scent of her shampoo mingling with my coffee.

Back at the bus, luggage was being stowed away, signaling the end of our brief escape. As we lined up to find our seats, Bailey's snicker was unmistakable. "Crew hooked up with twins last night," he said, nudging Parker with his elbow.

Parker shook his head, covering his face. "That's not a flex, that's deeply disturbing."

From his seat, Crew tipped his hat back, his grin all shades of sly. "I will neither affirm nor deny that accusation," he drawled.

"Reese hooked up with someone too," Parker continued, scanning the group. My gaze fell on Chandler, who quickly looked away, her expression unreadable.

"Whoa, jumping to conclusions, aren't we?" Reese countered, leaving everyone curious about the accusation.

"Actually, he's jumping to the right conclusion," Bailey interjected, with a grin. "The bartender said you already closed our tab then left with a blonde."

"Remind me to leave you with the tab next time," Reese shot back. "And when have I ever been with a blonde?"

"He's got a point there. He only hooks up with brunettes." Crew nodded.

"And where did you sleep, Bailey? There's no chance you made it to your own room," Reese asked, giving him a knowing look.

Bailey laughed. "I stayed in Willow's room. But behaving isn't really my style."

Parker paused for a moment, interrupting Bailey before he could speak. "Wait-—if you were in Willow's room..." Parker's eyes narrowed, then turned to Chandler, "...where did you sleep?"

Frozen, Willow and Chandler exchanged a silent conversation. I felt the weight of the moment settle over us.

"I let her have the bed in my room," I said, trying to keep my voice steady despite the hammering of my heart.

Relief washed over Parker's face. "Oh, thanks for looking out for her, man."

I nodded, the guilt gnawing at me. He had no idea what his sister and I had really done, and after last night, I knew I had to tell Parker how I felt about her.

Reese took a seat, shooting me a subtle smirk—just enough to suggest that he somehow knew what had gone down between me and Chandler. It felt like silent approval, even though I couldn't ignore the fact that he'd once had feelings for her. Maybe he still did.

The bus rolled into the Blue Devils' lot, the familiar sight of the field stirring everyone from their slumbers. Chandler shifted beside me, her head lifting from my shoulder where it had been resting during the ride. As if on cue, Bailey's eyes met mine from across the aisle, his expression a mix of amusement and annoyance. That glare could only mean one thing—I still owed him for the underwear fiasco.

"Sorry, man," I mouthed to him, offering what I hoped was an apologetic grin. He just shook his head, a smirk playing on his lips.

"Hey," I whispered to Chandler, leaning in so only she could hear. "I had fun with you this weekend, pretty girl."

Her tired hazel eyes gleamed as she turned to me, a soft smile curving her lips. "I did too."

The bus came to a gentle stop, and everyone around us began to stretch their limbs and gather belongings. Seizing the moment, I continued, "Are you going to dollar beer night tonight?"

"Possibly," she replied.

"Okay, Parker's going," I said, feeling the weight of the previous night's events pressing between us. "I think I might try to find a way to talk to him, if you're okay with it. After last night... I think he needs to know that I really do care about you."

She hesitated for a moment, biting her lip in thought, then nodded. "Yeah, I'm fine with it. Just not sure how he'll feel about it."

"Just leave it to me," I assured her, reaching out to tenderly rub her cheek with the pad of my thumb. Her skin was soft against the roughness of my hand.

As if on cue, everyone started to stand up. We rose together, caught in the flow of everyone eager to get off. "See you tonight, then," I said, stepping aside to let her pass.

"See you," Chandler echoed, her gaze lingering on mine before she turned to join the others.

Tonight was more than just dollar beers for me—it was about being honest with Parker, and maybe even taking a step forward in whatever this thing with Chandler was turning into. I just hoped he would understand.

Later that evening, Parker threw an arm around my shoulder as we made our way inside the bar, his laughter booming above the chatter and clinking bottles.

"Man, I missed doing this with you this past year," he said, scanning the crowd for our teammates.

"Same," I agreed, before signaling the bartender for a couple of beers.

Parker grinned, accepting the frosty bottles with a nod of thanks.

We navigated our way to the back tables where our teammates were scattered either playing pool or throwing darts.

"Reese!" Bailey called out, a lopsided grin plastered on his face. "You ever gonna tell us the details about this blonde you hooked up with?"

The room erupted into a mix of snickers and curious glances, everyone suddenly all ears.

"Bailey, why are you so obsessed with my sex life? You want to see my dick? Just ask," he quipped, taking a sip of his drink with a nonchalance.

"Maybe I am asking." Bailey shot him a nod, his smile never wavered.

Crew lined up his shot, a sly wink aimed at Bailey before the sharp crack of the pool ball echoed through the chatter. "I hooked up with two blondes," he boasted, chalking his cue after the successful pocket.

"Yeah twins, you sick fuck," Bailey tossed back, shaking his head but chuckling all the same.

I leaned against the wall, amused by the banter, watching as Parker wandered over, beer in hand, about to interject something in this ridiculous conversation.

"Speaking of hook-ups," Parker began, his gaze directed at Bailey. "What's the deal with you and Willow? Christ, were those her panties you wore at practice?"

Bailey sent a glare my way before he answered Parker. "Man, I wish I could say they were," he confessed. "But I can promise you those panties weren't hers. And we all know a gentleman doesn't kiss and tell, anyway."

"Here's to women Bailey hasn't hooked up with," I toasted, raising my drink with a small smile.

"Until they decide otherwise," Bailey chimed in, raising his bottle to join ours. The glasses clinked together as we continued on with our night.

"Hey, Park," I nudged him. He turned to me. "Could we talk? Out back on the patio?"

"Sure thing," Parker replied with an easy grin.

We made our way over to an empty picnic table on the patio. The wooden surface was worn smooth, and beyond the railings was a view of the lake.

Parker sat down across from me. "What's going on, man?" he asked, leaning forward with genuine concern etched onto his face.

"Being around you and the boys this summer has been good for me," I started, my fingers tracing the grain of the wood. "It's helped me clear my head, not focus so much on the bullshit stuff with my mom."

"Sometimes, that's all you need, right? A little distraction, some good company." Parker nodded, understanding flickering in his gaze.

"Maybe it was." I let out a breath I hadn't realized I was holding in.

Parker leaned back, the wooden bench creaking under his weight. He took a long swig from his beer, then turned to me with a small grin. "Missed the old Boston this year, man," he said, setting his bottle down. "I'm glad you're letting yourself have some fun again."

"Yeah, I'm trying," I replied, my eyes drifting toward the still water for a moment before meeting his gaze again.

"Listen, Parker, there's something else I need to talk to you about." My voice came out more uncertain than I intended. It was now or never. "I'm not sure how to say it, so I'm just going to—"

He raised an eyebrow, waiting for me to continue.

I drew in a deep breath, feeling the fresh air fill my lungs. "I really like Chandler," I confessed, the name feeling like a weight off my chest. "Like, I like her a lot and—"

"Boston, come on man, are you serious?" Parker interrupted me, sharp with disbelief. I was taken back for a moment, but I held his gaze steadily.

"Yes, I'm serious," I said firmly. "I wouldn't be talking to you about this if I wasn't serious about her."

Parker leaned forward, his elbows resting on the table, and he ran a hand through his hair. We sat in silence for a moment that stretched too long. Finally, he took a deep breath and exhaled slowly. "Fucking hell. We're really doing this." He glanced up at me, his expression unreadable. "Alright. I know you guys think I'm an idiot, but I knew—"

"Knew what?" I asked, my curiosity piqued despite the anxiety knotting in my stomach. Could he have known about everything that happened between me and Chandler this weekend?

"About all the times you passed her Monopoly money under the table growing up, or you'd sneak her your draw fours in Uno." Parker shook his head, almost laughing. "I knew there was no way she could have beat me at everything. But you did it for some stupid reason, and I saw that it made you smile to see her happy... so I always let it go."

"You knew about that?" I asked, taken back by his words.

"Hey, I notice more than you give me credit for." He smirked, then his face softened. "Told you, I'm not as stupid as I look. Look, Boston," Parker leaned forward, resting his elbows on the weathered wood of the picnic table. "I know you, man. You're like a brother to me. And I've seen how you are with her—always looking out for Chandler, even when she didn't notice."

I nodded, feeling a swell of gratitude for his recognition. Parker's gaze lingered on the surface of the water before he turned back to me, his eyes narrowing slightly as if weighing his words.

"But here's the deal," Parker continued, locking his gaze with mine, "if you take that leap, and you two decide to be together... Don't hurt her. I don't want our friendship to be over because things go south between you two."

"I'm thinking of her first, Park, always." I tightened my jaw, narrowing my eyes. "Hurting her is the last thing I want. I care about her more than I've ever cared about anyone."

Parker studied me for a moment longer, searching my eyes for the truth of my words. Finally, he gave a slow nod, a silent pact sealed between us under the night sky.

We both rose from the bench. Parker stepped in, wrapping his arms around me in a brotherly embrace. "Good talk. Love you, man," he murmured.

"Love you too, Park." I clapped him solidly on the back.

The bar was loud with laughter and the clinking of glasses as we made our way back inside. Chandler and Willow were sitting on stools at the bar drawing everyone's attention. Chandler caught my eye immediately, even in a simple tank top and shorts.

"Hey, beautiful," I said, sliding my hand around her waist as I approached. She turned, her hazel eyes lighting up, as she saw me.

"Hey you," she replied with a smile.

"I talked to Parker," I said, just loud enough for her to catch. "All good. He's not mad."

She turned to me with an expression that held a flicker of disbelief. "What, really?" Her eyes searched mine for confirmation.

"Yeah, it's all good," I said with a confident nod that I hoped would dissolve any lingering worries. Relief washed over her face.

"Can I get a round of shots?" Parker asked the bartender, as he motioned to our group.

"You're the catcher, right?" A girl leaning against the edge of the bar asked Parker.

"Depends who's asking, sweetheart," he replied, tossing back a flirtatious tone with a lopsided grin.

She stepped closer, as she said, "I'm asking." Her gaze dropped momentarily in a way that left little to the imagination, then snapped back up to his.

Bailey stood on the other side of Parker, eyebrow cocked. "Tell us," he said, with a grin, "why are you looking for the catcher?"

"Well," she purred. "A few of my friends and I couldn't help but admire how cute the catcher's butt looked in those baseball pants."

She tossed a nod over her shoulder, where a table of girls behind her waved and giggled.

One of the freshly poured shots was snatched up by the girl's hand. But before it reached her lips, Willow intercepted the glass with a swift motion.

"Sorry, honey," Willow quipped, her eyes sparking with possessive fire. The shot glass hovered at her lips for a second before she threw it back. "He might look good in a pair of baseball pants, but he's too good for some jersey chasers."

The girl's mouth twisted into a sneer before she folded her arms and marched back to her group of friends. Willow huffed angrily and took off, leaving the rest of us in a heavy silence.

chandler

"ARE YOU OKAY?" I asked Willow, watching closely as she stood on the back patio, chugging her drink.

She gave a short nod then sighed. "Yeah, Chandler, I'm sorry. I know it's your brother and it's weird, but it's annoying when he gives girls like that attention. He can do so much better."

My eyes narrowed slightly at her words. I was trying to figure out why she was so upset. "He deserves better, as in someone like you?" I asked, gently.

She hesitated before speaking. "I don't know... maybe. I guess... maybe I do still have feelings for him," she confessed, covering her face.

"Okay," I grimaced playfully, trying to lighten the mood. "Not gonna lie, it's kind of gross how you could see him in that way, but I get it." I paused, considering her situation with a more serious demeanor. "I think you should tell him, though."

Her eyes widened slightly. "You think so?"

"Yeah," I affirmed with a nod. "Trust me, he's not the sharpest crayon in the box—I'm sure he has no idea."

A small laugh escaped her, the tension in her shoulders easing slightly. "I'll think about it," she promised, and I could tell she meant it.

"Good." I grinned. "The look on her face when you took that shot was pretty funny, though."

"Wasn't it?" Willow chuckled, shaking her head. "She looked like she was going to murder me."

The laughter and excitement from our group was starting to get out of control. I watched as Parker made his way out onto the back patio to join us, choosing the seat right next to Willow.

"Word on the street is that I have some fans admiring my... assets in uniform," Parker teased.

"Please," Willow scoffed. "I heard it was actually the umpire they were admiring."

Parker chuckled, then turned to her with a tilted head and a half-smirk. "Just admit you check me out. You notice the goods every time I bend over. Don't you?"

Willow rolled her eyes but couldn't hold back a smile as she said, "I will admit nothing."

"We both know the truth, Sunshine," Parker replied with a small smile. He scooted just a bit closer to her, their shoulders nearly touching.

"Don't let it go to your head," she teased.

Caroline and her friends had joined us and started a game of truth or dare, eager to stir up some excitement, no doubt. The last time Caroline dared me to do something, it ended in me giving Bailey a lap dance, but it also was the reason Boston kissed me for the first time. They took turns, daring and challenging each person with something ridiculous and soon everyone was roped into the antics.

"Okay, Crew, your turn!" Caroline announced with a devilish grin. "I dare you to show a butt cheek to the girl sitting at that table over there!" She pointed dramatically at a nearby table where a group of girls sat, chatting to each other, oblivious of our antics.

Annoyance spread across Crew's face, but he lifted his tall and slender body up from his chair with a heavy roll of his eyes. A collective hush fell over the crowd as anticipation mounted.

"Fine, but y'all better get a good look," Crew huffed, and in one swift motion he turned and flashed a single butt cheek toward the innocent bystanders. The response was instantaneous—screams and cheers erupted from the targeted table.

"Of course you'd get that response, Crew!" someone shouted across the laughter, and it was true. I don't think anyone could be mad at that view.

The game spiraled on, dares escalating with each turn.

"Alright, alright, settle down!" Sam, one of Caroline's friends called out, giggling. "Who's next? Bailey!"

"You know I always take the dare, babydoll!" he said, taking a sip of his drink.

"Dare you to try to get the hot bartender's phone number," she said with a devilish grin.

Bailey stood up from his seat, a smile spread across his face. The group watched as he disappeared into the bar. Moments later, he emerged, phone held high.

"Got them digits, baby!" Bailey shouted, winking at the round of applause that greeted him.

It wasn't long before Caroline's mischievous eyes landed on me.

"Chandler, truth or dare?" she asked with a daring smirk.

"Truth," I straightened my posture.

"Who do you like more, Reese or Boston?" Her question hung in the air, halting any chatter or laughter.

I felt every eye turn to me, their stares weighing me down. Boston paused mid-sip, while Reese narrowed his eyes at Caroline.

"Caroline, stop," Reese said sharply.

"What? What's the problem?" Caroline feigned innocence, but her eyes gleamed with something else. "Didn't you hook up with Reese last summer? How far did you get? First base? Second? Did you go all the way?"

"Caroline!" Boston growled, raw and loaded with anger. "What the fuck?"

"What's the matter, Boston? Was she doing the same thing with you?" Caroline retorted.

I couldn't take it anymore. The weight of their stares, the whispers—it was too much. Wordlessly, I pushed back from the table and walked away, my footsteps quick and purposeful. I could hear Willow and Parker getting into it with Caroline but I was already gone, tears falling down my face as I leaned over the railing of the staircase that led to the lake. Alone in the dark, I allowed the tears to escape, tracing silent paths down my cheek.

The night air brushed against my skin, but it was Boston's presence that soothed me.

"Hey," he said softly, his arm finding its way around my waist. "Don't let her get to you."

I scoffed, a bitter laugh escaping me despite the tears that threatened to spill over again. "How am I supposed to not let it get to me? She's right." My voice cracked, and I hated how vulnerable I sounded. "Last summer Reese and I did do something."

"Chandler," Boston interrupted, his tone gentle yet firm. "You have nothing to be ashamed of. I mean obviously I don't want to hear about you and him, but..." he paused, his hand squeezed me tighter. "I have a past too. We all do."

"But Boston, doesn't that matter to you? He's your brother."

He shook his head. "No, that doesn't matter to me. You matter to me."

I turned to face him, his ocean blue eyes holding an intensity that made my heart skip. "But Boston, I—"

He cut me off with a shake of his head, his gaze never leaving mine. "Chandler, this is my fault. You have to know that. I didn't step up when I should have. I held back. It was all me."

My mouth opened to protest, but he continued before I could get any words out.

"Just let me own the past, okay? It was me pushing you away, I basically held the door open for you to walk right to him." His fingers brushed against my cheek in a slow, tender motion. "But the future... the future could be ours."

And in that moment, in the dark evening with the lake silently witnessing us, I absorbed the gravity of Boston's words. I found myself momentarily speechless, caught in the tangle of emotions that he had unraveled. He always looked out for me, protected me— and here he was, doing it again.

"I don't understand. I don't deserve the way you always take care of me, the way you always save me. You've been doing it since we were kids. Even the first time we ever met, and you didn't even know me."

Boston chuckled. "No, Chandler, you have it all wrong." His hand reached up to gently tuck a loose strand of hair behind my ear. "The moment I saw you, you saved me."

My pulse raced, every one of my senses dialed to his proximity, to the earnestness in his voice.

"I was a kid who spent the whole day watching my mom cry; she held it together around other people, but she let it out with me. And I was used to putting together some kind of meal for her that was probably like potato chips and ketchup. I was always so worried about her..." He shook his head, and then he spoke again. "And then there you were, the most beautiful thing I had ever seen. You gave me hope for the first time. You were a bright light in the darkness, and from that moment on, I always hoped that you would be my girlfriend one day."

I felt the tears trying to surface again.

"So the bracelet you gave me," Boston continued, a sheepish yet soft smile on his lips, "I'll never take it out of my glove. It's what reminds me of you. It's my hope, my luck—hopefully my future, everything."

Tears blurred my vision as my emotions surged, overwhelming and raw. Here was Boston Riley, laying bare his soul. And the worst part about it was that each time Caroline tried to embarrass me with this stupid game, it somehow ended up bringing us closer together.

"Fuck," I whispered. "What are you doing to me?" I knew at that moment, this whole trying not to fall for anyone this summer thing was crumbling—shattering, even.

Lifting my chin gently with his fingers, he met my gaze steadily. "I can't stand you crying," he said, his tone earnest and filled with emotion that made my heart swell.

With a calloused thumb, he wiped away a tear that had fallen down my cheek. Then he placed a gentle kiss on the other side of my face, removing another.

Without hesitation, I kissed him, our lips colliding. The kiss was different from any we'd shared before—gentle, but more intense. Boston's hand cradled my face tenderly as our lips and tongues moved at a pace that was both new and familiar. My hands found their way to his hair, the wavy strands slipping through my fingers like golden threads as I pulled him closer. Nothing else mattered in this moment— there was no more Caroline drama, no worries about what others thought, no barriers between us. Just Boston and me and the feelings I was finally allowing myself to explore.

boston

THE LOCKER ROOM echoed with laughter. Metal lockers slammed shut as we strapped on our cleats. I leaned back against my locker, shaking my head in disbelief at the locker-room talk. The events from last night's game of truth or dare had spiraled completely out of control.

"Man, you should've seen that girl's face when she had to suck Bailey's toe!" one of the guys hooted, slapping his knee.

"Hey, it wasn't so bad," Bailey shrugged.

Reese, leaning casually against the row of lockers, chimed in with a smirk. "Let's not forget how Bailey's dare was a complete failure."

The group snickered, but all eyes turned to Reese, anticipation hanging in the air.

"Apparently, she gave him Jim's Grocery's phone number instead of hers," Reese continued, trying his best to keep a straight face, but it was evident he was enjoying every second of it.

"Shut up, dude, she was probably just busy working and gave me the wrong number," Bailey retorted, trying to save face, but his cheeks were a telltale shade of red.

"Sure, Bailey," Crew chimed in, sarcastically. "She just wanted to get rid of you."

"Get rid of me?" Bailey scoffed. "No way. I'm irresistible."

"Speaking of irresistible," Parker said, nudging Crew with his elbow, "didn't you go home with the entire table of girls who you showed your ass to?"

"Hey, there's enough love to spread around," Crew boasted, puffing out his chest as if he were already a legend in his own mind.

"Wait a minute..." I cut in, trying to keep a straight face. "One of those women had to be in her eighties."

Crew shrugged, a wicked twinkle in his eye. "I don't discriminate."

Reese snickered, shaking his head. "Well, you fucking should."

The locker room filled with laughter again as everyone finished getting ready for the game.

"Alright, enough," Coach barked suddenly. "If you don't shut up and get to the dugout, I'm going to bench all of you. Get the hell out there."

The locker-room talk died instantly, each of us straightening under his tone. We knew the look in his eyes meant business with no room for delay.

"Let's move it!" he added, with a pointed glance at the clock hanging above the doorway to the field.

We filed out of the locker room, our cleats clacking against the concrete corridor that led to the bright open stadium. Once we ran onto the field, the noise of the crowd swelled around us—a living entity of cheers and anticipation. My gaze wandered over the bleachers, scanning faces until they landed on Chandler. Her wavy hair fell over her shoulders as she laughed at something said by the person next to her.

"Your mom's here," Parker whispered, tilting his chin toward where Chandler sat.

And there she was, right next to Chandler and Parker's parents. Mom's presence always brought a sense of calm over me.

Reese didn't mess around while on the mound. He was throwing fire today, each pitch more lethal than the last, his eyes fiercely locked onto Parker's signals. "Come on, Reese! Let's get this W, baby!" A voice from the crowd cheered.

Reese nodded once before winding up. The smack of the ball into Parker's mitt was almost simultaneous with the umpire's call. "Strike three!"

"Nice work!" Parker bellowed, clapping him on the shoulder as we jogged off the field.

We were down by one, last inning, with the weight of the game resting on our shoulders. The first two batters stepped up and were retired just as quickly—two up, two down. The pressure was on.

"Time to shine, Carrington," Coach yelled, his intense eyes shining beneath the brim of his cap.

"Always do," Reese said, swaggering up to the plate. With a crack that echoed through the stadium, he sent the ball whistling past the second baseman and into the outfield. The outfielder retrieved it quickly, holding Reese to a single.

"Keep it going, Riley!" Coach called out, reminding me this was it —my moment to keep us in the game.

I tried to shut out everything but the pitcher and the ball as I dug my cleats into the dirt of the batter's box. The pitch came in right down the middle. I swung with everything I had. The sound of the bat connecting with the ball rang in my ears, and I watched as the line drive soared straight to left field.

"Go, go, go!" Coach yelled.

I bolted for first, eyes locked on the left fielder who dove for the ball, missing by inches. The center fielder backed him up, holding me to first. Reese stopped at second. I turned to see Parker step up to the plate.

"Knock it out of the park!" Willow jumped up, her cheer unmistakable.

Parker paused, glanced back, and I swear I saw it—a wink aimed right at Willow. Then he turned his head back toward the pitcher.

The pitcher wound up, delivered, and Parker connected. I heard that unmistakable crack, and I knew without a doubt—it was gone.

Reese touched home, and I was right behind him, the roar of the crowd ringing in my ears. Rounding third, I saw Parker trotting the bases after me.

"Outta the park, Parker!" someone shouted, and I couldn't help but join in the chant as I crossed home plate.

"Home run, my boy!" I said, my voice nearly lost as the team swarmed us, celebrating the win. And just like that, it was over.

The crowd erupted with postgame chaos, and I followed suit as we lined up for the postgame handshake. When we were finished, my attention was snagged by Coach who had been pulled off to the side, engaged in a tense exchange with Reese's dad.

I couldn't make out the words, but the tight squint of Coach's eyes told me he wasn't happy about the conversation. Reese's dad exuded the same cocky confidence as Reese. He clapped a hand onto Coach's shoulder—and I watched as anger simmered on Coach's face when he turned away, jaw clenched.

I was packing up my bat, and helmet when his yell caught me off guard.

"Riley! Meet me in my office when you're packed up." His tone was gruff, lacking any hint of the joy from the win. No trace of a smile creased his stern features.

I gave a short nod, my fingers tightening around the strap of my equipment bag. Something was up, something stirred by that conversation with Reese's dad, and it left a taste more bitter than defeat in my mouth.

Coach's office door was open, and he was already inside. He was leaning on his desk with arms crossed—lost in thought. "Have a seat," he said, not quite meeting my eyes.

"There's something I need to talk to you about," he began, as he scratched the back of his neck. "You didn't do anything wrong this week..."

But even before he continued, I knew this wasn't going to be good.

"...but I need to give Smith a shot at shortstop next week." The words hung there, incongruous and unsettling.

Allan Smith was alright, no doubt, but shortstop was where I dominated. Everyone knew he couldn't play that position like I could. My pulse quickened, blood drumming in my ears as I fought to keep my expression neutral. It made no sense. Why sideline me now?

"Tomorrow at practice, he'll be on starting drills," Coach continued. And he'd be starting at the game this week—the very thought sent a surge of anger coursing through me.

"Then we'll plan to have you start normally next week." A temporary reassurance, perhaps, but missing the game next week was a big deal.

I wondered what he wasn't telling me as his gaze finally met mine. But he had already made his decision, and I wasn't sure anymore who was on my side.

"This week?" My voice cracked. "Everyone knows most of the scouts will be at our next game. Was that what Reese's dad was talking to you about?" I asked, the question slipping out, raw and unfiltered before I could stop myself. The image of Coach's red face after the pat on the back played back in my mind.

Coach's gaze, heavy with something unreadable, didn't waver. "I'm sorry, son," he said, but there was an undertone that suggested things were more complicated than he could explain. "Smith has been working hard at every practice. Let's give him this shot and see how he does."

Every fiber within me wanted to rebel, but there was nothing to do but nod, a silent acceptance of a decision that felt like a betrayal.

"Alright, Coach," I managed to say, though the words tasted like ash. I knew better than to let it consume me here, under Coach's scrutinizing gaze.

"Keep working hard at practice this week," he finally said, with a lighter tone. "And if Smith can't handle it, I will take his opportunity away without a second thought."

That small assurance did little to soothe my seething resentment. I nodded, not trusting myself to speak again, afraid that my voice would reveal the emotions swirling inside me—anger, determination, and the fact that this was completely unfair.

The door clicked shut behind me with finality, and the frustration was overwhelming. Hot and potent rage was a fiery companion to the cold confusion making my fingers tremble. I was pissed beyond reason, beyond the capacity to swallow back the bitter taste of injustice. It wasn't just about being replaced; it was the whispers between coach and Reese's dad, the sharp glances, the feeling that something more sinister was at play with Reese's dad and his smug assurance and influence.

I pushed through the double doors leading outside and made my way to the parking lot to see if Reese was still there. My hands clenched into fists at my sides. Confusion wrapped around me like a thick fog, clouding my judgment, making it hard to see the path forward. Why now? Why the most important week of the season?

Across the parking lot, Reese and Bailey's laughter was the last thing I wanted to hear. Reese lounged against his truck, his tailgate down.

"You knew, didn't you?" I shouted, tossing my duffle bag with a thud into the bed of my own truck. His smile was wide and untroubled. "Why coach just pulled me," I continued, "I'm guessing you know all about it."

Reese's laughter faltered, his eyes narrowing as he straightened up. "What are you talking about, Riley?"

I could feel the muscles in my jaw clench, the bitter taste of the accusation on my tongue. "You know exactly what I'm talking about. Your dad has a little chat with Coach, and suddenly I'm benched for next week's game?"

Reese's expression hardened, and he stepped closer—his gaze sharp and piercing. "If he's not playing you next week, it's because you suck. It doesn't have anything to do with my dad."

He knew how to push my buttons, what to say to make me snap.

But I refused to give him the satisfaction of seeing me unravel. I could play this game if that's what he wanted.

"You're just like him, you know." I stepped closer. "Lying, manipulative, using your last name to control whoever you want." I meant every word, and I know he felt it.

His jaw was set tight as if he was grinding down on the truth of my words. "And you're just like your mom," he shot back. "You need to take responsibility for your own shit. Quit playing the fucking victim."

I knew neither of us would ever budge on our stance, on defending the parent we grew up with. For a moment, it was just Reese and me, the two of us locked in a battle that might never end.

"Whatever makes you feel better for being a piece of shit, Reese," I spat.

"Be careful, Riley," he warned. "I should have never helped you. We all know you wouldn't even have a chance with Chandler if I hadn't stepped out of the way."

"Fuck you, Reese," I shot back. "I never asked for your help. And trust me, it would've only been a matter of time before Chandler really saw who you are and walked away on her own."

As I spoke, I clung to the truth. Chandler and I had shared something inexplicable from the very first moment our paths crossed—a connection, something special, inevitable. But still, a sliver of doubt wormed its way into my thoughts. Would they still be together right now if he hadn't bowed out? Did she still want to be with him?

That's when Bailey wedged between us, his hands pushing against our chests. "Stop it! Both of you!"

"Get out of the way, Bailey," Reese warned.

"We're done here, Riley," Bailey shot back at me, his gaze sharp.

With one last glare, we turned away. Doors slammed, engines roared to life as if echoing the tumultuous emotions that had just played out.

chandler

I CLUMSILY SCOOPED coffee grounds into the coffee maker. Sunlight was just beginning to sneak through the blinds. My eyelids were heavy, but Caroline's early morning emergency text shattered my slow morning plans.

"Willow," I called out, tapping on her door with my knuckles. "Caroline sent a text. She wants us there early today."

I heard a muffled grunt before the door cracked open. Willow emerged, backlit by the soft glow of her room. Her curly hair was wild, almost like she'd had a restless night.

"What kind of psycho wants us to be there so early?" she grumbled, rubbing at her eyes.

Shrugging, I poured the coffee into two mugs. "I'm the last person who understands the ways of Caroline," I admitted, handing her a cup as if it were a peace offering for the awakening.

Willow took a sip, her face scrunching up as the hot coffee kick-started her senses. We exchanged a look that said neither of us were excited for Caroline's demands.

"Fine," Willow huffed, setting down her coffee mug with a clink. "I'm taking a shower. Give me twenty minutes." And with that, she vanished back into her room.

The drive to the clubhouse was a quiet one, filled with yawns and the occasional sip of lukewarm coffee. Inside the clubhouse, everyone on the committee looked just about as excited as we were. Willow and I found refuge in seats in the back.

"Hey," Willow leaned in, giving me a serious look, "have you talked to Boston in a while?"

I shook my head, stirring the remnants of my coffee aimlessly. "No, I haven't seen him lately. Seems like he's been busy in the batting cages or at practice." My words trailed off as I thought about the past week. "He was also short with me when I asked him why he didn't play this week. I'm not sure if something is going on." I glanced at my phone, as if it might reveal some hidden message from him. "He texted me 'good morning' and 'good night,' every day but that's pretty much it."

Willow frowned slightly, twirling a strand of her blonde hair around her finger. "I wonder what's up. My dad has been off this week too."

"I'm not sure," I added, though a knot tightened in my stomach. Was it just the pressure of the season, or was it something else?

The murmurs in the room silenced as Caroline entered, her presence commanding attention without a word. She cleared her throat, and every pair of eyes locked onto her.

"If I'm not interrupting anything," Caroline lifted her chin, "I'd like to get started."

Caroline continued, her gaze sweeping across us. "The championship game is in three weeks, and we need to be ready for what comes next." She paused for effect, her eyes scanning the room. "Should our team win the championship, we will host an overnight lock-in with the players to decorate the parade float. And then," she drew out the word for emphasis, "The Bayside Ball is the week after."

A collective intake of breath filled the room, the weight of responsibility settled over us like a heavy cloak.

"Which means," Caroline went on, "we have a lot to do to make the end of this season better than it's ever been." She lifted a stack of binders from the table beside her, each one thick and bursting at the seams. "I've compiled a binder for each of you, filled with tasks. I expect them all to be completed."

She began passing out the binders, and when one landed with a thud in front of me, I couldn't help but let out a long sigh. Beside me, Willow did the same, and we exchanged a look.

"Any questions before we dive in?" Caroline asked, her tone suggesting she hoped there wouldn't be any. We stayed quiet, each flipping open our binders to a dizzying array of lists.

"Let's get started, then," Caroline announced.

I flipped through my binder and a page with a detailed timeline for the Bayside Ball caught my eye. My thoughts drifted. I wondered if Boston would ask me this year. It felt like ages ago when I was head over heels for Reese, and it was hard to believe it had been around the same time last year. Now, here I was, hoping to be asked by the boy who used to just be my brother's best friend.

I stepped out of the room and was met with players rushing through the hallways towards practice. Even through the chaos of ball hats and gym bags, I caught sight of Boston.

"Willow," I whispered, my heart doing an anxious little dance. "I'll meet you at the car."

"Okay, see ya in a sec," she nodded and continued walking, giving me a small, encouraging smile.

"Hey, you," Boston's voice reached me first. But the usual warmth that lit up his eyes when he saw me wasn't there today.

"Hey," I said, squeezing the binder tighter to my chest. "Haven't seen you since last week."

"I've been around," he replied shortly, and I found myself searching his face for something more, some hint of what was on his mind.

"Right." A pause stretched, and I decided to take the plunge. "We're starting to plan the Bayside Ball," I said, hoping it would spark something, a sign that he might ask me, anything.

His gaze shifted away then, down the hallway, as if he was trying to avoid the question. "Oh, that's cool," he said, casually. "Wish I could go, but I can't make it this year."

The words hit me harder than expected, a sting of coldness spreading through my chest. I covered the hurt with a half-hearted nod and forced a smile, though I could feel my hopes crumbling.

"O—oh," I stammered. I desperately waited for him to say more, to give me something to help me understand.

The silence stretched, until Boston broke it with a single phrase that caught me off guard. "Chicago."

"Chicago," I echoed, searching his face, confused.

"The Cubs are flying me out." He shifted his weight. "They want to meet, see if I might be a good fit for them to draft."

"Oh, Boston, that's amazing!"

"Yeah," he forced a smile, "but it's the same weekend as the Bayside Ball."

Suddenly I understood why he wasn't going to the ball. I tried to keep my face neutral, to hide the disappointment of knowing there was no chance we'd be able to go together. Boston's gaze lingered on mine, and I wondered if he was trying to decipher what I was really thinking. "Your future is way more important than some ball. Baseball is the priority. I get it," I managed to say.

"Chandler..." There was a hesitance in his tone.

"No, don't even think twice about it." I mustered a smile, even though a tiny part of me couldn't help but still feel the sting of disappointment. "It's a big opportunity, Boston. You can't miss it."

"Yeah, you're right," he nodded, before he glanced over his shoulder, a crease of urgency on his face as he looked toward the locker room. He leaned in swiftly, pressing a kiss to my cheek.

"I gotta get in there before coach notices I'm late and gets pissed," he said in a hurried whisper.

"Okay," I tried to sound nonchalant, even as my heart raced with disappointment.

He was already turning away when he yelled, "Team's doing karaoke tonight. You coming?"

"Karaoke?" The question came out before I could consider it. "Sure," I whispered.

Then he disappeared down the hall, leaving me rooted to the spot, confused. The warmth of his kiss still lingered on my cheek.

A few hours later Willow and I walked into the bar, arm in arm.

"Karaoke night, huh?" Willow asked as we stepped into the dimly lit bar. The overhead lights cast a warm glow on the small stage where the DJ had just called Parker up next.

"Can't wait to see this," she giggled, her eyes shimmering with excitement.

"Go grab us a spot. I'll grab the drinks," I told her, pushing through the crowd towards the bar.

"Two vodka lemonades, please," I shouted to the bartender. As I reached out to hand over my debit card, a firm hand blocked mine, pressing it gently back towards me.

"Put those on my tab," Reese ordered, his presence suddenly towering over me.

"Thanks, Reese," I said, turning to face him. "You didn't have to do that."

He gave a nonchalant shrug, his green eyes avoiding mine. "All good," he tossed over his shoulder, leaving a trail of moody energy behind. What was going on today? Was everyone in a weird mood?

I shook off the brief encounter and carried our drinks over to where Willow had secured a table, just as Parker took the stage. "I Want You Back" by *NSYNC blared through the speakers, and he belted out the lyrics with more enthusiasm than skill, holding a beer in hand.

"Where are you getting the dollar bills?" I laughed as Willow playfully tossed ones at him.

"Always got to be prepared for a random strip club night. Happens more than you'd think," she quipped, winking.

It was impossible not to snicker at Parker's performance. Off-key and overconfident, he was definitely putting on a show—if you could call it that. Suddenly, a familiar warmth brushed against me from behind, and before I could react, Boston's breath tickled my skin.

"Hi, pretty girl," he whispered, his lips grazing my cheek in a soft kiss.

"Hey, Boston..." I managed, turning to face him, my heart pounding a rhythm as chaotic as Parker's singing.

Bailey walked onto the stage with a swagger that had the crowd cheering before he even reached the microphone. The opening chords of "Wonderwall" filled the room, and to my surprise, his voice was actually pretty good—better than I had expected.

"You're gonna be the one that saves me," Bailey sang, his eyes locked on some distant point, lost in the music.

I was just about to comment on his surprisingly good performance when he abruptly punctuated the chorus with an unnecessary crotch grab followed by lifting his shirt up to flash his abs. A mix of cheers and laughter erupted from the crowd.

Willow snorted beside me. "Well, guess he had to ruin it somehow."

"He was doing so well," I sighed, rolling my eyes.

As the last note hung in the air, the DJ's voice carried above the applause. "Alright, we got a special request here! All Blue Devil athletes, get your butts on this stage, pronto!"

Groans and chuckles rolled through the group of athletes scattered around the bar. Bailey turned to them, a mischievous grin plastered across his face. "Nope, I don't want to hear it. Get your asses up here, boys!"

One by one, they ambled onto the stage, some more reluctantly than others. As they arranged themselves, I couldn't help but notice the glaring space between Boston and Reese. Their body language spoke volumes—they might as well have been on different planets. Boston leaned against the far end, his arms crossed, a forced smile not quite reaching his eyes. Reese stood on the opposite side, his hands shoved into his pockets, the usual cocky, laid back look on his face was replaced by cold detachment.

"Something's definitely up with Reese and Boston," I whispered to Willow, leaning close to share my thoughts with her.

"Yeah," she agreed, her attention fixed on the stage. "Something's off, and it's more than just bad karaoke."

Their performance was more shouting than singing, and it was bad—really bad. As the final notes were drowned out by the cheers and laughter, Parker hopped off the stage, the confidence in his step suggesting he was proud of that spectacle. He made a beeline to our table, sliding into the seat next to Willow with a wide grin.

"Alright, Will," he said, slinging an arm around her shoulders. "What did you think of my performance? Did it make you want to jump me on the stage?"

Willow tossed back her blonde curls, eyes sparkling with amusement. "Oh yeah, you stole the show, Parker. I laughed so hard I almost peed my pants."

"Good to know I still got it," he replied with a wink. Then, leaning closer with a cheeky glint in his eye, he added, "You know, I have one of your dollar bills in my waistband. Feel free to put your hand in my pants and take it back."

She burst into laughter. Just then, Boston pulled up a chair. With a small smile, he nodded towards Parker. "And there's the Parker we all know and love," he joked, but failed to hide the tension that seemed to be weighing heavy on him tonight.

Parker's laughter subsided, and he playfully punched Boston's shoulder. "At your service, baby," he quipped, trying to lighten the mood.

Boston shook his head and took a sip of his drink, his gaze lingering somewhere in the distance.

"Hey, Boston," I ventured, unable to shake the feeling that something was going on. "Do you wanna go somewhere more quiet and talk?"

His eyes met mine for a split second before he responded, "Sure." There was a hint of reluctance in his movement, as if for some reason he wanted to say no, but couldn't.

Boston led the way to the gambling machine area, away from the music and crowd. The dim lights flickered over the less crowded space, casting shadows that seemed to dance all around us.

"Okay, spill it," I urged, swirling my drink with the straw.

He swept his fingers through his hair. "About what?"

"Something is going on," I pressed, as I watched him closely. "You're acting standoffish.

Boston shifted uncomfortably, as the ticking sound of a spinning wheel played on the machines. "It's nothing," he dismissed.

"Does this have anything to do with why you didn't play this week?" I prodded.

He took a sip of his beer, the muscles in his jaw working silently. "Coach made that call," he said, but it felt like he wasn't telling me something.

I sighed, frustrated. "I just don't understand what's going on," I admitted. "Why you're in a mood... and why Reese is in a mood."

His eyes narrowed, the intensity within them turning dark. "How would you know Reese is in a mood? Why would you care?"

"Because I care about both of you," I breathed out.

He looked at me with those piercing eyes, "Be honest with me, Chandler. Do you still have feelings for him?"

"Boston, I don't know how to answer that." And I really didn't. Because when I saw Reese, I still felt a small attachment to him—did that mean I still have feelings? I wasn't entirely sure.

He nodded and I could see the hurt in his eyes. "That's what I thought."

I stepped closer. "But I know that you two have seemed like maybe you were on the verge of—"

"Of what?" He cut me off. "Being brothers? That's never going to happen." His hand tightened around the beer bottle. "We're never going to be some happy fucking family."

"Maybe?" I shot back. "Maybe start with actually trying to have a friendship?"

I reached out, my fingers brushing against the warmth of his hand. "He doesn't have to be the enemy anymore," I whispered, my voice barely rising above the sounds from the gambling machines. "He's not his dad."

For a moment, Boston's hand lingered in mine. But then, as if burned by the very idea, he pulled back. And that's when I felt it, and saw it written all over his face. He was pulling away and there was nothing I could do.

"How can you defend him right now? After everything?"

"I'm not trying to defend him," I said, softly. "I'm just trying to understand."

"Understand what?" His tone was sharper now. "Am I some test?" He asked, as he put more space between us. "To see if you like being with me better than him?"

The accusation stung, like a thousand tiny needles shoved right into my heart. It was as if he'd just thrown the thought in my face, the one I had fought so fiercely to keep hidden—even from myself.

"How can you even say that?" I stepped back, shocked in disbelief.

Boston's piercing blue eyes held mine with an intensity that seared. "What are we even doing, Chandler?"

It was the kind of question that demanded honesty, but my emotions were too scattered to be vulnerable. I was hurt by what he'd just said to me. The overthinking portion of my brain took charge, gathering all thoughts into one single, painful realization. Each moment longer I spent with him only tightened the knot in my chest; each laugh, each touch, was only leading me to one place—to him breaking my heart. That thought wasn't just daunting, but unbearable.

"You're right," I said, finally. "We should probably end whatever this is before it gets too complicated." I regretted the words as soon as they left my mouth. He didn't respond, but his eyes studied my face intently.

"We were just having fun, anyway." My own voice sounded hollow. But this was what I wanted, wasn't it? "I never wanted a boyfriend or a relationship, and that's what we did, we had fun." My gaze held his. "Once the summer is over, we can just go back to normal. You focus on baseball, and I'll be fine—like always."

He nodded slowly. "...Okay, but I wasn't just having fun with you," he admitted. "It was more than that to me. But, I agree. That's probably for the best."

For the best? I thought to myself as I watched him. The look on his face made me think he was carrying more than just the weight of my words—like maybe he had a lot more going on than he was letting on. How had I ended up here again, caught in the gravity of Boston's orbit? So close to him, yet feeling so far apart.

Then, he looked past me over the flashing lights of the gambling machines. "Can we just go back, please? Join the group?"

But the simplicity of his request couldn't erase the complexity of the moment, the depth of emotion that had been stirred up and left unsettled.

"Sure," I responded, more sharp than I intended. I turned on my heel and stomped away from him. I half expected him to reach out, to try and use that pull he so often had on me, but this time he just watched as the space between us grew. There was no gentle tug at my wrist, no whispered apologies against my lips, nothing to soothe the sting of our conversation. Just the sound of my own footsteps echoing my frustration.

I slid back into my seat at the table, still reeling. When I looked up, the sight before me took over. Parker and Willow's faces were contorted into expressions of pure horror, eyes wide, mouths open. Onstage, Crew was belting out a tune that could only be described as torture. It was like witnessing a car crash—you wanted to look away, but you couldn't quite bring yourself to do it.

Parker, ever the comedian even in the face of auditory assault, stood up slowly, his hand theatrically pressed to his chest. "I think I need another shot," he declared, grimacing as if the words pained him as much as Crew's singing.

"Take it easy," I warned, though my attempt at sisterly concern came out more annoyed than intended.

He shot me a mischievous grin and flicked my forehead as he passed by, heading toward the bar. He quickly returned to the table, downing another shot. "Okay, that's better," he sighed, placing the empty glass with a clink on the surface.

"Hey, Hartford!" The DJ approached, slapping Parker on the back with a grin. "You killed it tonight, man."

"Thanks for the assist, J-Bomb," Parker replied, raising an eyebrow at the nickname he'd stowed upon the DJ.

Just then, his gaze shifted to the stage, and he chuckled. "Oh, shit! D-Wagon is about to get on the stage."

Boston appeared behind him, clapping him on the back. "Parker is in the nickname stage of his drinking—that's our fifteen-minute warning before he passes out or pukes. Time to escort this guy home."

My irritation flared at Boston's words even though I knew he was right. "Maybe you should stop telling us all what to do and what's best for us."

"Whoa, calm down," Parker interjected, holding up a hand.

"Bro, don't you know never to tell a woman to calm down?" Boston fired back, shaking his head.

"That's not a woman, that's my sister," Parker quipped.

Willow, who had been quietly sipping her drink, suddenly choked on her laughter, spewing liquid across the table.

My eyes remained narrowed on Boston, unwilling to let go of the hurt I was feeling. I knew that I was the one who had made the decision, but I hadn't expected him to agree—not for a second. "You know what? You two should get out of here," I said, bitterly.

Boston reached out, his hand hovering near my arm, but I jerked away. "No, Boston. Please just go." I deliberately turned my body away from him, directing my attention to the next performer on stage, signaling the end of the conversation.

"Let me know if you guys need anything," Boston said to Willow.

"We'll be fine," she assured him, giving me a sympathetic glance.

As Boston steered Parker towards the exit, Parker called out to Willow, "Good night, sunshine!"

"Get out of here before I throw you out myself!" Willow retorted with a laugh.

"You're a mad woman, and I love it!" Parker's declaration echoed as they disappeared into the crowd, leaving me sitting there, arms still crossed, frustration lingering.

The sounds of karaoke night faded into the background, the off-key notes blurring into the distance. I sat at the table, laughter and cheering feeling like they belonged to another world—one where hearts didn't break and disappointment wasn't so familiar. I convinced myself that I wouldn't—couldn't—fall for someone this summer, I wouldn't let anyone hurt me, and here I was feeling like my heart was hardly even beating.

boston

.

EXHAUSTION HAD SEEPED into my bones, the same kind that weeks of two-a-days plus game days did to me. Coach had been brutal with us lately, and even though we were on a winning streak, he hadn't lightened up—not for a second. Muscles aching, I slid onto my bed and sent Chandler my habitual goodnight text. I'd barely seen her lately, but that didn't mean I wasn't thinking about her.

As soon as the message was sent my phone was ringing, and I was hardly able to keep my eyes to answer.

"Hey, Mom. What's up?"

"Boston, I know things have been... strained between us, but can you hear me out for a second?"

"Sure," I sighed, the weight of my exhaustion pulling me back against the pillows as I closed my eyes, bracing for whatever was coming.

"Every game this season, I let Reese know I'd be at Maria's Diner afterwards. Whether I could make it to the game in time from work or not, I'd go there, hoping he'd show up eventually." Her confession caught me off guard. "I know tomorrow is the championship, Boston. It's the last one, and I don't think he'll come, which is okay, I get it. But... would you come sit with me after the game and wait with me? Maybe share a milkshake?"

Despite the frustration she sometimes inspired, I couldn't say no to the vulnerability in her tone. "Yeah, Mom, I'll be there."

"Thank you, Boston. I'll see you then. Good luck tomorrow. I know you'll win."

"Thanks, Mom."

Morning came too early, my dream of playing in the World Series ruined by an unexpected soundtrack—Parker, singing some awful song. Groaning, I rolled out of bed and shuffled to the door, which creaked open just enough for me to squint at him.

"Why are you so happy? It's too early," I asked, barely able to keep my eyes open.

"Man, it's a good day!" Parker beamed. "It's championship day. We're bringing home the W, then it's all celebrations and no more stupid practice."

I leaned against the doorframe, crossing my arms as a thought occurred to me. "And you sneaking someone out early this morning doesn't have anything to do with your good mood? I swore I heard giggles and the front door close at like three a.m."

Parker's grin held steady, but a flicker in his eyes gave him away. "No, that was me," he insisted.

"Oh, you were giggling like a girl?" I raised an eyebrow, not buying it.

"Yeah, man, I had a really funny dream," he chuckled, scratching the back of his neck.

"And the pink lipstick I found in the bathroom last night. That was yours too?"

"Yeah, just trying something new," he said, trying to hide a smirk.

"Uh huh," I knew full well those giggles belonged to Willow. With a shake of my head, I retreated back to my room to gear up for the day.

The clubhouse was buzzing with nerves and anxious energy. We shuffled in, our cleats clicking against the concrete, each of us lost in our own thoughts. Coach was already there, pacing like a caged lion. His eyes were sharp as he checked his watch, and when he finally spoke, his voice silenced the room.

"Boys," he began, stopping to look at each of us. "We've had a hell of a season." His hands gripped his hips. "You've pushed through double practices, you've battled every inning, and you've earned your spot here today."

We paused, waiting for him to continue.

"Today's the day—the championship. Everything we've worked for all summer comes down to this. But remember," he said, softening ever so slightly, "it's still a game. Let's go out there, have some fun, and show 'em what we're made of."

Nods and hoots rippled through the team.

"Alright then," Coach gave a nod. "Let's do this."

We poured out of the clubhouse and stepped onto the field. I jogged between second and third base, taking my position as short-stop and readying for first pitch.

As the stands filled and the noise grew louder, I stole a moment to scan the crowd. I needed to see her—to know she was there. And then my gaze landed on Chandler. Even from a distance, I could see her smile under the stadium lights.

Beside her was my mom. They were both here—the two people I needed to see.

"Come on, Reese! Bring the heat!" Someone shouted from the stands as he took his place on the mound.

Reese nodded subtly, his gaze locked onto Parker behind the plate. With a fluid motion, he wound up and unleashed a bullet straight into Parker's mitt. "Strike!" the umpire bellowed.

"95!" someone yelled from the crowd, holding a speed gun, and a collective gasp followed. We may not have been on the best terms, but damn if I didn't respect his arm.

Reese didn't acknowledge the chatter about the speed or the awe. He narrowed his eyes, zeroing in on his target again. This time, he switched tactics. A changeup threw off the batter. The swing came too early, hopelessly out of sync with the ball's lazy arc into Parker's glove.

"Strike!" The umpire called out after the last pitch, the stands erupting as the batter slunk back to the dugout, shoulders slumped. Reese tipped his cap as the next batter stepped up to the plate.

"Alright, let's keep holding them off," Parker yelled, trying to keep spirits high.

The innings flew by, each team's defense refusing to give in. Third inning, nothing. Fourth, zip. The fifth rolled around, and suddenly we found our rhythm. A double here, a stolen base there, and before the other team knew what hit them, we'd racked up two runs.

"Keep it up, boys!" Coach commanded. "Don't let up!"

We couldn't hold them off, though, and they evened the score in the sixth. Our advantage slipped through our fingers, and the pressure began to mount. Heading into the ninth inning, we were deadlocked.

"Last chance," Coach said as we gathered our batting gear. "This is where legends are made. Let's make sure they remember us."

Bailey was up. He hit a ground ball and just barely made it to first base.

"Reese, let's go," someone yelled, as I fidgeted with my glove and bat in the on-deck circle. Reese stepped up to the plate, taking position. Everyone was on edge. Reese kicked the dirt, eyeing the pitcher with that cocky tilt to his head that said he wasn't worried for a second. His swing connected and the ball soared high and deep, right past the outstretched glove of the right fielder.

"Run, damn it, run!" The cheers erupted from our dugout as Reese tagged first and rounded towards second base, sliding in with a cloud of dust. Bailey rocketed to third.

"Alright, Boston," Coach shouted from the dugout. "You're up." I looked back and caught his gaze before stepping up to the plate.

"Make it count," Parker added.

"Always do," I shot back, trying to sound more confident than I felt.

I stepped up to the plate, the weight of the game bearing down on me. My first swing sent the ball foul. Taking a deep breath, I pictured Chandler's smile, her unwavering belief in me, and swung with all the pent-up frustration of the past few weeks.

"Come on, baby, come on," I whispered as the bat connected, sending a line drive zipping past the shortstop and deep into left field. Bailey, then Reese, then I sprinted home and scored before the other team could get the ball back to the catcher.

"THAT'S IT, BOSTON! THAT'S HOW YOU DO IT!" Parker cheered across the field.

Fireworks erupted overhead as the inning finished, but I could only think about one thing—seeing her. When my eyes locked with Chandler's, the shit going on between us didn't matter for a moment, and I could see the excitement and pride in her eyes. It meant a lot to have her there, and I knew she could see it reflected back in my gaze. Right then there were no complications, no thoughts about the situation between us—just her, there with me, and the fucking victory.

The field buzzed with excitement around me, pulling me back to reality—teammates rushed in, fans waved banners. It felt like a dream come true. The game, the field, this feeling—I wanted to soak in every moment. We shook hands with the other team, picked up our equipment, and walked off the field for the last time that summer.

The roar of the departing crowd was fading as something caught my attention—an out-of-place tone mixed with the excitement. It was my mom's voice, sharp and unyielding. I turned, my heart pounding unevenly. I saw her standing toe-to-toe with Reese's dad.

Her hands were balled into fists at her side, and even from this distance, I could see the fire in her eyes—I knew when her angry side came out it wasn't good, and it didn't happen often.

"Stay away from my son and continue on with your pathetic

little life," Mr. Carrington spat out. His demeanor was always so composed, so untouchable. He was a pillar of control, but the strain behind his narrowed eyes betrayed him. There was fear there, too, the kind that men like him tried to hide beneath layers of power and prestige.

Reese stood at his dad's side, a spitting image of the man. He was motionless, his gaze fixed on the confrontation, an unreadable expression etched across his features.

As my mom held her ground, I couldn't help but admire her strength, she was no longer hiding—and I think it even took Reese's dad by surprise. "It's been a long time. I'm not scared of you anymore," she hissed.

My hands clenched involuntarily as I inched closer.

Reese's dad cut in, his tone sharp and smug. "I would advise you to take your lies and allegations elsewhere."

"He's an adult now," my mom shot back. "He can make his own choices, and he deserves to know the truth." Her eyes, filled with pain, locked onto Reese's, pleading for him to understand.

"That's right. He's an adult. And you missed his entire life because you walked out," Ben Carrington said with a bitter laugh.

"Did you tell him?" She stepped closer, her hands trembling at her side. "How many times I tried? Did you let him see the letters, the gifts? Every birthday, every holiday..."

"Reese, do you remember a stuffed green dinosaur?" The question hung between them. "That was from me. It came with a letter, telling you how much I loved you."

I watched Reese take a step back, clearly shaken by the impact of my mom's words.

"Wait, Dad—the dinosaur?" Reese's voice held an edge, not an accusation, but a hint of betrayal. "That was from her? I thought that was from you. You know, the one I used to take everywhere—the one I have tattooed on my fucking arm."

His father, the epitome of tailored control, didn't so much as blink. His response was smooth, practiced. "Son, don't let her lies corrode your brain."

But Reese wasn't listening, not really. "But how would she know? And what letters?" he asked, angrily.

"Let's go, Mom," I said, the words barely escaping through clenched teeth. My hand found her quivering shoulder, guiding her away.

I glared at Reese's dad, letting the contempt I felt for him sear through my gaze. He stared back, his face an impenetrable mask. But beneath the surface, I sensed his unease. It was as though he could feel the shift in power.

We turned our backs to him, to the lies that had built walls around our lives. I walked her to her car. She was shaking slightly, whether from rage or relief, I couldn't tell. "I did it, hunny," she declared, "I finally stood up to him. I did it."

I saw her then not just as my mother, but as a warrior who had fought silently for every inch of ground, even when that ground seemed to crumble beneath her feet.

I shut the door and leaned in through the open driver's side window. "I'm proud of you, Mom. I'll meet you at the diner."

She nodded, eyes glistening with unshed tears. The corner of her mouth twitched upward, a fragile attempt at a smile. "Okay, hunny."

Pulling into the parking lot of the diner, I could already see the warm glow of the neon sign shimmer in the dark evening. Through the big glass window, I could see my mom sitting alone in a booth with a cup of coffee, her eyes scanning the menu.

I pushed open the door and the bell jingled, announcing my arrival. The smell of fried food and fresh coffee hit me. She looked up, then, her face lighting up as I slid into the seat across from her.

"Oh hunny, you were all so good tonight. I'm so proud," she squealed.

"Thanks, mom. Still feels unreal," I said.

She reached across the table, squeezing my hand. "Well, you've earned it. I saw those scouts in the stands."

"I know," I nodded. "The Cubs are flying me out this weekend. They want to get to know me, see if I might be a good fit for them."

"That's so exciting! Oh, Boston, they will love you," she said with unwavering confidence. "Everyone who meets you falls in love with you."

I cleared my throat, steering the conversation away from me. "So, he never shows, huh?"

Her expression faltered slightly. "No, but it's okay. I understand. All I can do is keep letting him know I'm here." She sighed, picking at the edge of a napkin.

I swirled the straw in my water, ice clinking against the glass, and let out a slow breath. "He may never be ready. This is a lot for anyone to process."

"Sweetheart, it's just..." she trailed off, her eyes searching mine.

The neon lights from outside flickered, pulling my attention away. I leaned back against the red vinyl seat, lost in thought about what family gatherings would look like—holidays, birthdays. The thought twisted like a knife. Holidays growing up were usually just my mom and me. She did her best to make up for the father-shaped void in my life, unspoken yet ever-present. Luckily, he left when she was pregnant, so I never had a chance to miss him.

How could Chandler ever fit into this broken picture? It was sad and pathetic. If Reese ever entered it, that would be an even worse shit show.

"What are you going to order, Boston?," she asked, nose in her menu.

Before I could respond, an unexpected voice interrupted me. "You gonna scoot over? Or you want me to sit at my own booth?"

I turned to see Reese standing there, hands tucked in the pockets of his leather jacket. We still hadn't talked since our last argument, and things were still rocky and unsettled. But at that moment, none of that mattered. Him showing up was far more important.

My mom's mouth fell open, a tear escaping the corner of her eye and falling down her cheek. Without hesitation, I slid closer to the window, making room for him in our booth. He slid in opposite of my mom, his presence filling the entire restaurant with an undeniable energy. The waitresses all paused, turning their attention to us, as if they knew my mom had been sitting alone here for weeks. But not tonight—tonight was different.

"So what's good at this place?" Reese asked, picking up a laminated menu and glancing over it, casually.

"Try the apple pie," my mom could hardly say, her voice quivering slightly as if the simple act of speaking to him held a crushing weight she'd carried for too long.

chandler

"WILLOW, have you ever done one of these overnight decoration things?" I hollered as I stuffed a pair of socks into my duffle bag.

"Yep!" Her reply floated in from the living room. "Not last year. No championship win, no parade. But the year before... oh, it was a blast!"

I paused, a t-shirt half-rolled in my hands. "What's it like?"

"Imagine this," she began, animatedly as she painted the picture, "the whole gym is ours, right? We're decking out the float, munching on everything in sight, sipping whatever we sneak in, and just chillin'. And when our eyelids get heavy, bam! We pass out whenever we want."

I sighed. "A sleepover with Caroline, her crew, and the entire Blue Devils' team—minus Boston of course—doesn't sound like a party to me."

"Do we need an escape plan?" Willow's lips curved into a grin, knowing all too well my history with Caroline.

"Absolutely." I nodded firmly. "A quick getaway could be essential for survival."

Willow snickered. "I got your back, girl," she called out, rifling through her closet with purpose. "Besides, I'm throwing a bottle of wine for each of us in my bag."

"Perfect," I yelled, tossing my striped pink pajamas into the mix of essentials spread across my bed.

As I zipped up my bag, sadness struck me knowing I wouldn't get to see Boston. He was getting on a flight, and things were still a mess with us. I shook my head, trying to dislodge the unsettling thoughts. What did it even matter? That night at karaoke, he had basically said this—we—would go nowhere. And the last few weeks he had been sending an obvious message, making it evident where we stood. Boston had never been an open book—he was more like trying to read a book with most of the pages torn out. I sighed and glanced at the mirror, catching a glimpse of my own anxious eyes staring back.

When we arrived, the auditorium doors swung open with a creak, revealing a crafter's dream. Cots were stacked up against the walls, and the barely started float sat in the center, begging for deco-ration. Surrounding it were tables cluttered with ribbons, paper flowers, and glue guns.

"Looks like Caroline's been busy," I said, nodding towards the organized chaos.

"Or she's just good at delegating," Willow quipped from beside me, her eyes scanning the room.

I weaved through the room to claim a cot, draping my overnight bag over its metal frame. It was then that Parker strolled in.

"Are you people sure you want my help?" he asked, eyeing the float skeptically. "I failed art. Always more of a sports guy."

"Failed art? How is that even possible?" I asked, incredulous. My hands paused on the zipper of my bag.

"Told you, I'm a sports guy," he reiterated with a nonchalant shrug. "Skipped it to have two P.E's instead."

I shook my head. "You're ridiculous, Parker."

He grinned, flashing his set of pearly whites at me. "Hey, if it's any consolation, I'll be your muscle for the heavy lifting tonight."

"Hey, crank up that volume!" someone called out from across the auditorium. The speakers buzzed to life, and soon the room was pulsating with music. Everyone seemed to move with a new energy, their hands reaching for streamers, glue guns, and glitter.

"Pass me those ribbons, will ya?" Willow asked, juggling a stack of construction paper under one arm. I tossed a spool of shiny blue ribbon in her direction.

Reese strolled in, then. His casual demeanor stood out, surrounded by the frenzy of activity around him. Caroline, ever the taskmaster, didn't miss a beat. She thrust a pair of scissors and a stack of cardstock into his hands. "Glad you could join us, Reese."

He smiled and got to work. As time slipped away, our collective efforts began to resemble something parade-worthy. The float was taking shape. Then, without warning, darkness swallowed the room.

"Nobody panic," Caroline yelled. "This happens sometimes when we use the speakers. Let's find the breaker box. Also, pizza is on its way, so it's a good time for a break."

"Thank you, pizza gods," Bailey yelled, somewhere near the back.

"Alright, let's split up. We'll find that box quicker. I'm going to call maintenance while we're looking," Caroline directed before she quickly dialed a phone number and left the room.

Everyone quickly scattered in different directions, while Caroline's friend Sam rushed to hand out flashlights from a box she'd grabbed from the auditorium closet.

"Willow, you're with me," Parker declared in amusement. "Because you're scared of the dark."

"I am not. Watch, I'll even lead the way," Willow teased, her tone light.

"Of course you will," Parker admitted. "Because you're my sunshine."

"Ugh, puke," I interjected, unable to resist the jab at their cheesy exchange.

But they were already moving off together, their laughter fading into the shadows. That's when I realized there was only one person left behind me. I turned to Reese.

"Looks like you're stuck with me again," he said with a grin. "Want to take the other hallway?" he nodded toward the left.

"Sure," I replied, rolling my eyes.

"Here, take this," Reese said, handing me a flashlight. I nodded, gripping it tightly and pointing it toward the shadows ahead.

"So, what's been going on with you, Hartford?" Reese asked.

I flashed him a smirk, my flashlight casting shadows on the walls as I moved it from side to side. "Oh, you know, never a dull moment. Just the way the universe thinks I like it."

He flashed one of those dimples of his, barely visible in the dark. "I know a thing or two about that," he said smoothly. There was always an ease about him—a dangerous charm that always somehow drew you into him.

We continued down the narrow, dark hallway, the silence punctuated by the sound of our footsteps. Reese's flashlight beam danced across the walls. As we rounded a corner, the circle of light landed on a colorful poster plastered on the wall.

"Looks like we're at a dead end," I slumped my shoulders.

"Seems that way," Reese responded, but he didn't move the flashlight away from the poster. It was decorated for the Bayside Ball, with swirling fonts and bright pastels.

"It's tomorrow. You excited?" he asked.

I shrugged, feeling the furthest from excited. "Nah, I don't think I'm going."

His steps faltered, and he reached out, his fingers gently tipping my chin upward to meet his gaze. "Why not?"

The warmth from his hand radiated into my skin, making me acutely aware of how dangerous it was to be close to him in the narrow space. "It's not as fun when you have to go alone," I confessed, the words tumbling out before I could stop them.

He dropped his hand, but his eyes remained locked on mine. I continued before he could speak. "I mean, I could still dance, and steal Willow from Parker, but..." my voice trailed off. I looked down again, unable to look him in the eyes any longer.

I couldn't tell Reese how I had hoped Boston would ask me—that this whole summer I wanted to go with him. But Boston was miles away, swept away in a world where I wasn't sure I belonged. So I swallowed the confession, letting it sit heavy on my tongue.

"Let me guess, because you want Riley to take you?"

I clutched the flashlight like a lifeline. "It doesn't matter," I said, blowing it off. "He's hundreds of miles away, doing bigger and better things."

The past few weeks our lives had synced, and I found myself on the edge of daring to believe in something more. But I was no longer sure if this summer meant anything at all to Boston.

"It does matter, Chandler." There was something about the way he said my name—not Hartford, but Chandler—that seemed to reach out and wrap around my ribs, squeezing until I could hardly breathe.

I leaned against the cold wall of the hallway. "Why?"

"Don't do that," he shot back.

"Do what?" I asked, trying to read his expression.

"Act like what you want doesn't matter." There was no mistaking the intensity in his green eyes, even in the darkness.

I shifted uncomfortably, my mind reeling. "What if I don't know what I want?" The question came out more vulnerable than I intended.

He narrowed his eyes at me, before turning away to scan the darkened corners around us. "You know what you want," he said, with a confidence that I envied. "And I think all you have to do is say the word, and he'd drop everything for you."

"It's not that easy, Reese," I shook my head. "I think I really upset him and messed things up, things are... they're complicated."

"Look at me," he commanded softly, and I raised my gaze. "Do you think I've ever let 'complicated' stop me from getting whatever I want? I like a little challenge. Makes things more interesting."

There was something in the way he said it—so assured, so effortlessly Reese—that was sort of comforting. I envied the way he seemed to move through life unscathed by complexities that could so easily take down anyone else.

The moment was interrupted by the newly awakened fluorescent lights overhead.

"Chandler!" Willow's voice echoed down the hallway, shattering the fragile stillness between me and Reese. "Hurry up and come eat before all the pizza is gone!"

"Let's go, Hartford," Reese said, flashing me a wink.

The auditorium buzzed with chatter, punctuated by the occasional burst of laughter. We sat cross-legged on the floor, paper plates heavy with slices of pepperoni and cheese pizza balanced precariously on our knees. I picked at the toppings. My appetite had fled during my earlier conversation with Reese.

The night continued on for what felt like forever, and we snacked on chips and sipped sodas, voices growing quieter once exhaustion set in. Eventually we retreated to our cots, the lights dimming to a soft glow that barely reached the corners of the room.

I lay there, staring up at the ceiling, the sounds of steady breathing around me. My thoughts were a tangled web of conflicting emotions. I had told Boston that everything was okay, that what we had was just summer fun. But I hadn't been honest—not with him, not with myself.

There were a few empty cots on my right, which made me wonder if one was meant for Boston. I wondered where he was, if he was thinking about me. And then there was Reese, on the left, his presence like a shadow, filled with mystery. How could two people who were so different both have a place in my heart?

I shifted restlessly, pulling the thin blanket up to my chin. Maybe it was the nostalgia of the passing summer or the vulnerability of the night, but I couldn't shake the feeling that something real was slipping through my fingers. Was it possible to hope for more with

Boston, even as part of me still clung to the hurt and memories of my past with Reese?

A sigh escaped my lips, unheard in the silent expanse of the auditorium. I felt like I was standing at a crossroads, with my future more uncertain than ever before. Whether it was fear of the unknown or the pain of letting go, I wasn't sure. All I knew was that deep down I hoped for something beyond the simplicity of "just having fun."

My eyelids grew heavy as the minutes ticked by, images of Boston and Reese blurring together until they were indistinguishable. In the depth of the night, I finally succumbed to sleep, my dreams a tangled mess, leaving me to wonder if the morning would bring clarity or even more confusion.

boston

A WHIRLWIND of lime green flew past me in the form of a family decked out in matching vacation shirts. "On your left!" they chirped almost in unison, and I ducked out of the way. I luckily avoided a collision and reached my gate in the terminal.

I slung my duffle onto an empty chair as I sank down beside it. I relaxed for a moment, taking in the scent of overpriced airport coffee and fresh magazines. My fingers fumbled for my phone, as I waited for the alert to start boarding. The screen lit up, and I saw the notification for messages waiting in the group chat.

PARKER

Boston wtf how'd you get away with ditching the lock-in?

BAILEY

Not like coach can make us run laps anymore

CREW

So we didn't have to go? Shit. My back hurts from those stupid cots.

ME

Told coach I had to be at the airport early,
couldn't risk it.

PARKER

Genius

BAILEY

You know what's not genius? Me, at 6'3,
trying to sleep on a 4 ft cot

REESE

There's no way you're 6'3

BAILEY

Am too

CREW

My ass. But we love a short king.

REESE

BAILEY

Fuck you all

My head snapped up as I realized I had missed the announce-ment and boarding had already begun. With a quick press of the side button, my screen went dark, and I hurried to take my seat just before we ascended into the sky. I slouched in the stiff airplane seat, my eyes tracing the rolling clouds. I closed my eyes briefly, only for the image of Chandler to float behind my eyelids. I forced them open, shaking my head.

Stepping off the plane, the airport buzzed with a tornado of people sprinting in all directions. My eyes scanned the arrivals crowd until they landed on a driver holding up an iPad with "Boston Riley" across the screen.

"Mr. Riley?" he asked as I approached.

"Call me Boston," I replied with a nod, following him to the sleek black SUV waiting outside.

"Please make yourself comfortable," he said, gesturing to the interior where bottles of water, chips, and peanuts were neatly arranged. "Help yourself to anything."

"Thanks," I said, settling into the plush leather seat.

The city passed by in a blur as we drove to the hotel. I could imagine the possibility of living there, seeing the view everyday.

We pulled up to a hotel downtown and a doorman greeted us with a bright smile. The driver retrieved my suitcase from the trunk.

"Thank you," I said, glancing at the intimidating hotel, feeling out of place in such luxury.

"No worries, sir. I'll be back bright and early tomorrow to pick you up for your day," he assured me.

"See you then."

The comfort of the hotel bed was heaven compared to the stiff, small airplane seat. I was ready to get to bed early and let my body sink into the mattress.

Just as I lay down, my phone started to vibrate and I glanced at the screen. Reese's name flashed in bold letters. It had to be a mistake—I wondered if it could have been a butt-dial.

"Hello?" I answered, rougher than I'd intended.

"Hey," Reese's tone was casual, but there was something underneath it—something more serious.

"What's up?" The question came out hesitant.

"Can you talk for a sec?" he asked.

"I guess." My voice still carried an edge.

"I'm not calling to talk about us," he started cautiously. "I'm calling to talk about Chandler."

The mention of her name made me tense, every muscle coiling like a spring. I sat up straighter in my bed, the sheets pooling around my waist. "What about her?"

The silence between us stretched, and I could tell he was measuring his next words. My throat tightened as I waited.

"Relax," Reese said, finally. "It's about you and her."

I shifted on the bed, resting my elbows on my knees waiting for him to continue.

"Ditch the stupid meeting and take her to the ball," he continued, his words creating a mental picture of Chandler in her dress, her eyes searching through the crowd for someone to dance with. I would have killed to be the one to save her in that moment, no matter where we stood.

The ball was the next day. The thought of her going alone, or not going at all, twisted something inside me. I couldn't even imagine thinking about her going with someone else. I didn't even have to see her to know she'd be the most beautiful one there. I should've been the one taking her. Instead I was gone, covered in sheets way too soft for the harsh reality that I might have lost her.

"She's not going because she wants to be there with you." He seemed genuine which caught me off guard. But I still couldn't trust him and he didn't understand how big this meeting was for me. I wasn't like him—no one handed me opportunities.

"What is this?" I snapped, my pulse quickening with the rush of adrenaline. "Another plan you and your dad have to sabotage me again?"

The accusation hung in the air, and silence followed—a heavy, expectant pause. I waited for whatever sharp remark he was about to toss back at me.

But instead of anger, there was only the exhale of a sigh before he spoke. "Despite what you might think, my dad and I are not the same person," he said, pausing before continuing. "You were right about him—he was keeping shit from me. And I... I should have been more open to hearing you out."

He had thoroughly shocked me with that response, and I let out a breath, the tension in my shoulders easing ever so slightly.

"Thank you," I said softly, feeling a genuine shift between us for the first time. "I shouldn't have blamed you for anything he's done— I know you're not him."

"Riley," Reese said smugly, "If you're about to apologize and say you love me, I might actually puke."

I couldn't help but laugh. "Not a chance," I shot back, grateful for the brief break from all the seriousness.

"Anyway," he continued, letting out a sigh, "there will be more chances and other opportunities. Who knows how many chances you'll get with Chandler? So find a way to get back before the ball."

I closed my eyes, the weight of his words settling around me.

"It's not that simple," I explained, knowing I wouldn't be able to make that happen.

"You'll find a way," Reese said, and I could almost see him rolling his eyes. "Don't be stupid. Just get back here and get the girl."

"Never thought I'd hear those words come out of your mouth," I said with a small chuckle betraying my amazement.

"Yeah, me either," Reese replied, before I heard Bailey yell his name in the background. "I should probably take it all back, but you're lucky I have to go. Remember what I said, Riley."

"Bye," I said, then ended the call.

In the quiet that followed, Reese's advice weighed heavy on my mind. I was highly aware of the pulse in my veins, the dull ache in my chest where something vital strained against my ribcage. Chandler, the ball, my future—all of it hung in the balance. But I'd already made my choice. I was here, and I couldn't turn back.

Sunlight pried my eyes open before the alarm could. Once it went off, I bolted to get myself ready.

I showered and threw on a crisp button-up, then stepped into dress pants. I adjusted my collar with an air of finality. It was show-time. I had to play the part—tell them exactly what they wanted to hear, hoping they'd like me.

With a last look around the room, I grabbed my essentials and headed downstairs where reality—and my driver—awaited.

"Good morning, sir," the driver said kindly as I slid into the back-seat. "You ready for a big day ahead?"

"Yes, sir," I managed, my nerves starting to get to me. The car moved smoothly, parting through the morning commotion, and soon the Wrigley Field loomed before us.

Wrigleyville was full of life—restaurants and shops were filled with people inside and out. We passed it all, slipping into a private entrance that granted us access inside the field.

"Here we are," the driver announced, bringing the car to a graceful halt.

I stepped out to a welcome committee dressed in blue and red— the team colors. The coach was there—I remembered shaking his hand at one of our games—alongside the assistant manager and several other staff members.

"Big day planned for you, man," Coach Colin greeted me, extending his hand.

"Can't wait," I responded, shaking his hand firmly. But then, caught in such a big moment, I saw her—Chandler—flash before my eyes. Her image clung to me like a stubborn shadow as I tried to anchor myself in the GM's words. Nodding along, I pushed thoughts of her away with all the strength I could muster.

They ushered me through the halls. Fluorescent lights overhead punctuating all of our movements. The smell of fresh coffee and sizzling bacon drew us into an area laid out with a catered breakfast. People were spread around and introductions followed as we settled at a large conference table.

"So tell us all about yourself," The GM prompted, all eyes turning my way.

Who am I? I wondered silently, feeling suddenly small. My gaze swept over the expectant faces and I couldn't shove away what I was feeling any longer. I was an idiot. That's what I was. I finally had a good thing—the girl I'd always wanted—and I'd just let her go.

A profound thought struck me as I sat there, unable to speak. What the fuck was baseball without someone to share it with?

I swallowed hard, trying to force my focus back to the pivotal crossroads that could lead to my future. This was the chance I had worked for, sweated for, bled for. But as the silence stretched on, realization struck hard. Yes, this was an opportunity that could make all my dreams come true. But the undeniable truth was that I should have fought harder for her. Baseball was my dream, but Chandler... She was my heart. And in a moment of piercing clarity, I realized the choice wasn't really a choice at all.

I stood up, the chair scraping against the floor. My palms were slick against the polished wooden table, my heart pounding louder than I ever thought possible. "Baseball... it's been my life," I began, forcing the words out. "But if there's one thing I've learned, it's that your passion means nothing if you have no one to share it with. It means nothing without a home. And she... she's my home." The confession hung in the air, as I took in my own words.

"Thank you," I continued, "for everything you've done, for bringing me here." Around me, the coaches and staff looked back at me in confusion and concern. But none of it mattered. "You probably won't consider me after this, but if you do, I will never let you down again." I paused, a lump forming in my throat. "And I'm sorry, but there's somewhere I need to be. I hope you all understand."

The room fell silent, thick with unspoken questions and judgments. The coach's stern eyes watched me as he rubbed his chin—thinking about what I had just said, no doubt. But no words came from him; he simply waited, as if anticipating my next move.

It was the assistant coach who finally broke the stillness, standing up with an ease that seemed out of place. "Son," he said, his voice begging me to reconsider. "I can tell you that you don't want to throw this opportunity away. Is there anything we can do to get you to stay?"

"No," I affirmed. "There isn't."

"Then I guess you've made the decision for us," he said with a note of finality.

I nodded and left the room, closing the door behind me and

sealing away the future I would have once done anything for. There was a possibility this didn't just ruin this opportunity, but could ruin my reputation across the board. But she mattered more than any of that. I had to get to her. I had to make things right.

The driver was waiting in the lobby, his expression curious as I panted out instructions. "Hotel. Then airport. It's urgent."

"Right away, sir," he said, and we were off.

In the backseat, my fingers fumbled over my phone, checking flight times, searching for the fastest way back to her, back to everything that mattered. Back home.

I fired off a text to Bailey.

ME

Need a favor

BAILEY

Don't you still owe me from the last favor?

ME

I need another. It's important.

BAILEY

I'm listening

ME

Can you get Chandler to the ball? Make sure she goes. I'm going to do my best to try to make it there and surprise her.

BAILEY

Maybe I have a date

ME

Do you?

BAILEY

No. I had two dates until about two hours ago. They found out about each other and decided to go together instead

…Without me

ME

Perfect

BAILEY

Fine but you owe me double. Guess I can
manage showing up with a baddie on my
arm.

ME

Touch her and I'll kill you

BAILEY

Relax man I got it

Sinking back into the seat, I allowed myself to finally let out the breath I'd been holding.

The plane's tires screeched against the tarmac, jolting me from my restless thoughts. Around me, passengers rustled in their seats and the cabin filled with the clatter of opening overhead compartments.

"Please remain seated until the seatbelt sign has been turned off," the flight attendant directed through the intercom.

Her words did little to keep me in line. I stood up, ignoring the sideways glances as I edged into the aisle. The wait seemed endless, a barricade between me and the girl I desperately needed to get to. I checked the time on my phone with nervous energy, knowing the ball was about to start. My fingers drummed against the handle of my carry-on bag. Every second felt like an eternity.

I finally began to move, each step towards the exit a step towards hope. Each moment bringing me closer to seeing the girl I loved, the one who'd been right in front of me all this time. I may have been a dumbass when it came to her, but I was hoping from this moment on I could get it right, or keep trying to make things right as long as she'd let me.

"Thank you," I whispered to the flight attendant as I stepped off the plane, sprinting through the airport terminal. Urgency propelled me forward until I finally reached my truck.

"Come on, come on," I said to no one, jamming the key into the ignition. Tires screeched against asphalt as I peeled out of the parking lot, hoping traffic on the way would be kind to me just this once.

chandler

I GASPED, almost choking on hairspray as Willow was getting ready in the bathroom. The counter was a mess of curling irons and mascara wands. She paused her eyeliner in mid-stroke and let out a sigh. "I can't believe we're already at the end of summer."

"Tell me about it," I replied, leaning against the doorway. "I always say it flies, but this one really did." I caught her reflection in the mirror—eyes bright, lips curved in a knowing smile.

She twisted a lock of her curly blonde hair around her finger. "Who would've thought I'd be going to the ball with your brother?"

"Oh, I had a feeling," I said, rolling my eyes playfully at her through the mirror.

"Can you blame me?" she teased, her cheeks glowing with a flush of excitement. "He's hot, funny, a badass catcher."

"Please stop before I get sick right here," I groaned, half-serious and half-amused by her recent infatuation with Parker.

Despite my happiness for her, there was also a twinge of disappointment there. I was genuinely happy for her, yes, but I couldn't ignore the fact that I wasn't going to the ball. Half of the excitement was getting ready, and getting picked up by the hot guy.

A knock at the front door echoed through her apartment,

signaling that it was time for her to go. "That's got to be Parker," I called out to Willow, who was adding the last touches to her makeup. "Finish getting ready and make your grand entrance when you're done."

"All of my entrances are grand," she teased.

I made my way to the door, ready to tease Parker with some kind of joke about whatever he was wearing, like usual. However, Parker wasn't on the other side of the door. It was Bailey, looking unexpectedly dapper in a suit. Something I would never admit aloud to anyone.

"Ugh, can we help you?" I asked.

Bailey's response came with an easy smile and a wink. "I can do you one better, darlin'," he drawled. "I'm gonna take you to the ball."

I couldn't contain my laughter. "Absolutely not. You can go on your way now." I started to close the door, but Bailey was quicker, wedging his foot firmly in the gap.

"Please," he said softly, in a way that made me pause, then added, "We can go as friends. Heck, I'll even wear a sign that says 'platonic dates' if that'll sell it for you."

My mouth quivered into a reluctant grin. I wasn't sure what Bailey was up to, but if he didn't have a date then going to the ball as friends was a better plan than sitting in bed and eating ice cream all night.

"Fine," I sighed, giving Bailey a stern look. "But if you try anything funny, or so much as think about touching my butt, I will pepper spray you. I carry it in my purse. It looks like lipstick, and I'm not afraid to use it."

Bailey held his hands up in surrender, the corners of his mouth twitching into a smile that was trying hard not to turn into a full-blown grin. "I come in peace," he assured me.

Opening the door wider, I motioned toward the living room. "Fine. I guess I need to get ready, then. You're welcome to wait on the couch."

As soon as the word "couch" slipped past my lips, Bailey recoiled as if I had suggested he sit on a bed of nails. He hissed dramatically. "Have I ever told you how much I hate couches? Especially ones that turn into beds."

From the bathroom, Willow's laughter echoed through the apartment. She would forever be responsible for Bailey's aversion to sleeper sofas, which was still endlessly hilarious.

"That couch doesn't turn into a bed, you're in the clear," I assured him, rolling my eyes at the absurdity.

"How do you not have a date?" I asked before I could stop myself.

He laughed. "I lost 'em both, Chan."

"Both?" I asked.

"Both of my dates." He shrugged as though it was nothing more than a minor miscalculation. "Figured two was better than one, but they didn't think so when they found out. You know how it goes."

"I'm not sure I do," I said, unable to stop a smile.

Bailey grinned. "Hey, I learn from my mistakes! Women want me all to themselves, I get it."

"That's the lesson you learned?" I said, but it was sort of sweet that Bailey had thought of me. Even if it was only so he didn't have to go alone.

Willow's face appeared just outside the bathroom door frame, waving me toward her. "Why is Bailey here?"

"Guess he's my date," I said, reaching for the makeup bag. "He lost both of his."

"EEK!" she shrieked. "I'll grab you a dress. Thank god I prepared for moments like this."

Another knock on the door interrupted us, and I pointed toward it with a smile. "Now that has to be Parker."

I made it halfway there when I noticed someone beat me to it. Bailey, already lounging like he owned the place, swung the door open as he leaned against the frame.

"What the fuck. You're not the hot blonde I expected," Parker grumbled, his face momentarily sour before breaking into a teasing grin.

"Ouch, that hurts," Bailey shot back.

"She's almost done getting ready," I interjected, hoping to diffuse any tension before it could start.

Parker shifted his weight, his gaze sliding past Bailey to find mine. "Why the hell is Bailey here? Is he lost?"

"Still figuring that out myself," I replied, meeting Parker's raised eyebrow with an innocent shrug.

"I'm here to take your sister to the ball, if you must know." He gave Parker a challenging smirk.

Parker's protective glare was obvious even from several feet away. Then he turned to me. "Chandler, how many times do I have to tell you? Stop dating my teammates."

I opened my mouth to protest, "Parker, I'm not dating—"

But that's when Willow chose to make her grand entrance. She stepped out of the bathroom, the light catching the sequins on her dress and making her shimmer. Parker's jaw practically unhinged, and he quickly sidestepped.

"Peasants, out of the way—she's coming through."

Despite the eye roll I couldn't suppress, a proud smile crept onto my lips. Willow did look stunning, and somewhere between Parker's dumbfounded expression and Bailey's intrusion, I knew it was going to be a great night. They patiently waited for me to get ready before we took off.

I knew how stunning the ball would be since Caroline had worked us tirelessly to get it finished. It was magic—-glimmering lights and swaying bodies. Bailey extended his arm to me as we entered, a grin spread across his face. I hesitated, my hand hovering over it like a bird uncertain whether to land or fly far away. Finally, I let my fingers rest lightly on his sleeve. It wasn't as if I had many options, and besides, I was determined to enjoy the night—even with him.

For a moment, my mind drifted to Boston, how good he would have looked in a tux, his perfectly tousled hair that always reminded me of every hot lifeguard at the beach. His tux would have somehow showed off his broad shoulders and muscles. But he was miles away from this small town, probably lounging in some upscale suite, surrounded by people wooing him with talk about his pro career—a world apart from me.

Bailey interrupted my thoughts when he tapped me on the shoulder. "I'm gonna go grab us some drinks."

"Make it a strong one," I quipped, watching as Parker clapped a hand on Bailey's shoulder, the two of them disappearing into the crowd.

Willow linked her arm with mine as we navigated towards our table. "This is it, the last hoorah before our summer responsibilities are over," she sighed.

"Then real life kicks in," I whispered, my gaze scanning the room. I wondered how Reese was doing. He had brought me to the ball last summer, and although we were both in different places now, I thought I might always have a soft spot for him.

Reese was impossible to miss when he wanted to be seen. Yet there was no trace of him.

"Think Reese will make an appearance?" Willow asked, following my line of sight.

"Of course. He wouldn't pass up a chance to bask in his own glory." My words carried a hint of sarcasm.

"Oh, there he is." I followed Willow's gaze across the room. The khaki suit he wore looked like it was custom made. His dark hair and those enigmatic green eyes were in deep contrast against the light fabric. He laughed at something the Coach said and I remembered how that effortless charm had both intrigued and infuriated me last summer.

The chatter around started to quiet as Caroline took her place at the front, tapping the microphone.

"Good evening, everyone! If I could have your attention, please," she said. "We're going to begin the awards shortly, so if you could all find your seats, we'll get started."

Soon, the room settled, excited faces turning toward Caroline as she beamed back at them.

"Welcome to the annual Blue Devil awards night—a celebration of our team's hard work and dedication this summer," she announced. "Let's give these players the recognition they deserve!"

Applause erupted. My gaze found Reese again. He was headed in our direction. He took the seat opposite Parker, and Bailey slid into the seat beside me.

"Here's a vodka lemonade for my date," he teased.

Across the table, Reese's eyes flicked up, a slight eyebrow raised in response to Bailey's claim.

The excitement in the room grew with each award announced as the evening progressed. Applause rippled through the room, punctuated by the occasional cheer as the players were recognized for their accomplishments.

"And now, for best batting average..." Caroline's voice boomed through the microphone, her pause drawing out the suspense before she finally declared, "Boston Riley!"

A round of applause erupted, though not as thunderous as before—Boston's absence was evident. "Unfortunately, Boston couldn't be with us tonight, but we'll make sure he gets this award," Caroline added, prompting nods and understanding from the crowd.

I felt a pang in my chest—a mix of pride and disappointment—and I discreetly pulled out my phone. I typed out a quick message to Boston. "You were recognized for best batting average. Wish you could've been here."

No response, no typing—nothing. With a sigh, I pocketed my phone, trying to shake off the feeling of insignificance that crept upon me. Perhaps this little gathering seemed trivial in the grand scheme of things to someone like Boston, who was already moving onto bigger and better things.

The crowd hushed again as Caroline took to the podium once more. "And now," she began, the weight of the moment palpable, "the award we've all been waiting for—the Most Valuable Player."

Bailey's grin was infectious as he kept holding up the award he'd won. Parker, too, seemed proud, medals adorning his chest with his awards. And Reese... Reese had a collection of trophies by his side.

"It's Reese again—no surprise," Bailey whispered.

"The MVP goes to... Boston Riley!"

A collective gasp cut through the room before the applause. Out of habit, my eyes darted to Reese, expecting his usual cool smirk, but instead, I saw him straighten up, as he adjusted his tie.

Silence settled over our table as Reese quietly stood, and then slowly made his departure from the room. The echo of the double doors closing behind him seemed louder than the applause, and even Caroline's confident voice hitched for the briefest of moments.

Bailey half-rose, concern etching his features.

I shook my head slightly, placing a hand on his arm. "I got this," I whispered, offering him a reassuring look.

With careful steps, I slipped out of the room, following Reese's path. The back patio was covered in moonlight, but Reese wasn't there. I followed a path from the patio that led out to a dock. He was there, leaning back on his hands, gaze focused on the shimmering lake.

I sat down beside him, trying my best to fold my dress underneath me. The gentle lapping lake water against the shore offered some comfort—it had always been one of my favorite things. "Could your ego really not deal with that?" I asked, taking in the view alongside him. "How many times have you won that award?"

Reese's gaze remained fixed on the distant ripples on the lake's surface. "It's not about the award."

"Then what is it about?" I asked.

"Everything else this summer." His words were heavy, carrying more than just disappointment. "I've been distracted with my real mom, with other shit going on... I let myself slack on the one thing that really does matter."

"Slack?" I turned to look at him. "If this year was you slacking, then I am terrified of what you're going to do when you go pro and you're on your game."

That earned me a glance, finally. Reese's lips curled into a smile, the one that disarmed every situation. "It's always so simple with you," he said, shaking his head.

"Reese, you were meant to play baseball—that is simple, yes," I said. "But everything else isn't. Life is far from simple."

He was silent for a moment, contemplating something. "Yeah, I finally decided to meet with her," he admitted, almost to himself.

I turned to face him fully, surprised. "Cindee?"

"Yep." He shrugged. "Don't even know how I found myself there, but... it felt like some kind of step. Still a million miles to go, though."

I reached out, placing a tentative hand on his arm. "That's okay, Reese. Go at your own pace. Don't push yourself if you're not ready." I paused, finding the courage to add, "I grew up next door to her, and I've seen how big her heart can be, though. I promise you, it's there."

Reese ran a hand through his dark hair. "Speaking of hearts," he said, obviously deflecting, "how's that hot girl summer going? Going the way you planned?"

I let out a dry, bitter chuckle and tucked a strand of hair behind my ear. "I tried," I confessed, staring at the ripples in the lake. "I tried to be careful, not to dive into anything too deep. I told myself I wouldn't get hurt again this summer... I guarded my heart." I drew in a deep breath. "But here I am. Hurt."

"Chandler," Reese said softly, "hearts aren't meant to be guarded. No matter how much we try to control them, they're meant to be stolen—whether we allow it or not."

I couldn't help but let out a soft sigh. I wouldn't admit it, but I knew he was right. The tension in my shoulders eased as I leaned sideways, resting my head on his shoulder. The fabric of his suit was soft against my cheek, and for a moment, all the chaos of summer seemed to fade into the background. We sat there, together, sharing the silence that felt like genuine understanding. I knew in that moment exactly who I wanted to be with, exactly who had stolen my heart.

Before I could respond, the quiet of the night was interrupted by the sound of someone clearing their throat—an unmistakable, deliberate noise designed to grab attention. My heart leaped into my throat as I straightened up and Reese shifted beside me.

Standing a few feet away from us was Boston. His blue eyes were sharp, focused intently on us.

boston

HER HEAD WAS RESTING COMFORTABLY on his shoulder, and her soft laughter reached me even at a distance. But, it didn't matter. I was here for one reason, and one reason alone—to fight for her. As Reese's eyes met mine over the top of her head, they flickered with an understanding that didn't need words.

In a single, fluid motion, Reese untangled himself from Chandler and stood. "I've got somewhere I need to be," he said to her, then stood.

"About time you showed up," he said to me, walking away with his hands shoved into his pockets.

Taking a deep breath to steady my thoughts, I walked over and sat beside her on the weathered dock. Our silence stretched out like the water's surface—calm, yet hiding so much beneath. I dared to glance at her profile. The breeze toyed with her hair, the moonlight painting her features in a soft silver glow that made my heart clench.

"Chandler, do you remember when you'd come over for frozen pizza?"

Her eyebrows shot up in surprise. "Boston, you're talking about frozen pizza right now?"

I nodded, swallowing the lump in my throat. "I used to hate it."

"You hated when I came over?" There was hurt in her voice, as she stared down at her hands.

"No. Well, sort of," I said. My words tumbled out as I tried to open up to her the best that I could. "I hated it because dinners at your house were perfect. You had both your parents and Parker at the table, your mom made a home-cooked meal, your dad helped do the dishes when it was done..." I trailed off, lost in the memories of her family, an extreme difference to my own reality.

"And when you and Parker used to come over," I continued, my eyes locked on the dark water, "Mom would throw a cheap frozen pizza in the oven." I hesitated, unsure if I should say more, but the stillness of the evening pushed me forward. "With my mom, it's complicated. I'll always love her and want to protect her, but it's never been easy. I guess I've been distant because I thought keeping you at arm's length was a way to protect you from the mess I'm dealing with. Every time I pulled away, it was because I didn't want you getting dragged into it, too."

There was a long pause, and I braced myself for her response to the raw edges of my insecurities.

"Boston," she said softly, turning to face me, her eyes reflecting the twilight sky. "I don't remember frozen pizza. I remember the belly laughs we had at your house." A small smile graced her lips as she continued. "I remember your mom turning all the lights off and us playing hide and seek. I remember all the fun we had." She reached out tentatively, her hand brushing against mine. "I didn't care what was on the dinner table—or how many people you had around it. I liked spending time with you... and her. I just wanted to be with you. No matter what that looked like."

I realized then that it wasn't the perfection of the surroundings that mattered—it was the imperfect realness of being together that had etched those memories in her heart. And maybe that could be enough for me to accept too.

"Chandler," I whispered, my voice barely rising above the gentle lap of the lake against the dock. "I'm sorry for letting you walk away." I paused. "I'm sorry for accusing you of comparing me to him."

The silence that followed felt heavy, filled with all the things I'd left unsaid over the years.

"Reese and I," I continued before she could respond. "Things will probably always be complicated. But I know he's a good guy deep down. I know there's a side to him that not everyone gets to see, and I understand why you care about him. Even if I'm not who you want, if you don't choose me, I'll walk to the ends of this earth for you. Today and always." I swallowed hard, trying to push away my ego.

Her eyes searched mine as she tilted her head to the side. "You're right, Boston," she agreed. "He is a really good guy deep down. Reese doesn't let many people see it, but there's so much more to him."

I felt my jaw involuntarily tick, listening to her go on about the great things about him—the way he listened when she talked, how he was smart, driving in deep the point she was trying to make.

She paused, her gaze still lingering on the dark waters as if they held the answers to our tangled hearts. "But unfortunately, there's a problem..." her voice trailed off, her eyes holding mine with a new intensity.

"He's not you," she said simply.

I felt like I could breathe for the first time that day. My heart hammered, daring to hope for something I thought I'd pushed too far away.

"See, unfortunately for me, my heart has always belonged to the boy who grew up next door." She paused, and then turned toward me. "You captured my heart the same night you captured those fireflies."

I struggled to process her words and she continued. "No matter how many times you tried to push me away, I knew one day we'd find our way to each other. And I'm sorry, too. For everything I said. I didn't mean it. We weren't just having fun. This is so much more than that."

It was as if oxygen had rushed back into my lungs, sweet and life-affirming. My hand found her cheek, almost instinctively, and she nestled into the warmth of my palm.

"It is more than that," I said earnestly. "You're the only thing that has ever truly made sense to me." Tears welled up in her eyes as I spoke. "When everything around me falls apart, when my world is spinning out of control, you're the one constant thing that I've always been sure about."

Slowly, I leaned into her, closing the space between us. When our lips met in a kiss, it was like a reunion of souls, a remembrance of the perfection we'd been denying ourselves.

Chandler's breath caught, eyes wide with a mix of confusion and surprise as she pulled away. "Wait a minute," she whispered. "I thought you were in Illinois until Sunday."

"I was supposed to be," I admitted. "But I should have been here. Baseball is important—it's going to be my future, and I'll figure it out. But you," I said, cupping her face gently, watching as her hazel eyes searched mine for certainty, "you are my home, Chandler. And honestly, I'd give it all up for you."

Then, slowly, she slid her arm around me, her head coming to rest against my chest.

"Wait," I murmured, just as I remembered something. "I got this for you." She sat up then, curiosity lighting up her features as I fished to my pocket, fingers closing around the small gift I'd picked up on my layover.

"I made it at the airport," I said, placing the delicate friendship bracelet into her open palm. "I didn't have many options, so don't ask me how many bracelets I had to buy and take apart to make one say what I wanted..." I trailed off, watching as her fingers traced over the beads that spelled out "I love you."

A glistening tear streaked down Chandler's cheek as she looked up from the bracelet. "I love you too, Boston."

I wiped her tear away and held her for a while, soaking up every moment of having her in my arms finally. She was mine.

"Hey," I said, breaking the silence. "You wanna go back inside the ball? I've got some dance moves that I can't wait to show off." I gave her a playful wink, hoping to see the sparkle that always danced in her eyes when we were on the brink of adventure.

She laughed, and it was like music to my ears—the sound I'd been missing without even knowing it. "Let's go," Chandler giggled, her smile so wide it could outshine the moon.

I stood up first and reached out to help her to her feet, our hands lingering in the space between us. As we walked back toward the glittering lights of the ball, Chandler started chatting animatedly about the baseball awards I had won, recounting each with a pride that made my chest swell.

"Seriously, Boston, when they said your name—" she mimicked Caroline, nearly tripping over her own feet as she did. This night, this girl—everything felt like it was falling into place.

"Promise me one thing, though," she said, her tone shifting to something more serious as we neared the entrance.

"Anything," I assured her.

"Promise you won't break my heart. We will do this together from now on—no matter how hard or tough it might be."

"Cross my heart," I replied, drawing an invisible X over my chest. "I'll never let you go, I'll never push you away. I'm all in when it comes to you. Now come on, let's show them how it's done."

And we spent the rest of the night on the dance floor, enjoying every moment to the fullest, as if every step, every turn, every shared glance was a testament to a love between us that had been waiting patiently to take center stage for most of our lives.

THE NEXT MORNING I slipped on Reese's jersey, which was way too big for me. But it was the only clean top I had left to wear. Willow was out, so I was doing laundry and cleaning alone. The clinking of dishes filled the quiet apartment. Sudsy water swirled around my hands as I scrubbed the last of the breakfast plates. The washing machine was running, too, whirring from the other room. In just a few days, I'd be trading in this lake town for textbooks and lecture halls.

The sharp ding of a text message jolted me from my terrible singing. I dried my hands on a nearby rag before sliding up the screen. It was Kristina.

KRISTINA

Okay, so. I have a confession...

ME

Spill it

KRISTINA

I went out with Papi Likes Butts

I blinked at the screen, my jaw nearly unhinging.

ME

Kristina!

KRISTINA

I know, I know, but the options were limited
on the app, and I figured why not? Plus, he's
hilarious, Chan. I peed my pants!

ME

Oh, we have a lot to catch up on when I
get back

Setting the phone down on the counter, I shook my head, still snickering. With one final glance at our conversation, I turned back to the sink and plunged my hands into the warm water.

Then a knock on the door made me pause. I turned off the faucet, my hands dripping water as I reached for the dish towel again. With a quick swipe across my hands, I headed to the door and pulled it open.

"Morning, beautiful," Boston greeted me with a grin, holding two to-go cups. "Figured you'd need coffee after last night."

"Aw, you read my mind," I squealed, taking the cup he offered.

He stepped inside. As I closed the door behind him, his body stiffened, narrowing his eyes. "Are you wearing Reese's jersey?"

"...sorta," I admitted, a sheepish smile tugging at my lips. "Laundry day left me with limited wardrobe options." I gestured vaguely to the chaos behind me, where the washing machine had a load running and a full basket sat next to it.

He placed his coffee on the counter, then threaded his fingers through his hair, pushing it back in a gesture that was both casual and disarmingly attractive. Leaning back against the counter, he watched me with a curiosity that was new—not angry but more mischievous.

"Want me to take it off?" I asked, half-expecting him to make it a bigger deal than it was.

But then he shot me a dangerous half-smile, his gaze suddenly burning with a heat that sent a thrill down my spine. "Nah, keep it on," he demanded, closing the distance between us. His hand found my hip, fingers gripping tightly and pulling me closer. Fisting a hand in my hair, he gently tugged. My head went back slightly and he leaned in, lips brushing against my ear. "I'm going to fuck you in it. So the next time you try to put this jersey on, you'll be thinking about me."

His breath was hot and heavy, making my skin prickle with goosebumps. I quivered as his fingers roamed up my body, tracing the outline of my breast. My nipples hardened under his touch, straining against the jersey fabric.

He pulled back slightly, then, gazing into my eyes as his hand slid down to the hem of my jersey. With a slow, deliberate motion, he lifted it up, exposing my stomach and the waistband of my panties. His fingers traced along the edge, teasing me before finally dipping below the waistband.

"Oh god," I gasped approvingly as he touched me, his fingers exploring my wetness.

"Fuck, you're dripping wet." He groaned in response, his own arousal evident as he pressed himself against me.

"Mhm," I moaned, his fingers starting to move over my clit.

"Tell me you're mine," he demanded. His eyes were dark, fathomless, clouded with desire. "Tell me you belong to me, Chandler, not him."

I licked my lips before replying in a breathy whisper. "I'm yours. I belong to you."

He crushed his mouth to mine, swallowing my soft moan as he lifted me off my feet. My legs wrapped around his waist instinctively before he set me on the counter. The taste of his desire lingered on my lips, fueling my own need for him.

He lifted up the jersey, his eyes devouring my nakedness underneath. He leaned down, taking one nipple into his mouth as his hand teased the other. I moaned in pleasure, arching my back as his tongue flicked and swirled around the sensitive bud.

His hand slid down my body as he slowly peeled my panties down my legs, his touch sending waves of desire crashing over me.

"Spread your legs for me," he growled, his voice low and husky. "Let me see that pretty pussy."

I obeyed, my heart pounding in my chest as I spread my legs wider, revealing myself to him completely.

"That's my girl," he groaned approvingly. "You're so fucking beautiful."

He slipped two fingers inside as he continued to torture my clit, his touch sending waves of pleasure coursing through my body.

"I'm your girl?" I managed to ask. His eyes blazed with lust and possessiveness. He didn't stop for even a second to answer the question. Instead he continued curling his fingers, moving them in and out of me. The sensation was already almost too much to handle. I never wanted him to stop.

He leaned in closer with an arrogant smile. "You've always been my girl."

I wrapped my arms around his neck, pulling him closer until our lips crashed together, grinding my hips against his hand.

"Oh, fuck." I moaned in pleasure as his fingers continued to work their magic, teasing and stroking my swollen clit until I was gasping with need. Just as I was about to come, he pulled away, leaving me aching for more.

"Not yet," he whispered and stood up, peeling off his shirt. His muscles looked even more defined and toned from the sunlight peeking through the windows. My heart raced at the sight of him. He reached down, undoing his pants and freeing his throbbing cock before sliding on a condom.

He positioned himself between my legs, his hardness pressing against my entrance. His lips devoured mine in a possessive kiss before his teeth grazed my neck, sending shivers down my body. He achingly teased me, tracing circles around my swollen clit with the tip of his cock.

"Boston, please," I gasped. "I need you inside me."

He growled. "Tell me how much you want me, that you feel what I feel."

I whimpered. "Boston, I want you, I need you, I fucking love you."

I could feel my body trembling with anticipation as he pushed inside, pressing his hips slowly but relentlessly against me. The sensation was incredible, his size filling me. I moaned in response, and he captured my sounds with his lips.

"Fuck, you feel so good," he grunted, lifting up one of my knees.

His thrusts were slow and deliberate to start, slowly building up speed. I clenched around him, my body responding to his every movement.

"Fuck," I whimpered, his hands holding my body tight, his fingers digging into my hips, pulling me closer as he thrusted deeper and harder.

The tension was building, my orgasm approaching quickly. He must have sensed it because he suddenly changed his angle, hitting that perfect spot.

I moaned, "Oh god, Boston, holy fuck, don't stop."

I dug my nails into his back as he pounded into me relentlessly, each thrust sending waves of ecstasy coursing through my veins.

"That's it, pretty girl," he barked, his own orgasm building as he pushed deeper into me. "Come for me."

"Boston," I whimpered, my breath hitching. "I'm.... going to... oh god..."

I came with a cry, my body convulsing as pleasure washed over me.

"Fuck," he roared, his own release triggered by mine as he came. I could feel his cock pulsing in me as he let out a breath. "I'll never get enough of this," he said, then picked me up and carried me before we collapsed in a heap on the couch, our bodies spent and satiated.

As we lay there, panting and sweaty, I couldn't help but feel the satisfaction flow through me. I knew he'd just accomplished what he wanted with the jersey. There was no way I'd ever forget what we'd just done—and on Willow's kitchen island at that.

"So summer is almost over," he flashed that charming grin at me. "How many points have I scored with you so far?"

I couldn't help but smile. "Infinity, Boston," I rolled closer and rested my head on his chest. "Infinity."

His smile widened, and he dipped his head closer to mine. "Good answer." Then his lips captured mine in a kiss.

That moment—it was everything I'd ever wanted. The boy who raced ahead of me on his bike, who threw acorns at my window to get my attention, who made every birthday wish seem possible, Boston Riley—was all mine. I still saw the shadow of the boy I'd grown up next door to in his smile. That smile that dared me to dream bigger than our small town.

If I could have spoken to my younger self, I would have whispered with a smile, "We got him—he's all ours." The boy who captured our heart the moment we first saw him. That night, under the stars, we didn't just exchange a jar of light or a simple friendship bracelet—we exchanged our hearts. Despite the distance, the missed chances, and the imperfect roads we traveled, we still found our way back to each other.

boston

THE SHARP DING of my phone pierced the quiet as Chandler and I sat on the dock, me silently admiring her while she took in her favorite view. I sat up reluctantly, stretching out to grab my phone, and I couldn't help but smile as I read the messages.

BAILEY

One last end of summer celebration?

CREW

I call the twins

PARKER

Once again, no one wants that freak show.

CREW

As long as you know that freak show is
all mine

BAILEY

What kind of celebration are you guys
talking about? A fucking orgy? I just want to
drink together. You know, hang out, maybe.

REESE

Like you'd ever say no to an orgy

BAILEY

Can one of you idiots just answer my
question?

Chandler looked up at me, her hazel eyes catching the amusement in mine. "What's so funny?" she asked, tucking a lock of hair behind her ear.

"It's just the boys' group chat," I replied, watching her curious gaze turn into a playful challenge. "It's unhinged, you don't want to see it."

"Oh yes, I do," she countered, the corners of her mouth lifting in a mischievous grin. "We don't keep secrets."

"Is that so?" I teased, knowing full well I loved the thought of sharing every part of my world with her. "You'll never look at us the same."

I didn't care about her seeing the chat, and truthfully, I wanted her in every part of my life—the mundane, the exciting, and even the unhinged boys group chat.

I tilted the phone her way, and she snagged it out of my hand.

"Let's see this infamous chat," Chandler said, thumbing through the messages with a look of apprehension that quickly dissolved. "Crew? Twins? I can't believe what I'm reading right now."

"Hey, you can't judge," I protested with a grin. "There is no judgment in a group chat."

"The male group chat is a scary place."

"You asked for it," I joked, smiling at her appalled expressions.

"I'll never ask to look again—I wish I could take it all back," she snickered.

"Also," I added, watching her expression shift back to normal. "He managed to convince Willow to throw the party at her place."

"Really?" Chandler's eyes widened. "How did he manage that?"

"Charm and the promise of cleaning up afterward," I replied. "But I think he just wants to crash there so he doesn't have to drive home."

"Smart," she nodded. "And convenient for us, too." A conspiratorial glint was in her eyes.

"Very," I agreed, leaning closer. "Means we can go to bed whenever we want."

"One last time?" I winked at Chandler.

She nodded, knowing exactly what I was asking without me having to say it. "I mean... we have to, right?"

Laughter echoed off the water as Chandler and I jumped into the lake. When we rose back up for air, her waves were catching the light, hazel eyes sparkling. Parker and Willow were in their own world, splashing around without a care.

Reese, my mom and I... Well, we weren't quite there yet. But right then everything felt at peace. I finally had the girl, and if she was all I'd have in this world, I could live with that, for the rest of my life.

When we got to Willow's place later, Parker and I hauled coolers onto the deck, ice cubes clinking as we dumped them over cans and bottles.

"Quite the turnaround since June, huh?" Parker slapped me on the back, grinning broadly.

I grinned, tossing a few extra beers in the cooler. "Never thought anyone could lock you down. Now look at you."

Parker smirked, "didn't think there was a woman out there that could handle all this."

We shared a laugh before pride crept into his voice. "And the championship, man. Someone also got MVP this year. Speaking of, any news from Chicago?" he asked, popping open a bottle and taking a swig.

"The GM called," I said, fiddling with a bottle cap. "Wants Chandler and me to go back for a game."

"Doesn't sound like he's holding any grudges," Parker observed, eyebrows raised.

"Apparently he pulled a similar stunt for his wife," I replied with a shrug.

Parker leaned against the railing just as a group of people made their way up the drive. "You know," he began with a small smile, "if you and Chandler tie the knot, that makes us actual brothers. And you'll never get rid of me."

"Get rid of you?" I scoffed playfully, shaking my head. "Parker, even if I tried, it wouldn't happen. But seriously, what kind of life would that be without getting to laugh at you every day?"

"Hey now, you mean laughing with me, right?" He grinned and took another sip.

"No," I said, grinning back at him, "I said what I said." We snickered, our laughter mixing with the commotion of arriving guests. Soon enough, clusters of people were on the yard, some lounging on the patio, others mingling by the open door.

Catching sight of Chandler among the crowd, I could feel the corners of my mouth lift involuntarily. My heart soared with her laughter. She was the prettiest smile I had ever seen, the most incredible person I had ever known. She caught me looking and sent a quick smile my way.

"Blue Devils, assemble!" Bailey commanded, grabbing the attention of those around him. Our teammates began to shuffle around, forming a semicircle in the yard gathering around Bailey.

"Come on, we've earned this," he shouted with a grin as wide as the lake we'd spent many of our days in.

"Here's to a badass summer," Bailey raised his cup high, "and to bringing home the championship!"

"Cheers!" we echoed, clinking cups, followed by cheers and whistles.

As the huddle broke and everyone dispersed to continue celebrating, I slipped through the crowd, making my way to Chandler.

"Hey there," I said as I wrapped my arms around her from behind, feeling her lean back into me.

"I like boyfriend Boston," she teased, turning in my embrace to face me, her eyes sparkling with warmth. "Did I ever tell you how much I like you cooking for me and bringing me coffee?"

"I like the way you say boyfriend." I leaned down, brushing a soft kiss on her forehead.

Parker was laughing next to us. He had that look in his eye—the one that meant he was about to give someone shit—and tonight it was directed at Bailey.

"Come on, Bailey," Parker could barely get words out through his laughter. "Tell Crew what username you use on that dating app." He leaned back, arms crossed over his chest.

"Shut up, man," Bailey retorted, but there was no real anger in his words. He looked away in defeat. "I can't go by my real name because all the ladies would want me for my status."

I couldn't help but snort at that comment. "What status is that?"

"Yeah, what status, dude?" Parker added. "An average third baseman?"

"Okay, but what's the name you use?" Crew asked eagerly. "Can't wait to hear this one."

Bailey let out an annoyed sigh. "It doesn't matter," he finally grumbled. "He only knows because he was being a creep and looking over my shoulder."

"Fine," Parker said with a grin. "I'll do the honors since our star player here is suddenly shy. It's 'Papi Likes Butts.'"

Chandler stepped back like she was struck by lightning. Her drink became collateral damage as it fell from her hand, liquid splashing on the ground before her. A choked gasp escaped her lips before she scrambled down to pick up her cup. She stared wide-eyed at Bailey, who hardly noticed her reaction because Parker was still giving him shit.

"Shit," I murmured, a frown creasing my forehead. "You okay? What was that about?"

"Walk with me?" she asked, her hand already tugging at mine, eager for movement. "I need to grab my lipgloss from Willow's bathroom, and you're not going to believe what I'm about to tell you."

"You want me to go with you for lip gloss and gossip? Shouldn't you be doing this with Willow?" I groaned, but I couldn't resist her pull.

"I don't know where Willow ran off to, but I have to tell this to someone."

"This better be good," I joked.

"Papi Likes Butts, Boston. How did this happen? I never would have put it together," Chandler whispered in a rush, as she pulled me inside and we navigated the crowded hallway toward Willow's room. The thrumming bass of the party music seemed to fade into the background, as I focused on what she was saying.

"Put what together?" I asked.

"He's the guy..." she shook her head. "He sent her feet pics." Her lips curled into an amused smile as we walked through Willow's room toward her bathroom.

"Okay, not where I thought you were going with this. Sent who feet pics?" I asked just as Chandler's hand found the doorknob.

I was so focused on what she was saying that I didn't pay attention to what was happening around me. I ignored the first warning sign that should have made me stop her from opening that door—a pair of heels carelessly discarded on the floor. A picture frame had fallen from the wall, landing face down on the carpet, almost as if someone had knocked it down. That was the second sign, and I'd once again failed to recognize it in time.

She pushed open the door mid-sentence and her next words caught in her throat.

The unexpected sight before us stole the air from our lungs. His body was pressed against hers, his hands possessively sneaking under her shirt. Their lips were locked on each other, frozen suddenly by the creak of the opening door.

"Reese?" Chandler's voice was a breath, still trying to decipher what she was seeing.

In that split second, as the two of them broke apart, I realized who he was with. "Caroline!" I blurted out. There she was, her blonde hair tousled around her flushed face, lipstick smeared.

"Uh—" I stuttered, my brain short-circuiting.

Chandler's hand flew to her mouth, stifling a gasp, her eyes wide with shock. For a lingering second, nobody moved—time itself seemed shocked by the discovery.

Then, with a swift, reflexive motion, Chandler slammed the door shut. The sound echoed through the stillness.

"I don't need the lipgloss," she whispered in disbelief. We stood there, hearts pounding, the secret scene burned into our minds.

acknowledgments

To my husband - Thank you for supporting this crazy dream of mine, for helping wrangle the children on a daily basis, and for your jokes and comments that often end up in my stories.

To my children - May you always fight for your dreams and what makes you happy! You can do anything you dream of.

To my parents - Thank you for all the lessons you taught me, and for introducing me to magical stories through movies and books growing up, it created this imagination of mine.

To Sam & Dan - Thank you for your constant support, kindness, and always being there for us. Here's to many more rounds of Sevens! So grateful for you!

To Cindee - The worlds best SIL. You are the opposite of the character in my story - you're a momma bear to your core and you protect and stand up for all of us. I am so lucky I was finally blessed with a sister, and one who is always there for me. Atticus & Arlo - proud of you who you are! Can't wait to see the amazing things you do in the world.

To Gina & Jerry - To my incredible in-laws, thank you for your support and love. Your kindness and generosity has meant more than words can express. I'm so grateful to have you as family, and the babies are even luckier to have you as grandparents.

To Nana & Grandpa Seeds - Your stories, support, and kindness mean so much to me. Nana's hugs and laughter have a magic that could heal the entire world, and I'm so grateful for you both.

To Nana Bryson - The Nana with the sharpest wit and unwavering kindness and support. Thank you for the joy of your yearly birthday serenades, and for the story I'll never forget — "eggs and bacon, hold the bacon."

To my friends - To my amazing friends who have supporting me through this writing dream of mine, thank you for being my cheer-leaders, and constant sources of encouragement. Your support has meant the world to me.

Ruth Gough - You are not just a phenomenal alpha, you're also now a close friend of mine. You helped push me through Rival Summer when I wanted to give up and you've believed in me on days when I struggled to believe in myself. I'm endlessly grateful for the joy and light you bring to my life. The world is not ready for the day you publish your first novel because it will be a masterpiece.

To my Beta and Alpha Reads - Thank you for being my first audience and for diving into these pages with such enthusiasm and kindness. I'm forever grateful for your time, support, thoughts, and belief in my work.

www.ingramcontent.com/pod-product-compliance
Lightning Source LLC
Chambersburg PA
CBHW020131310726
48970CB00006B/1814